FREE LUNCH
IN
NEW YORK CITY

Matthias Drawe

D.A. Publishing
228 Park Ave S #24579
New York, NY 10003
Tel.: + 1-212-486-8049
info@da-publishing.com

Editor: René Alfaro

ISBN: 1534774459
ISBN-13: 978-1534774452

CONTENTS

1.
THE NEW LOCK

"Open the damn door, or I'll kill you!" Bill threw himself against the door with all his might. "Open up, you son of a bitch, I know you're in there!"
Trembling, Hardy stood with his back against the wall, clenching his hands around the baseball bat. He had changed the lock overnight.

If Bill managed to kick down the door, there would be a fight to the finish.

Once more, Hardy's former friend thrust himself against the massive wood of the old entrance door. The hinges slightly gave way, but the door held firm.
Bill cursed. "I'll get you, you scumbag. Just wait and see." He ran down the stairs muttering something under his breath
Hardy's heart pounded in his temples. He would be done for if Bill could get the guys from Avenue B on his side. Together, they would certainly be able to break through.

Tammy lay in a drunken stupor in her room, snoring. Obviously, she would be of no help.
Hardy called Loraine but only got the machine.

Suddenly, she picked up, sounding sleepy and annoyed. "What is it now?"
"He tried to kick in the door."
"Where's Tammy?"
"Passed out."
Loraine moaned. "Okay, I'll come by."

Hardy rummaged through the trash, fished out a cigarette butt and lit it. He took a few puffs and coughed. Bronchitis. He had started smoking again after months of abstinence. He wanted to stop but couldn't. Not now.

He glanced into the mirror over the sink. His face was bloated, his dry lips cracked open, his tongue coated white. Bizarre. He suddenly resembled Otto Steinhagel, the screwed-up gravedigger in *Cryptic X.* — Damn, his film! Bill knew where the can was hidden.

Hardy rushed to his room. His bed was made up of upturned milk crates and a mattress he had found on First Avenue. He pulled the dented can from behind the bed and pressed it to his chest. Where could he hide it? Where would Bill never look?

Hardy opened the door under the kitchen sink. A few cockroaches scurried into nooks and crannies. One fled into the open, and Hardy killed it with his shoe.
No, he could not leave the can under the sink. The moisture and the cockroaches could damage the sensitive film material. Hardy made a mental note: *Get duct tape and seal the can!*
When he shut the closet door, a water bug flew into his

face. Hardy screamed, sending the film can smashing to the ground. The lid rolled off to the other side of the kitchen.

The water bug sat still on the floor. Hardy nailed it against the wall with the edge of his shoe. The bug wiggled its legs a few times, and a yellow liquid oozed out from under its shell.

The filmmaker quickly reassembled the can and hurried through the apartment. Tammy lay on her bed, snoring. She was naked, except for the headscarf concealing her unkempt hair. One of her thin, black legs hung over the edge of the mattress, twitching — a tic that drove him crazy when they slept in the same bed.

He stared at her shaved pussy. It turned him on. She had shaved it for him — as a gift for his birthday.

Where the hell was Loraine? Hardy pushed the can under Tammy's mattress and peeked through the curtains. A Puerto Rican guy pulled a sled with shopping bags through the thick snow. Even the burned-out car wreck at the corner of Avenue A was snowed in, which transformed the rundown street into a fairy tale landscape.

Hardy heard a vigorous knock on the door.

He hurried back to the entrance peering through the peephole: Loraine. At last! She was completely different from Tammy: tall, robust and feisty. Colorful beads dangled from her braids, and enormous breasts bulged under her African robe. Almost unbelievable that she was Tammy's sister.

Loraine grinned when she saw the new lock and gave the thumbs up. "Good work. Let the black prince piss in a bucket from now on."

She couldn't stand Bill and therefore called him *the black prince*. When Hardy had moved in, Bill had battled a drug problem for years, although he concealed it well. In the beginning, they hit it off, drinking red wine and listening to the Jazz station from Newark, but after a while Bill's condition deteriorated. Maybe he had taken the wrong pills. He talked haltingly, uttered complete nonsense, and constantly forgot to lock the door.

There was a subtle knock, and Loraine peered through the peephole. "The cops!"

One of the officers was black, the other white. Snowflakes melted on their caps. Bill stood right behind them. He was rail thin, his upper body slightly bent forward. As always he had his magical glass sphere dangling on a leather strap around his neck.

"Are you the tenant, Miss?" the black cop asked.

Loraine shook her head. "I'm her sister."

"Where's the tenant?"

"Sleeping."

"Wake her up."

After Loraine had shaken her vigorously, Tammy came to. She put on a long, worn-out sweatshirt, yawned, and shuffled to the entrance.

The black cop pointed at Bill. "He says he's your roommate, and you don't let him use the bathroom."

Tammy scratched her head and groaned.

Loraine stepped in. "Let me help ... This black prince lives over there!" She pointed across the hall to Bill's shack. "My sister has allowed him to establish himself in this storage closet so he has a roof over his head. He doesn't pay a single penny, and it was pure charity to let him use the bathroom once in a while."

"Charity my ass!" Bill exclaimed, pointing at Tammy. "She gets more food stamps because of me."

"Why don't you let the gentleman use the bathroom?"

Tammy shrugged.

"Why, why ..." Loraine waved her arms. "Because he constantly leaves the entrance door open, and quite a few valuables have gone missing, that's why. He needs to stay in his damn closet."

"This one ..." Bill pointed his thin index finger at Hardy. "He's the one to blame, the sneaky bastard. He's the one who changed the lock."

Bill stuck his finger further out, as if he wanted to pierce it into Hardy's flesh. "He's not even American. He's illegal. He snuck in here, trying to take over. But I won't have it. Arrest him, and take him away!"

Hardy froze.

He had feared that it would come to this. Over some wine he had told Bill his story, a huge mistake as it now turned out.

So far Hardy's papers had never been checked. Only once had he come close to detection, as he had

11

worked at the vegetable market in Hunts Point. Two plain clothes guys appeared and wanted to see work permits. Having been warned just in time Hardy had hidden in a crawl space with an illegal Mexican.

"Listen, sir," the black cop said. "We are the NYPD. The INS decides about immigration status, not us. We would only be responsible if there is a formal deportation order."

"Very well," Bill exclaimed. "Then I formally demand as a rightful citizen of the United States of America that you officially deport him. Immediately!"

"Wait a minute," Loraine said. "I have a better idea. Why don't you look deep into the eyes of this gentleman? You might notice an enlargement of his pupils. Why don't you also have a quick look into his shack over there, just to make sure he doesn't store any illegal substances?"

Bill threw Loraine a venomous look. "This is an absolute impudence. I am a freelance artist and a law-abiding citizen of the United States of America. I've never done anything wrong."

Tammy giggled. So did Loraine.

The two policemen exchanged a meaningful look. They were dealing with a couple of lunatics again!

"Listen, sir," the black cop told Bill. "There is a crucial question here. Do you have a lease, anything in writing?"

"Sure," Bill said triumphantly. "Of course!" He went into his shack and rummaged through a box. "Here!" He held out a piece of paper. "Here it is!"

"A phone bill?"

"That's right. In my name."

Bill had a phone in his shack. But for fifty bucks you could get a connection almost anywhere, even under a bridge.

The police radio beeped. The black cop turned away and muttered something into the microphone.

"Listen, Mr. ..." The white cop looked at the phone bill. "Mr. Williamson ... I suggest that you contact public assistance. Keep to your space for now. We don't want to come back, okay?"

The cops turned and walked down the stairs.

Loraine slammed the door in front of Bill's face. "Good bye, you bum."

"Scumbags, you damned scumbags!" Bill screamed. "This is not the last of it, just you wait and see!"

2.
THE EXPERT OPINION

"So, did you read it?"
Francisco nodded, sipped his coffee, and leafed through a few bills. His tiny office in the Lumière was cluttered, a poster of *La Dolce Vita* hung on the wall. Francisco was Colombian and in his late forties. Short, round-faced, and pot-bellied. Even though he ran an art house cinema, you could have mistaken him for a bus driver.

The telephone rang. A call from Iran. A documentary filmmaker had problems with his visa.

Hardy sat on a metal chair next to the desk and examined a flyer with the program: European classics, Asian avant-garde, Australian underground — most of it crap.
Through the open office door Hardy could see into the foyer. A few people stood in line for the next show. A freak with dyed blue hair, an elderly couple in trench coats, a woman with a tattooed tear beneath her eye.

It smelled of buttered popcorn.

Hardy had a five-inch kitchen knife in his pocket. Not

exactly the best defense but better than nothing. Bill would not give up easily.

Francisco was done with his phone call. He had promised to give Hardy's script to producer Floyd Burns: *Chaos in Kyrgyzstan,* a surreal road movie.
"What's the word from Floyd?"
"Haven't passed it on yet."
Hardy felt queasy. "How so?"
"Because he's in Toronto right now. Besides ...," Francisco rummaged through his drawer and pulled out Hardy's screenplay. "... it's too European. You want American money, you need an American plot."
He put on his reading glasses and looked at the comments he had scribbled in the margins. "But I think you can make it work. Kyrgyzstan becomes Mexico, we turn the German fellow into a New York Jew, and the Turkish guy could be a Puerto Rican. Vodka becomes tequila, Stalin's limo becomes Kennedy's Cadillac, and the hilarious scene in the chicken coop can stay as is — chickens are nearly everywhere ... Title: *Mayhem in Mexico* - What do you say?"

Hardy stopped breathing. With a few casual strokes Francisco had wiped off months of work.

"Why a New York Jew in the lead? That's not exactly my background."
"Because it shows your range, Hardy. It makes you great as a screenwriter, don't you understand?"
Francisco was Hardy's main contact in New York. They knew each other from the San Sandoval Film Festival, where *Cryptic X* had won the Newcomer Award.

15

Francisco took a few photos from the drawer and slid them across the table. A forty-year-old guy with an eye-catching, Jewish nose and a receding hairline.

The sinking feeling in Hardy's stomach grew stronger. "He's much too old."

"Only because of his roles. He looks younger with the right makeup."

"Never heard of him. What's his last name?"

"Feinstein. He stars in *Boston Law* and *Carmine Medical Center*. And he plays on Broadway."

Jimmy stood in the doorway: an Asian-American with tattoos on his forearms, wearing his baseball cap backward. "The freakin' projector bulb blew again."

Francisco unlocked a small safe and handed him a twenty.

Why a New York Jew? Hardy did not understand why on earth Francisco was pushing Feinstein.

"Because he's perfect for the role, Hardy. It all fits together: Avi, Floyd, low-budget shoot in Mexico ..." Francisco snapped three times with his fingers. "Once the script is done, we will get financing in no time."

Mayhem in Mexico. Hardy closed his eyes, imagining the frail Jew Avi Feinstein in the lead and shifting some of the key scenes from Kyrgyzstan to Mexico. It was incredibly difficult, if not impossible.

"I know what you think. You think Avi is a bit, how should I say it, too delicate for the role, not macho enough, right?"

"Right."

"Wrong! Forget the crappy TV shows, you have to see him on stage. He has an insane range, believe me. One minute you laugh yourself silly, and the next your blood will freeze ..."

Francisco pulled out a theater ticket. "Okay, it's an off-musical, but Avi is excellent. He sings, tap dances and plays the mandolin. I guarantee that you'll get goose bumps at least five times."

Hardy looked at the ticket: *The Kalashnikov Concert.* "What is it about?"

"He plays a melancholy mafia boss. A very strong part."

Francisco stood up and spread his arms. "I really have to go, my dear, the damn visas for the Iranians are driving me crazy."

They embraced, and Francisco patted the back of Hardy's head.

Hardy remembered the boozy opening night of *Cryptic X* at the San Sandoval Film Festival, where they had become friends. Francisco was so drunk that he had given Hardy a wet kiss on the neck. The Colombian was married, but it was an open secret that he also liked boys.

Hardy pulled away from him. "When do I have to deliver the rewrite? When can you give it to Floyd?"

"I suggest you write the intro, the magic moment in the chicken coop and the conclusion. That should convince Avi."

"Avi? We show it to Avi first?"

"Sure. Avi is the godfather of Floyd's son."

The phone rang. Francisco took the call, waving Hardy good-bye.

Outside the cinema Jimmy swapped photos in the showcase. The Asian tried his hand at filmmaking as well but so far had only completed a two-minute short on Super 8. Hardy did not like him and knew that Jimmy disliked him just as much. If they met somewhere on the street, they ignored each other.

Hardy pulled up the collar of his pea coat and trudged against the icy wind through the East Village. Hardly anyone was on the street. Christmas lights blinked in the windows, and a few cars drove slowly over the slippery First Avenue, their headlights projecting cones into the snowfall.

Hardy turned onto East 2nd Street and noticed dim lights behind the sleazy curtains of Bill's shack.

The filmmaker lit a cigarette butt he had saved in a small plastic bag, took a few puffs and threw it out into the snow. He slipped into the foyer, pulling out his knife.

He heard the squeak of a door and paused. Was Bill hiding somewhere in the hallway?

Hardy cautiously walked up the stairs, the knife at the ready. Bill's door was closed. He had placed two bowls of salt in front of the threshold, and a piece of cardboard read: *Depart from me, Lord of Darkness!*

Hardy slipped into Tammy's apartment and bolted the door.

3.
BY THE SWEAT OF THY FACE

Hardy sat in front of a computer he had purchased for fifty bucks at the flea market. It had come with a black and white monitor and a junky nine-needle printer. The screen darkened occasionally but lit back up if you banged your fist on the top edge.

Hardy paced back and forth in front of the table. His room was tiny — not much larger than seventy square feet. A bed, a desk, a chair. That was it.
His only decoration was a photo of a Mexican *soldadera* cut out from a newspaper. She wore men's clothes, a sombrero, and a colt tucked into her belt. The resolve in her black eyes and her pouty mouth were sexy. It was rather odd since he had hung the photo a week before Francisco suggested Mexico. Was this an omen? Maybe.

But why on earth Avi Feinstein?

Hardy's original hero was tough, athletic, and in his mid-twenties. Avi Feinstein was frail, delicate and in his forties. Would anyone believe that he could lift a limousine from a muddy ditch?
Hardy imagined Feinstein wearing a baseball cap. This would at least cover his receding hairline. No, a baseball

cap wouldn't work. If he'd wear headgear, it had to be a small hat, similar to that of Yogi bear. Feinstein would look younger this way.

Hardy stared out at the snow-covered park of the retirement home on Houston Street. His window, leading to the fire escape, was secured with a locked sliding grate. For added security, he had installed a deadbolt inside the door jamb.

Tammy was probably drinking in a nearby bar, as always. Although she was past forty, she could still look pretty good if she fixed herself up.

Thirsty, the filmmaker went into the kitchen, noticing a mouse on the table with the hotplate. It scurried down to the floor, disappearing behind the fridge. Bingo!
Hardy smirked. He pulled out the glue trap from behind the fridge, and sure enough, he had caught the mouse. The little critters always used the same escape route, so it was not difficult to find the ideal place to set the trap. The mouse tried to wiggle out of the glue, but its tiny feet were stuck.

Hardy opened the window and ejected the trap with a Frisbee swing into the park.

He sat down at his desk again and stared at the computer screen. He had not written a single line yet. Could it be that the tiny room suffocated him?
He went into the living room and walked in circles around the shabby sofa and the old TV set, which was

missing the dial knob. You needed a pair of pliers to change the channel.

The golden holiday decoration from the previous year still hung above the fireplace: *Merry Christmas and a Happy New Year!* Sort of neat since next Christmas was approaching fast.

Should he skip the intro for now and warm up with a scene in the middle, where the hero was stuck in the Sierra Madre? Maybe that would do the trick!

Hardy hurried back to his room. Pressing his tongue between his lips, the filmmaker typed a few lines and saw the barren Sierra Madre: At the side of the road lay the broken-down jalopy that Feinstein had bought to track down Kennedy's Cadillac. It was extremely hot as he fanned his face with the Yogi bear hat. No, no, stop. This didn't work because of the receding hairline. Feinstein had to wear the hat at all times.

Hardy was sweating. The damn radiator was running on full steam again. Not adjustable, it was either boiling hot or not working at all.

He opened the window but soon closed it again — too cold. Anyway, a little sweating wouldn't do him any harm. Far from it, it set the right mood for the Sierra Madre.

He took off his sweater and imagined the scene in which the gangsters set the trap. What would he call the boss of the villains? Hardy recalled an Argentine acquaintance nicknamed Lugo. Lugo sounded fine. It was no ordinary name and had a nasty ring to it. Lugo,

Lugo, Lugo. Hardy hammered a few lines into the keyboard — the scene slowly took shape.

Suddenly, the computer went dead along with the desk lamp. Hardy cursed and rushed to the peephole. The hallway was clear. He cautiously opened the door and looked at the ceiling. Some scumbag had cut the extension cable. Maybe the Chinese landlord? No, it could only have been Bill because his own cable was still plugged in.

The power had been turned off months ago because Tammy had not paid the bill. To get around the lack of juice, while still buddies, Bill and Hardy had tapped the hallway light. At each 99 cents store you could buy a fixture adapter with two power outlets. You just took out the bulb, screwed in the adapter, and consequently had two outlets while keeping the bulb in place. Bill and Hardy had laid the extensions discreetly along the ceiling. One led to Bill's shack, the other to Tammy's place.

Hardy noticed a strange smell: Bill had injected Super Glue into the new lock!

Hardy rummaged through the kitchen drawer and found the benzene. He dribbled a few drops on his key and inserted it into the cylinder. Gradually, the glue dissolved, and the lock turned again.

Hardy was close to kicking in the Bill's door, but this was exactly what the scumbag wanted. Then he would call the cops again.

The filmmaker fetched the ladder, climbed up to the hallway ceiling and peeled the plastic coating of the cut cable. He carefully inserted the blank wire into the outlet, and Tammy's lights came back on.

Hardy bolted the door, lit a half-smoked cigarette, and sat on the chair with the broken armrest. He coughed, staring into the void.
The computer worked again, but Hardy, drained as he was, could not continue writing. He could not think clearly in this shitty place. Something new cropped up every day, with no apparent end in sight! Would Eisenstein have been able to write a screenplay in this environment? Certainly not.

Suddenly, Hardy remembered Steven C. Cornfield.

Ironically, it had been Bill's idea when they were still friends. At the time, it seemed far-fetched, but why not give it a try? What did he have to lose?
Hardy went to Tammy's room, sifting through her drawers. Steve's papers had to be somewhere in there!

4.
A WATERTIGHT SYSTEM

"If you want to smile, do it now."
Hardy put on a forced smile as the DMV photographer pressed the shutter button. The office was on the 8th floor of a commercial building in midtown. Next to the elevator stood a beefy security guard in uniform.

I am Steven C. Cornfield, born in Hartford, Connecticut,
I am Steven C. Cornfield, born in Hartford, Connecticut.

Hardy had read that spies used self-suggestion when taking on another identity. Maybe it would work for him as well.
The photographer slid the print across. "Sign on the dotted line."
Hardy scribbled Steve's signature on the form. It had taken him quite a while to fake it properly.

I am Steven C. Cornfield, born in Hartford, Connecticut,
I am Steven C. Cornfield, born in Hartford, Connecticut.

Hardy sat down in the waiting room, nervously fumbling with his wait number. What would happen if they caught him? Would he go straight to jail? Maybe.

Hardy felt the sudden urge to smoke. He pulled out a plastic straw, which he had cut in half, and sucked on it. Supposedly, some guys in Texas had kicked the habit this way. The cut straw had the same size as a cigarette, except that you sucked in air instead of smoke. Amazingly, it helped. When you vigorously sucked on the straw and held your breath for a few seconds, the urge subsided. Sure, it looked silly, but it was worth a try.

Since his arrival in New York, Hardy had kept afloat with odd jobs: removing debris, refurbishing apartments, stacking boxes at the market in Hunts Point. When he got home, he was half dead. But without papers, it was impossible to get a better job.

I am Steven C. Cornfield, born in Hartford, Connecticut, I am Steven C. Cornfield, born in Hartford, Connecticut.

Steve's story was mysterious. As a metal worker in a large factory, he had an accident when he was thirty-seven: multiple herniated discs and a neuropathy in the left arm. In early retirement, he spent his money on drugs and alcohol. Eventually he met Tammy, moved in with her, and at some point began to peddle cocaine. One evening he just did not come back. Perhaps a deal had gone wrong and someone had killed him. Since that day his papers had been sitting in one of Tammy's drawers, unused.

Hardy was sweating. Almost all public offices in New York were overheated. He opened his jacket and sucked on the straw.

Ding-dong! — The board showed Hardy's number.

The official's name plate read *Michael T. Snyder*. He had a harelip and grown-in earlobes. He wiggled a pen between his fingers.

Hardy slid Steve's social security card and birth certificate across the table. Those two were genuine. Everything else was forged.

Snyder stared at the worn social security card. "Is this a three or an eight at the end?"

"Eight."

"What did you with the card — put it in the washing machine?"

Snyder shook his head and punched in the number. He leaned closer to the monitor, studying the information. Had Steve been reported dead?

Hardy was sweating. Why was it so damn hot?

"Have you ever had an ID of the State of New York?"

"Uh ... no."

Snyder clicked with his mouse. "Did you ever have an ID of the State of Connecticut?"

"Yes."

"Where is it?"

"Lost."

"Did you report the loss?"

"Sure did."

Sweat ran into Hardy's eyes, and it started to burn.

"How did you report the loss? Over the phone? You should have received a confirmation in the mail."

"I didn't."

Snyder shook his head. "Connecticut ...! Where is your proof of address?"

Hardy showed him the tinted plastic envelope with the forged electricity bill. He had inserted Steve's name using a color copier. It looked almost perfect, but the paper had a slightly different consistency than the original bill. It was thicker.

"Take that thing out of the dark sleeve. I can hardly read a thing."

Snyder looked at the address on the bill and then at the back of the page. The filmmaker had scribbled a shopping list on the reverse side and crumbled the sheet, so it looked more authentic.

Snyder sneezed. He held his breath for a moment and sneezed again. "Damn allergies." He slid the bill back and wiped his nose with a paper tissue. "Let me see your passport. Military ID, veteran's ID, disability ID: a card with a picture on it."

Hardy held Steve's disability ID against the window. He had glued his photo over Steve's and then plasticized the card a second time. If Snyder demanded to see it up close and touched the photo, he would notice the forgery.

"So young and already handicapped?"

"Multiple herniated disc. Very painful. Can't lift more than one pound. Also a neuropathy in the right arm." Hardy put the ID away and awkwardly moved his fingers in front of the window, demonstrating his disability. "Can't feel much with this one."

Snyder typed something into his keyboard and nibbled on his lower lip. Finally, he hit the return key.

Nothing happened.

Snyder raised his eyebrows and looked at the printer. "Hm, it doesn't print, but why?" He studied the monitor. "Oh ..., yes of course. What's your mother's maiden name?"

Steven C. Cornfield, froze. He had no idea. How could he not know his mother's maiden name?

"Without it I can't close the window. What's your mother's maiden name?"
Hardy was paralyzed, his mouth dry. He swallowed.
"You are very pale," Snyder said. "Not feeling well?"
Hardy touched his back in pain. "Ah, the disc, this damn pain. Always strikes without warning." He squinted, breathing heavily. What should he do now? Jump up and run?

Snyder impatiently tapped his fingers on the table.

Hardy racked his brain. What the hell was Steve's mother's maiden name? He had seen it somewhere, but where?
Snyder had an inspiration. "Here," he said, pointing to Steve's birth certificate. "Here it is. Rickert," he muttered to himself. "Rickert ..."
Of course, Rickert! Now, Hardy remembered it. He kept on groaning anyway, since his fake back pain could not have gone away so easily.

Snyder hit the return key again.

Nothing happened.

"I don't get this, George ...," Snyder turned to his colleague at the next desk. "I entered the maiden name, but it just won't print."
"F5 and delete section seven."
Snyder complied and once more hit the return key.

Still nothing.

Hardy held his breath. What the hell was wrong? Snyder and his colleague stared at the screen in disbelief.

Suddenly, the printer reacted and spat out Hardy's confirmation.

"A glitch in the software," Snyder said apologetically. "You need to give it a little twist sometimes."
He came closer to the window and lowered his voice. "People think that our computerized system is waterproof, but you know what ...? This is just between us, don't tell anyone, okay, but if you came in here on a very busy day with a few, uh, let's just say cleverly manipulated documents, you might as well walk out with a ..." Snyder paused, waiting for Hardy to complete the sentence.
"... you don't say ...?" Hardy whispered in disbelief.
"Exactly."
Hardy shook his head. "Impossible!"

Snyder grinned. "I know, it should not happen, and on my watch, it won't, but you know what? It could happen, it really could."

He slid the confirmation across the table. "You are done, Mr. Cornfield. In about two weeks you will receive the card in the mail."

Hardy walked along Broadway. A cold, sunny day. At the corner of 32nd Street he stopped for a moment, blinking into the sun. The area was full of street vendors selling Christmas accessories, cheap jewelry, and trinkets. It smelled of toasted almonds.
Most vendors were immigrants without papers. Poor suckers who lived from one day to the other. Up to this point, Hardy had been one of them. But not any more.

He pulled out the confirmation and held it up. The sun illuminated the paper from behind, circling the data like a spotlight. From now on, he was Steven C. Cornfield, born in Hartford, Connecticut.

5.
SMOKE SIGNALS

"Damn, hurry up, something's wrong!" Bill stood in front of Tammy's door, sniffing the air.
As Hardy opened the door, a dark cloud of smoke hit him. He slid open a window and gasped for air. Tammy had started to boil rice and forgotten about it. The electric plate was red hot, the table underneath charred. He juggled the pot with the burned rice into the sink and opened the faucet. Dark steam billowed, hissing loudly.

Bill stood in front of the fridge, his arms folded across his chest. "She's a security risk, man. Could've burned down the entire house. The Chink would have loved that."

Hardy rushed into the living room. Tammy was sitting on the rocking chair by the window, asleep in a drunken stupor. Her head was tilted to the side, her mouth agape. She had traded her food stamps for alcohol.
He grabbed her by the arms and shook her. "Wake up, dammit!"
She came to, looked at him with glassy eyes, and mumbled something.

Hardy remembered his film. Bill was still in the apartment and could grab the can with the 16-mm print, Hardy's most valued possession!

He ran to his room, took the picture with the *soldadera* off the wall, loosened the bricks and reached into the cavity. He let out a sigh of relief. The can was still in its hiding place. It contained the only existing print of *Cryptic X.* Sure, there was the negative in a Berlin lab, but Hardy had no access. He had shot the film on credit, and a considerable bill remained unpaid.

If Hardy lost the print of *Cryptic X,* it would be almost as if he'd lost his child. At the premiere in San Sandoval there had been standing ovations. The press had compared him to Eisenstein, which was surprising, since until that point he had not watched a single work of the Russian master.

Hardy heard a loud fart. Bill was in the bathroom, sitting on the toilet.

The filmmaker grabbed his baseball bat. He knew how to defend himself come crunch time. He had been in fights with his brother or with rivals in school, and during his time as a squatter in Berlin he had fought off the cops. But that was a long time ago. He had not been in a physical altercation in years.

Hardy was raised in a small West German town near Kassel. He did not get along with his father, and shortly after his eighteenth birthday he moved to West Berlin to escape conscription. The wall city teemed with artists and colorful birds from around the globe. Rent was cheap, booze was cheap, and a lot of love was in the air. Hardy had lived in a squat and played guitar in a punk-rock band.

Eventually, a Super 8 camera had fallen into his hands. When he projected the first images of his own creation onto a white wall, playing a tape of "O sole mio" along, he was immediately hooked. He had created something magical with a daring close-up montage of a kissing couple. It looked just like a movie on the big screen even though he had shot it on Super 8. From that moment on he knew that he would be a filmmaker.

Bill came out of the bathroom, tightening his belt. He sat down at the table and rolled a smoke. "Give me the key."

"I thought we had resolved this."

Bill lit his cigarette and leaned back. "Okay, I can wait."

Bill was well over fifty but looked younger. His skin was very dark, and if you looked at him from a certain angle he resembled Chuck Berry. He claimed to have started the sit-ins in North Carolina way back when, but Hardy doubted it.

In the style of an African American Chagall, Bill painted surreal scenes from the rural South and the industrial North. A busty blonde angel, wearing a see-through dress, graced almost all his canvasses. Bill claimed to see her almost daily. If he found anything of value on the street, he said: "My angel sent it to me."

At some point Bill's life had been going down the drain, though. After an early success with his paintings his career wasn't going anywhere, and he started experimenting with drugs.

The door opened with a squeak. Bill had left it slightly ajar, as always.

"What the hell is going on? It reeks of smoke." Mickey Doggy Style held his nose. "Terrible stench, man."
Mickey was bloated and in his mid-forties. He wore a scruffy baseball cap and brown tortoiseshell glasses. He did drugs and stole everything that was not nailed down. He lived on the 3rd floor with his older brother and a German shepherd. When his brother was in the hospital due to hip surgery, Mickey Doggy Style sold half the furniture and blamed it on a burglar. Allegedly he banged the German shepherd, and that's how he got his nickname.

"Can I roll one?" Mickey asked.

Bill slid the tobacco across the table. Mickey quickly and artistically rolled one with his fat fingers. He lit the cigarette with a battered Zippo, blowing the smoke into the air with relish.

Suddenly, Tammy appeared, wearing only her large sweatshirt and socks. "What's going on? It smells funny."
She discovered the pot with the burned rice. "Holy shit!"
Looking at Bill and Mickey she motioned toward the door. "Get out!"

"Only if you give me the key," Bill said.
Tammy grabbed the iron poker from the fireplace and held it up to Bill's face. "Get out!"

"Okay, okay. Stay cool." Bill grabbed his tobacco and left.

"Thanks for the hospitality," Mickey said and vanished as well.

6.
A SAFE HAVEN

Francisco sat at his desk, sipping a coke. Two stacks of film cans were piled up behind him: the documentaries from Iran.

"Don't know what to do with your print, Hardy. Just look at what's going on in this place. I mean, you can leave it here, but I can't guarantee anything."

Hardy held *Cryptic X* under his arm. It was not safe in its hiding place. In a real fire, the film would melt.

Francisco could not lock up the can, and Hardy didn't want it lying around in the cinema. Film cans were constantly mixed up or just disappeared. And then there was Jimmy. The bastard could simply destroy *Cryptic X* out of pure spite.

"How's *Mayhem in Mexico* coming along?"

Hardy had printed the scene where Feinstein tried to heave the limo out of a muddy ditch. The scene was almost entirely silent. Only occasionally Feinstein talked to himself out of despair, which made it funny.

Francisco put on his reading glasses and read into the scene. His face lit up. "It's really, really good. I told you that Mexico would work. But it would be even funnier if, at the end, a bird shits on his head."

Hardy burst out laughing. The idea was great.

The telephone rang. Francisco took the call and made a cross in front of his chest. "Talebi finally got his visa."

Hardy stood in front of the cinema with the can under his arm. Where could he possibly store it, where would it be safe?
It snowed. A cloudy, gloomy day. A few cabs crept along Second Avenue, headlights on. Hardy pulled up the collar of his coat and trudged toward Avenue B.

Loraine was wearing a red bathrobe and red socks. She seemed surprised to see Hardy at her doorstep. Her doormat had a strange style. *Welcome* was crossed out, and right below it read: *Get lost!*
They sat in the kitchen and drank lukewarm tea from a thermos. A tiny black and white TV was tuned into a cartoon show.

Loraine lived in public housing. Even though illegal, she had rented one of the rooms to a student from NYU. Earl, her son's father, did not pay alimony. Yet, he occasionally appeared when he had nowhere else to go.

Hardy slid ten bucks across the table. "Ten per month until I pick it up, okay?"
Loraine opened the nightstand in her bedroom. It was the only cabinet with a key. Unfortunately, the can, being too wide, did not fit in straight.
Loraine took out a shelf, inserted the can diagonally, and stuffed the gaps with her private things, including a few condoms and a tube with lube.

"I got some leftover chicken and rice. Want some?"

Loraine put the food into the microwave. Her roommate Kristen appeared in the kitchen door. A frail blonde in a baggy jogging suit. "Just wanted to let you know that I'll pay the rent on Monday, okay?"

Loraine frowned. "Again? This really needs to be the last time, honey. We've settled on the first, as you know."

Kristen nodded and disappeared.

Shortly after, Hakeem, Loraine's son, came in. He was tall for fourteen and wore dreadlocks. "I need some dough, mom. Can I have an advance?"

"Again?"

"There's a party at the club today. I am the only one who has no money."

Loraine reached into her robe and gave him the ten she had received from Hardy.

7.
LOVE THY NEIGHBOR AS THYSELF

"Eighty-seven, who's number eighty-seven?"
The woman at the information desk looked through the waiting room.
"You called eighty-seven already, honey," shouted a guy in the back row. "Call eighty-eight, damn it!"
Tammy had number 126. The glare of the neon light was harsh, the chairs uncomfortable. A sign on the wall read: *No Alcohol, No Drugs, No Exceptions.*

Tammy filled in a form, chewing on her pen. Hardy had joined her to make sure she wouldn't quit.

In anticipation of his ID he had waited for the mailman every day. The lock on the mailbox was broken, and he feared that Bill would skim the mail. The ID hadn't arrived yet but a letter from welfare. A final warning. Tammy had ignored all requests to appear, and they stopped paying the rent. The Chinese landlord had initiated the eviction process.

Hardy pulled out his custom-made straw, inhaled deeply, held in the air for a while, then exhaled. The urge slowly subsided. He hadn't smoked a real cigarette for days.

"No smoking, sir." A welfare worker stood next to him.
"I'm not." Hardy held up the straw.
"You're smoking a straw?"
"Sure, why not?"
The guy shook his head and moved on.

Tammy grinned. "You look like an idiot with that straw, but if it helps, fine."
Tammy was clearly an alcoholic, but she did not smoke. Her family came from Alabama, and as a child she sang in the gospel choir. When she was fourteen her father landed a job with a construction company in New York, and the family moved to the city.
After high school, she had worked at an AT&T warehouse and pursued a singing career on the side. As the lead singer of The Chanderellas she had recorded a single at a small label in Brooklyn: "If I only knew the crazy things you do." It was a catchy doo-wop song. With a little luck, it could have been a hit.

"What does it say right there?" Tammy held out the form. "It's printed so damn small I can't read it."
She had left her glasses at home.
"They ask if you want to apply for emergency food stamps."
Tammy checked the box.

Hardy glanced out the window at the snowed-in landscape. It was an exceptional winter. He had never seen so much snow.
He pulled out the postcard for his mother. A panorama picture showing the Statue of Liberty and the imposing Manhattan skyline. Inserted in the picture, a Santa with

a reindeer sleigh and the caption: *Merry Christmas from the Land of the Free!*

Hardy had searched quite a bit, and that was exactly the card he wanted. He began to write:

Dear Mom,

From the snowy, enchanting New York at Christmas time, I am writing to you in the best of spirits. The city is a great inspiration and my film project looks promising. Better yet: I am in love ...

Tammy pushed back her wool hat and scratched her head. Her kinky hair was matted. She desperately needed a hairdo.

Hardy continued:

I can't promise anything, but maybe I can send some good news soon. I think my girlfriend is pregnant ...

Hardy nibbled on his pen. Damn, now he had gone too far. Anyway, it was exactly what his mother wanted to hear.

And there's more! Guess who I saw a few weeks ago on the street? Hold your breath! Yes, yes, yes, it really was him: Robert De Niro!

Hardy was not sure, but the guy who had stepped out of a limo in Tribeca looked very much like the movie star. Some bystanders even cheered and clapped, so it must have been him — or a damn good impersonator.

I am sending you a big hug and many kisses for Christmas.

Your loving son, Holger.

Hardy's real name was Holger. H O L G E R. It sounded like a mushy, half-melted chocolate bar.

As a squatter in Berlin he had simply called himself *Hucky*. Razor sharp and a perfect fit for a punk rock guitarist. It did not work for a filmmaker, though. The name sounded too childish and smacked of *Huckleberry Hound*.
Hardy on the other hand sounded fine, cinematically, and went well with *von Hachenstein*. The name had panache and stood on a level with *Vittorio De Sica, François Truffaut,* and *Sergei Eisenstein. A film by Hardy von Hachenstein* — this sounded great!

Hardy read through the card. He had forgotten the others and scribbled an addition into the margin:

Merry Christmas also to Heidi and the rest of the family.

Heidi was his sister, and the rest of the family were his father and his younger brother, Helge. The relationship with his sister was okay, but he had not spoken with his father and brother for years.

"The vibe in here makes me sick," Tammy said. She crossed her legs and nervously rocked her foot. "I need something to drink."

The others in the waiting room threw them glances. Hardy was the only white. All others were black or Latino.

Tammy headed to the exit, and Hardy ran after her.
"What if they call you?"
"Get me something to drink."
"No."
"Okay then, I'll get it myself."
She walked past the security check into the open.
"I'll get you some vodka. At least that won't smell. If they call you, we'll lose our spot."
"I'll go with you to the liquor store."

They trudged through the snow. A few children with sleds passed.
Hardy bought a flask of vodka, and Tammy gulped down half. Had he not pulled the bottle, she would have finished it all.

Going back in they were searched again by security. The burly officer discovered the flask in Hardy's pea coat.
"Have you been drinking?"
"No, only took in a bit of fresh air."
"Why's the bottle half empty then? We have strict instructions not to let drunks into the building."
"Do I look drunk?"
"Breathe out for me, please."
Hardy breathed on him.
"Again."
He breathed out again.
"Okay."

He turned to Tammy.

"Have you been drinking?"

Tammy shook her head.

"Breathe out for me, please."

Tammy breathed on him ever so slightly. The officer hesitated. Vodka was hard to smell. He waved them through. "The bottle stays here. When you come out, you can pick it up, okay?"

They went back into the waiting room. A welfare officer pushed a shopping cart with files. A baby cried.

Hardy pulled out his small notebook. To get ahead with the rewrite he had to take advantage of every free moment and therefore always carried the booklet with him.

He closed his eyes and let his thoughts wander to rural Mexico — a grain field in the early morning sun. Camera from above: a secret track between the tall wheat ...

Hardy felt an uncomfortable pressure in his stomach. The diarrhea had started in the morning. Probably some virus.

He hurried to the bathroom and got there just in time. He barely had his pants down when his stomach emptied in a gush into the toilet bowl.

Hardy sat on the bare edge, because there was no lid. Also no door, only two side walls. On the opposite wall was a sink. An artist had immortalized himself where once must have hung a mirror. He had created a magic funnel:

F U C K
F U C K
F U C K
F U C K
F U C K
F U C K

A skinny Puerto Rican came in and used the urinal. He smiled at Hardy, lacking the upper front teeth. He took out his massive member and relieved himself with a powerful, splashing jet.

"I like it here," the guy said as he looked at the artwork. "It's so cozy."

"Right," Hardy said. "Almost like home."

The Puerto Rican grinned. He put his member back in and returned to the waiting room.

Hardy was done, but he had a serious problem. No toilet paper. The only option was his notebook. There were a few blank pages left, but he did not want to use them. He had already typed the pages at the beginning. Those he could use, but of course it was a little questionable if you looked at it symbolically. Anyway, he ripped out the first few pages of the book, cleaned himself, washed his hands, and dried them on his pants. He recorded the experience in his notebook. *Wipe butt with thoughts!* He had to put this somewhere in the script. It was a powerful image, cinematically.

When Hardy came back to the waiting room, he froze: Tammy was gone.

The Puerto Rican from the bathroom smirked. "Don't worry, man, she didn't quit. They called her up."

8.
A WINTER WONDERLAND

The bus rumbled through the Upper East Side, the richest part of town. A beautiful wintery landscape. The luxury stores were decorated festively and had Christmas trees in their windows. Women in furs and men in cashmere coats strolled along the streets.

The bus needed an hour to the East Village, and Hardy and Tammy drank the rest of the vodka. The booze took effect instantly. Hardy felt relaxed. Everything seemed to be easy all of a sudden.

Tammy had shed some tears at the welfare office. They would continue to pay the rent and had even approved emergency food stamps.

Hardy didn't know when something had gone wrong in Tammy's life. Probably her first husband, an Irish-American mailman, was to blame. Seamus, a violent drunkard, was twenty years her senior. After he died of a stroke, Tammy's alcohol intake doubled. Two unsuccessful withdrawals later, the phone company fired her. A psychological assessment classified her as unfit for work, and she started receiving public assistance. After that she lived with several men she had met in bars. The latest in this long line was Hardy.

The bus drove slowly through the snowy streets. A fat Santa sat next to a fake reindeer in front of a toy store, and children pulling sleds walked toward Central Park.

Hardy wondered if his road movie would ever see the light of day? Maybe. Or maybe not. It seemed to drag on for ages. But there was hope. Not too far away he would attend the premiere of *The Kalashnikov Concert* and deliver the most powerful scenes to Avi Feinstein. Maybe it would all fall into place after that.

The bus stopped with a cold draft sweeping through the open door. The driver lowered the lifting mechanism and transferred a man in a wheelchair into the car. Nearby played a Salvation Army brass band with a choir: *I serve a risen Savior, I see his loving care ..., and though my heart grows weary, I never will despair ...*

Tammy and Hardy moved closer together. She had beautiful eyes. Deep black and somewhat sad. They kissed.
The bus doors closed, the music faded and Tammy fell asleep on Hardy's shoulder. He pulled out his notepad and continued to write on his screenplay.

9.
DEADLINE, INC.

The lobby of Deadline, Inc. had no windows, the gray carpet was worn and stained. Some candidates completed tests on workstations in a small subsection of the cramped space. The agency specialized in subletting office personnel.

"Social security and ID, please."

Hardy slid the cards across the counter. The shiny, new ID had finally arrived and smelled of fresh plastic, contrasted by the worn social security card that looked as if it had been buried under rubble for half a century. The receptionist stared at the social security card. "Very hard to read. What did you do with it?"
Hardy used Snyder's explanation. It was a good one.
"Put it in the washing machine. By accident, of course."
"Is this a three at the end, or an eight?"
"Eight."
"Okay. I'm going to make a copy real quick."

"Hm, German, French, and Spanish ... How good is your Spanish on a scale from one to five, if five is tops?"
"Four."

Bob Crevitz, the agency's boss, made a note on Hardy's application form. His wavy hair was mousy, and he had a wart on his nose. His office wasn't a real room — it was merely a cubicle in one corner.

"French?"

"Also four."

"German?"

"Five."

Bob raised his eyebrows. "Five for German? Not bad." He called his secretary. "The linguistic tests, please. Spanish, French, and German."

Hardy felt queasy. Occasionally he spoke Spanish in New York, the city being full of Latinos, but his French was rusty. The last time he had spoken the language extensively was twelve years ago at a student exchange in a small town near Paris. Most of his vocabulary came from Lucky Luke comic books — a gimmick at French gas stations at the time.

"We're not digging terribly deep here," Bob said. "But it helps to separate the chaff from the wheat. What do you want first?"

"German."

Bob slid a page across the table.

— *Wo ist die Bilanz für das Steuerjahr 1991?*

— *Im letzten Quartal haben die Aktien stark fluktuiert.*

— *Der Apfel fällt nicht weit vom Stamm.*

The third phrase was folk wisdom and a trick question of course. Hardy translated it as *Like father, like son.* Bob went over the answers. "Okay. You got that one."

He handed over the Spanish page.

— *¿Cuánto cuesta el vuelo a México, D.F.?*
— *El precio del crudo ha caído en los últimos meses.*
— *No es oro todo lo que reluce.*

Obviously, the third phrase was folk wisdom again and no problem: *All that glitters is not gold*. Hardy also got the gist of the first two sentences, except for two words: *D.F.* and *crudo*. *Crudo* meant *raw*, but it just did not make sense in this context. He translated it as *raw meat* and simply ignored *D.F.* The sentence made sense even without it.

Bob pouted when he saw the result. "Mr. Cornfield those are not four points for Spanish, those are not even three. I hope you realize that we have a reputation to maintain. We cater to some of the most prestigious companies. Do you still claim four points for French, or would you rather tell the truth?"
"Okay, two point five."
Bob looked at his watch. "Well, I have little time today, so I will just take your word for it." He scribbled a note on Hardy's application form.

"I need to step out soon, so let's get to the core, Mr. Cornfield. What about your computer skills?"
"Very good."
"Would you be willing to take a test?"
"Sure."
"I'm sorry, but it kind of smells funny, here. It smells of burned food or something."
"Burned food?"

"Yes, as if somebody had left something on a stove."
"I don't smell anything."
Although Hardy had aired his jacket extensively, it still smelled of burned rice. But it was the only jacket he had.

The first test program was Word. The initial questions were simple. *Cut and paste, search, find and replace.* But then came *mail merge, templates, table functions, insert objects, auto format ...*
After a few minutes, Hardy received the result: forty-three percent.

Bob wasn't exactly thrilled.

"How about Excel and PowerPoint?"
"Basic command."
Bob sniffled at Hardy's jacket. "I think it's you."
"Me?"
"The smell, it comes from you."
Hardy sniffled at his jacket. "Well, maybe the dry cleaning?"
"Be sure to change your cleaner."
Bob slid Hardy's application into a folder. "Come back after you have practiced a little, Mr. Cornfield. We can't place anyone who does not have at least sixty percent on the computer test."

10.
SILENT NIGHT, HOLY NIGHT

Tammy kept a plastic Christmas tree in the closet and a few lights, but she could not find the rest of the decoration, so she turned tinfoil into tinsel. She wore a red, skimpy dress and a Santa hat. The kitchen table stood in the living room, now, and they had lit the fire place with scrap wood. The radio played "White Christmas."

Just in time, a letter from Hardy's mother had arrived.

Dear Holger,
Now, during the holidays, my thoughts are with you, naturally. Unfortunately, we have no Christmas weather at all. It's cloudy and gray in Bad Wildungen and drizzling constantly. A festive atmosphere will simply not come up like this.
I still remember when I brought you into this world on a very cold November morning. It was a difficult birth, but I was overjoyed when I finally could hold you in my arms. You were such a pretty baby! And you turned into a very smart little boy. Can you remember, what you wanted to be when you grew up?

Tammy took a sip of beer and turned in a circle, arms outstretched. "How do I look?"
She threw him a sexy glance over her shoulder and smiled. Despite the booze she was slim and had a pretty face. Only her teeth were a bit rotten.

Architect is what you said, dear Holger. Yes, you wanted to be an architect! And to hear that from such a small tot. Oh, how we laughed. Where did you get that word being barely five years old?

Hardy knew the story. His mother had told it many times.

Unfortunately, you never followed up on that early vision. I recently met Trischa Warncke at the health food store. She just delivered her second child. I am enclosing a photo from the Bad Wildunger Anzeiger.

The photo showed Trischa with husband and baby at the annual flower parade. She had been Hardy's first love. The first real kiss of his life in Warncke's party room in the basement. She still looked good, unlike Tommy Köhler, who already had a bald patch.

Trischa always asks for you, and when I told her you are in America, she was shocked. What drove you there, we all wonder, Holger? You could have had it all right here.

Hardy took a sip of Puerto Rican rum. Tammy had traded the emergency food stamps for booze.

Well, I have gotten used to you being somewhat different by now. But where did you get it from? Not from me and certainly not from daddy. Anyway, we all greet you warmly and send you our love. Hugs and kisses, mom.

P.S.: Please be careful. I have sent a bit of money through the same route as last time. Daddy mustn't know it. And one more thing: A short while ago Farben Winkler had an opening for a well-paid job in sales. Since I go bowling with them, you could have started immediately, but now the position is filled of course.

Hardy neatly folded the letter and put it in the back pocket of his pants. He was surprised that his mother did not relate to his postcard. Probably she had not received it yet.

He thought about his screenplay. Mexico was almost completely Catholic, and Christmas in Mexico could be incredibly appealing, visually. What if the story was set during the holidays? Feinstein had to steal back the limo during an unbearably hot Mexican Christmas, which stood in sharp contrast to his departure from icy New York. A Christmas lights fade-over would make a very elegant transition from New York to Mexico. Actually, it was awesome, cinematically. Why hadn't he come up with this before? Hardy made a mental note: *Research Christmas in Mexico: customs, processions, songs.*

Tammy leaned over from behind and caressed his chest.

"Do you want me?"

"Now?"

"Sure, why not. Christmas makes me horny."
"Loraine will be here, soon."
"So what?"
She leaned forward, securing herself on the back of a chair, and pulled up her skirt. She wore no panties.

Hardy gently ran his hands over her little ass. Tammy's black and his white skin stood in stark contrast.

While doing it, Tammy's Santa hat bobbed up and down, and the radio played: *Jingle bells, jingle bells, jingle all the way ..., oh what fun it is to ride in a one-horse open sleigh ..., hey ...*
Hardy looked at the crackling fire and the blinking Christmas lights. It was romantic, somehow.

A loud knock on the door: Loraine.

"Don't stop, now," Tammy whispered. "I'm almost there!"
Loraine knocked on the door again. "Hey, what's up, it's me!"
Tammy cursed. "Damn, she always shows up at the wrong time." She pushed Hardy back and pulled down her dress.

"Why did it take so long to open the door?"
"We were in the living room." Tammy straightened her Santa hat.
Loraine put the duck on the table. It was wrapped in tinfoil. She had brought Hakeem along. Although only fourteen, he smoked.

"Okay, let's eat." Loraine divided the duck and distributed the pieces. The meat was somewhat dry.

A knock on the door.

Tammy went to the peephole. "Oh God!"
"Who is it?" asked Loraine.
"Earl."
Loraine screamed. "Don't let him in. I don't want to see him.
Earl was Hakeem's father. He knocked again.
"I am leaving if you let him in. He's the biggest jerk ever. I don't want to see him."

Tammy let him in.

Earl was all smiles. His flat cap sat askew. One of his canines was made of gold and blinked in the light.
"Hi, dad," said Hakeem subdued.
"I don't want to see you any more," Loraine screamed. "When will you ever get it?" She threw a fork at him, but he artfully dodged it.
Earl had brought a large, elongated package and a small square package. He put the presents under the tree and sat down.
Earl looked fine. His dark brown skin had a soft shine, and several rings adorned his slender fingers. He was past fifty but looked younger.
"Do you want a piece of duck?" Tammy asked.
"He's not getting anything — that's my duck." Loraine threw a napkin on her plate and left the room.

The burning scrap wood crackled in the fireplace.

Earl devoured a piece of duck. "Delicious. Well, maybe just a little dry."

Omar lit a smoke. "Okay, when will do the thing with the presents? My homies are waiting for me."

Earl handed over the big package, and Hakeem unwrapped it: a semi-acoustic electrical guitar. Used but in good condition.

Hardy hadn't touched a guitar in years. With his band back in Berlin he had played covers and a few compositions of his own. A wild time with booze galore, groupies, and all the trimmings. But there had been too many similar bands. T.T. Embargo didn't really have a distinctive style, and they ended up disbanding.

Hakeem strummed on the guitar but could not play. Earl took over and hammered out a Christmas song. His fingers wandered elegantly over the fret board as he sang: *It's Christmas ..., a merry, jolly Christmas ...*

Tammy and Loraine came back into the living room. Loraine had tear-stained eyes. "Stop the damn music. It's a nice song, but it won't work this time. How about paying your damn alimony arrears?"

Earl slid the small package across the table. "Don't you want to open your present?"

"I want no presents from you," Loraine said. "You really got some nerve showing up here."

Tammy took the package and opened it: a green, oval stone.

"A moonstone from Sri Lanka," Earl said. "A magical energy stone — it heals everything."

"Bullshit. The stone is bullshit, just like you." Loraine brought it to her forehead, then close to her heart. "This thing doesn't do shit. I am feeling just as bad as before. But thanks anyway."
She hugged Earl, and his flat cap fell to the ground.

Tammy climbed on top of her chair and whispered: "Silent Night ...!" She started singing:

Si-i-lent niiiight, ho-ho-ly niiight, all is calm ... all is bright ...

It was magical. Tammy's angelic voice was as soft as silk. Hardy had tears in his eyes, and Loraine and Hakeem were close to crying as well. Earl played some subtle chords on the guitar, which added to the beauty of the song.

... round yon virgin, mother and child ... Holy infant so tender and mild ...

Tammy slowly sang louder and ended in a crescendo:

Slee-eep in heavenly peeeace ..., sle-eep in heaaaavenly peaaaace ...

Hardy was floored. He had to put the song in the script! But with a twist, naturally. Wouldn't it be most interesting if crime boss Lugo, of all people, sang the song with an angelic voice?
Hardy made a mental note. *Research Spanish lyrics for "Silent Night."*

Hakeem wiped tears from his eyes. "My homies are waiting, mommy. Can I go now?"
"Okay, get lost."

He grabbed his guitar and disappeared.

11.
CODENAME *PAPILLON*

Danny Moran brushed a lock of hair from his forehead, and grinned. "First rule: Cool, calm and collected. Second rule: We have to be really fast anyway. Third: Nothing, absolutely nothing must leak to the outside, but that's obvious anyway, after all we are all professionals. Any questions, I'm sitting over there." Danny pointed to a desk on the opposite side of the room. Moran was in his forties, had acne scars, and wore an old-fashioned tweed suit.

After passing the agency's test on his second try, Hardy had been sent to Harper & Morris, an international law firm. The project bore the code name *Papillon* and was strictly confidential. Perhaps that's why they had moved it to the deep reaches of the basement. Twenty translators were sitting at workstations, arranged in a square, so they could all see each other.

Hardy's first document was a German email from a Swiss department head. Dr. Schürli suffered from digestion problems and asked a colleague for a good laxative. Hardy thought for a moment and then entered his summary: *Private matter — digestive problems.*

He flipped through the oncoming docs: pages seven and nine of a contract, a spreadsheet with historical exchange rates, a presentation regarding feldspars extraction, and an email regarding a fishing trip near Vancouver. It was a hodgepodge of paper that made little sense.

"Hm, how would you handle this one?" Hardy's neighbor showed him a letter. "I really don't get what the guy wants to say: bauxite, aluminum, okay ..., but I have the feeling that they communicate in a kind of code." He looked over his glasses at Hardy. "How can I summarize something that I don't understand?"
The other translators also had difficulties and started whispering to each other.

Hardy coughed. The air was incredibly dry.

His neighbor stretched out his hand: "Rainer from Munich."
"Steve," Hardy said.
"Steve or Stefan?"
"Steve."
"Ah, you're American, then," Rainer said. "I would have thought you're German, actually."
Rainer was half bald, wore horn-rimmed glasses, and had a slight gap between his upper front teeth.

Hardy preferred to leave his background in the dark. Steven C. Cornfield had German ancestors and was brought up partially in Germany. That had to suffice.

Danny came back, handing out vouchers for lunch.

"Hah, free lunch," Rainer said and put the voucher in his shirt pocket. "Not too bad. I am starting to like it here."

Hardy worked his way through endless emails. Most had something to do with aluminum production and how the company could increase efficiency.

Finally, it was lunch time. Hardy and Rainer took the elevator to the 40th floor.

The cafeteria had huge windows in all directions, overlooking the entire city. The interior was all white and shiny. The sole decoration: large plants in terracotta pots and an oversized photo of a bear catching a salmon.

Despite the Christmas season, the cafeteria was crowded. Most of the lawyers were Jewish. The kitchen was closed, though, and only sandwiches were available.
After just one bite, Rainer pulled his sandwich apart.
"I think this is supposed to be chicken breast, but it's appallingly dry."
"Mine too," Hardy said.
"Can only be saved with ketchup. If at all."
Rainer squirted a good load of ketchup into the sandwich and took a bite. "Okay, now it's bearable but just barely. Where the hell did they find that chicken, and who prepared it?"

Hardy looked at his watch and went to the bathroom. The job messed up his writing schedule. If he did not set aside any free moment, he wouldn't be able to complete the scenes on time for *The Kalashnikov Concert*.

He sat on the toilet lid, pulled out his notepad and worked on the Christmas scene with Lugo.

12.
FIRE!

"Stay clear — you can't get in here!" A cop was blocking Hardy's way. "Can't you see there's a fire?"
The windows of Tammy's apartment were smoldering black holes. Three fire trucks and an ambulance stood in front of the house, lights flashing.
The block was crowded with onlookers. Several people gawked out the housing projects across the street.

The ambulance drove off, its siren wailing.

Bill sat on the roadside on an upturned crate, his face buried in his hands. Beside him lay a few belongings and half-burnt canvases. "It's all over," Bill said. "I'm done."

"Where's Tammy?"

Bill pointed toward the ambulance.
"What happened?" Hardy asked.
"I don't know. She probably cooked again."
"Did you smell anything?"
"Wasn't home. When I arrived, it was all up in flames."
Hardy ran toward 14th Street. It had become warmer, and the snow had turned into dirty slush. Ice water slowly seeped through his shoes.

"Where's the emergency room?"
The receptionist of the hospital pointed behind her. "But you can't just walk in, sir. What is this about?"
"My girlfriend. The fire on East 2nd Street. Can I see her?"
"Not today. Come back tomorrow."

Hardy stood in front of the hospital. Traffic on 14th Street had come to a complete standstill. Headlights pierced through clouds of exhaust fumes. It was odd, but just a few yards away stood a salvation army band with a choir, singing: *I serve a risen Savior, I see his loving care ..., and though my heart grows weary, I never will despair ...*
It seemed like it was the exact same band he had seen in midtown with Tammy. Was this a coincidence or were they following him around?

Hardy pulled up the collar of his coat and walked to Avenue B.

"It had to come to this one day, it was obvious!" Loraine gave him a blanket, a pillow, and a bedding sheet. "But it seems she was lucky again, somehow she's always lucky. At home we called her *the princess*. She was daddy's favorite."
Loraine seemed strangely cold, as if she was hardly interested in her sister's fate. "You don't really know her. You have no idea what I've been through with her."

Loraine's room was decorated with pictures of African warriors and a black Madonna with a golden halo.

Hakeem had connected the electric guitar to his stereo and fiddled around in his room. It sounded terrible.

Kristen stood in the door, holding an envelope. As always, she looked frail. Her hair was greasy. "Here's the rent. Sorry for the delay."

Hardy made his bed on the couch. Since the incident with the burned rice he wore all important documents on his body, including the flash drive with his screenplay. His computer was gone now, but the piece of junk was no good anyway. He would try to secretly write in the office.

Loraine lay on her bed, watching a black sitcom with an annoying laugh track. She wore her red bathrobe and the red socks.

Hardy's couch stood close to the bed. The room was bedroom and living room at once.

Loraine giggled along with the sitcom, but Hardy didn't find it funny. Her bathrobe slipped, revealing her thigh, and she quickly covered herself.

"Want to join me on the bed? It's better for watching TV."

Lying beside Loraine, Hardy noticed a large mirror on the ceiling. For a split second they looked at each other in the reflection.

The star of the sitcom tried to undress his girlfriend on the couch but did everything wrong and destroyed a flower vase. Loraine laughed, and her big breasts wobbled. Her nipples were discernable even under the coarse fabric of the bath robe. Hardy imagined what it would be like to suck those long nipples. The thought

66

turned him on, and a massive erection bulged under his pants.

Hakeem still fiddled around with his guitar, as Kristen listened to Indian sitar music in her room.

Hardy felt that Loraine watched him through the mirror. Had she noticed his erection? Certainly.
She switched off the TV and turned her back on him. "Good night!"
Hardy's erection remained. But it was unthinkable to touch Loraine under the circumstances — he just couldn't do it.
He lay down on the couch, turning against the wall. He couldn't stop thinking about Loraine's breasts, and his erection just wouldn't go away. But if he masturbated, Loraine would surely notice. He started counting sheep and slowly drifted away ...

Hardy is wandering through the rural South: birds chirping, butterflies fluttering from flower to flower, small fish cavorting in a crystal-clear creek. It is unbearably hot, and he jumps into the cool water of the creek.
He discovers a black woman downstream washing clothes. Her top is wet and shows two enormous breasts with protruding nipples. It is Loraine.
She spots him, and he says softly: "Don't be frightened, my black pearl, I am the forest spirit and will bring you bliss ..."
"Bliss," Loraine says. "What kind of bliss?"
Hardy swims on his back, and his enormous erection sticks out of the water.

Loraine scratches her head. "Bliss is a WHITE COCK?"
"It's my magic stick. It'll make you happy. Come on in!"
Loraine looks around. No one in sight. She slips into the creek, and both frolic in the lukewarm water. Hardy indulges in Loraine's breasts and Loraine plays with the magic stick until it erupts.

13.
NEW ENGLAND CLAM CHOWDER

Hardy coughed. The air was terribly dry in the basement of Harper & Morris, and his throat itched. He sucked cough drops. It was the only thing that helped. The others also coughed occasionally.

Rainer typed a summary, and his glasses slightly slipped down his nose. He was incredibly fast and hit the keys as if he was playing the piano.

Rainer had studied philosophy in Munich, driving a cab on the side to make ends meet. At a friend's party he had met Linda, an American photographer and visual artist ten years his senior. The two had married, and Rainer was a proud holder of a green card.

Hardy kept thinking about his dream with Loraine. Never before had he ejaculated in his sleep. Was it like real sex? Not quite but close.

"Okay, folks." Danny held out a stack of documents. "I need a few candidates for full translations. No summaries but full-fledged translations, folks. The firm pays double time, but you need to stay as long as it takes."

69

Rainer grinned. "Double time ... I'm starting to like it here." He coughed. "If only the damn air was not so dry."

Hardy translated an email from department head Dr. Schürli to his colleague Dr. Landeck. Schürli appreciated the great time in Vancouver and the fishing trip. Then he got to the point: The competition planned a coup, trying to take over the South American market.

Eventually, after what seemed like an eternity, it was lunchtime.

"Oh, no," Rainer groaned. "Sandwiches again." He pulled one apart. "Chicken breast!"
The kitchen was still closed.
"Okay, I'll try mustard today." Rainer squeezed a good load of mustard into his sandwich and so did Hardy.

It didn't help.

Suddenly, Danny showed up, a laptop and papers under his arm. "Just had a meeting with the emergency team."
He slid a printed email chain across the table. "We need a translation of this one. Perhaps you can split it up, so it's faster."
Rainer frowned. "In the lunch break?"
"It's urgent."

"Okay," Rainer said. "Just one little question: Why do we get the same sandwiches every day?"

Danny nodded. "I know. But in the kitchen almost everybody is Puerto Rican and Catholic. Tomorrow everything should be fine."

Rainer pulled his sandwich apart. "I am not even sure if this is chicken."

"I have an idea," Danny said. "Why don't you start, and I'll get you something yummy. The soup kitchen at the corner serves an exquisite New England Clam Chowder today. How does that sound?"

The email chain revolved around the South American market. Dr. Landeck proposed to make the Brazilians an offer they could not refuse. If that didn't work, the team would have to pull the emergency brake, or they would have to torpedo the Argentines where it hurt the most. The managers' internal communication was odd, but if you were familiar with the matter, you would get the gist of it.

When Danny returned with the chowder, Hardy and Rainer had already translated the email chain. Danny hastily read it. "Wow," he said. "Really, wow!"
He grabbed his laptop and quickly vanished.

The clam chowder came in two large paper cups with packaged crackers on the side. Rainer took a good spoonful but halted. "Hm, funny. It tastes a bit flat. They didn't put any salt in."

The chowder tasted bland indeed.

"I'm not even sure if those little pieces are clams," Hardy said. "They seem more like flower lumps to me." Rainer nodded. "If those are clams, it's definitely a strange breed."

They put the chowder aside and only ate the crackers.

14.
TRANQUILA

Tammy's roommates were an obese woman from the Dominican Republic and a toothless Russian granny. The granny was sleeping, and every time she exhaled, her flabby lips produced a flat whistle.
Tammy had bandages on her lower legs and on her right hand. Otherwise, she looked fine. The cramped room had barely enough space for the three beds. The neon light was harsh and unpleasant.

"What happened, why was there a fire?"
"No idea."
"No idea?"
"When I woke up there were flames all around me, honey, so I ran and got out."
"Did you cook again?"
"No."
"Why the fire, then?"
"Don't know. Maybe it was the Chinaman."

Tammy came closer. "Did you bring me something to drink?"
"Sorry."
"At least give me a kiss."
Hardy gave her a kiss. She smelled of ointment for burns.

Hardy took off his jacket and sat down. They were holding hands.

"So, did you do her?"
"Do who?"
"Don't act stupid. Loraine, of course. You smell of her. She always uses this cheap perfume. And you have it on you."
"I'm sleeping on the couch."
Tammy laughed. "Yeah, sure ... She always tries to steal my men. With Steve she tried too!"
"Steven C. Cornfield?"
"Exactly. God have mercy on his soul, wherever he is now. She shamelessly threw herself at him, whenever I was not around. She simply uses her big boobs in a suggestive way, and most guys fall for it. Don't tell me you haven't noticed her big tits."
"Not directly."

Tammy laughed out loud.

"So did you do her or not?"
"I did not."
"Swear."

Hardy pondered a moment. Wet dreams were no sexual act. Erotic fantasies were just that: fantasies. He was therefore innocent.

Tammy pulled out a flask of rum under her pillow and took a swig. "Want a little bit?"
"Where did you get that?"
"Carmelita has helped me. We're buddies."

Carmelita pulled a chocolate bar from under her pillow. "Want some?"

The door burst open. Carmelita's family. They bantered in Spanish and played *Bachata* on a tape recorder. The Russian granny woke up, looking puzzled.
Tammy waved at her. "Hello Natasha, everything all right?"
The granny nodded.
"She doesn't speak English, but she's cool. Her son will bring me vodka next time."

The tape recorder played "Tranquila" by Luis Vargas. Carmelita's family members started dancing. It was amazing what they were able to pull off on a space that was barely bigger than a quarter.

Natasha clapped along and laughed, exposing her toothless gums.

The song by Vargas gave goose bumps, and the trumpet solo was world class. Somehow the piece transformed the simple hospital room into something noble and beautiful.
The song had to be in Hardy's film. Okay, it was no Mexican song, but it was Spanish and fit into the concept. The song immediately created images in Hardy's head. When Feinstein stole back the limo, the song would be just perfect. Maybe "Tranquila" could even become the film's signature song. Hardy made a mental note: *Check copyrights for "Tranquila."*

"When will you get out?"

"Don't know," Tammy said. "They want to do some tests. Something to do with my heart."

15.
THE NEW YEAR'S ORACLE

December 31, shortly after 8 p.m. Five translators remained at their workstations, Hardy and Rainer among them.

The reduced troops looked tired and worn.

"I think I can dismiss you, now," Danny said. "As you know, today is our last day. The deadline is at midnight, and after that it's in the hands of the authorities."
Hardy did not know what this meant since nobody had ever filled them in about the details.

The translators packed up their things, and Rainer wrote down his number. "Let's keep in touch." He pulled a few small lead bars from his pocket. "Bought them in Chinatown. I've got plenty. Want two?"
Hardy put the bars in his pocket. He had always liked lead casting.

Rainer struck his forehead. "Ah, I almost forgot ..." He took a note from his wallet. "Got it from Linda. She designed an album cover for the guys."

The note read: *BYRDSEED, 242 W 30 St, 15th floor.*

"It's a room in a loft. Just for one person and only on a temporary basis, but maybe it helps you out."
"How much?"
"Five hundred, I think."

Hardy stood in front of the law firm, waiting for a cab. The Financial District was deserted, and a freezing wind blew through the high-rise canyons.
Suddenly, Hardy remembered his flash drive. He searched his briefcase and pockets but couldn't find it. He had left it in the office computer!

He hurried back into the building. A guard sat at the darkened lobby, watching TV.
"Need to get back in real quick."
"Where's your keycard?"
"Returned it. The project is over."
"Then I can't let you in."
"Why not? I just walked out."
"Nobody gets in without a card."

It was a disaster. Undoubtedly, someone would discover the flash drive, exposing Hardy's fraudulent use of company time. But even worse: The device contained the only copy of his script. He cursed himself for not having made a backup.
"Why don't we go in together?"
"Can't leave my post."

Hardy pulled a twenty out of his pocket. "I left my car keys on the desk. Couldn't we just pretend that I didn't step out yet? I'll just pass behind your chair, and nobody will ever know."

The guard pocketed the bill. "If you take more than five minutes, I will sound the alarm."

Hardy hurried down to the deserted basement. There was only emergency lighting by now. Suddenly, he heard a loud snoring noise. Danny Moran was still at his post! He had fallen asleep at his desk with his head tipped over on a stack of documents.

Hardy tiptoed up to his workstation and quickly pulled the flash drive.

Back on the street, Hardy was in luck and found an empty cab. Twenty minutes later he arrived on the Lower East Side, eager to take a drink.

"Lead casting?" Loraine asked. "I've never heard about this. How does it work?"

"The lead is heated and then poured into water," Hardy said. "Kind of an oracle."

They sat in Loraine's living room, occasionally glancing at the TV, which showed a program about recently deceased celebrities.

Loraine wore a small silver cylinder and her wide African robe. Kristen sported a golden face mask, and Hakeem had a flashing string of lights in his dreadlocks, powered by a battery hidden in his shirt pocket. He had wanted to spend the night with his buddies, but Loraine did not allow it.

Hardy cut the two lead bars with a knife, so each had their own piece. Using a spoon, they heated the lead over a candle and dropped it into a bowl of water.

Kristen's oracle looked like a crooked heart, Hakeem had something like a fish, and Loraine had a spider.

79

Hardy's piece was a strange, elongated block that ended in a sphere.

"Yikes, I have a spider," Loraine screamed. "I hate spiders." She dropped the piece on the ground.
Hardy picked it up and turned the spider around. "Now it's a fruit bowl."
"True, true!" Kristen clapped her hands excitedly. "It's a fruit bowl, it's a fruit bowl."
"Yes, well, okay," Loraine said. "And what does it mean?"
"It probably means that it will be a fertile year for you."

"Fertile? You mean I'm getting pregnant again?"

"It could also be a financial gain. Or a job."
"Bullshit," Loraine said. "I've been out of work for three years and never won anything." She took the piece out of Hardy's hand. "But okay, better than a spider."
"And me?" Kristen held out her piece.
"It's a heart," Hardy said.

"A heart, really?"

"Sure, it's a freakin' heart," Loraine said. "And what does it mean? It means, that a freakin' prince on a freakin' white horse will appear and do you real good. That's what it means."
Kristen frowned. "This is not fair. Why do you have to drag everything in the dirt?"
"Okay, well, sorry," Loraine said. "We all need a little love, that's right. Agreed. Check. What does Hakeem have? I would say he has a fish."

"Yes," said Hakeem. "It's clearly a fish, but what does it mean?"

"A fish means luck," Hardy said. "And spiritual development."

"Spiritual development is not really that big of a deal for me," said Hakeem. "The most important thing would be the final exam. Does it mean I will pass?"

"Could be," Hardy said. "Yes, absolutely."

"Bullshit," Loraine said. "He will only pass if he sits down on his ass and studies, instead of smoking pot in the park with his buddies."

Loraine took a sip of champagne. "Okay, we're done with the fish. Fish means, sit down on your ass and study. Check. Now only one question remains: What did Hardy get? I would say it's a vibrator."

Suddenly, all were silent. On TV they played a medley of the hits of the year.

"What's the matter with you today, mom?" Hakeem said. "Everything okay?"

Loraine had tears in her eyes. "Yes, damn it. Everything okay, everything fine, everything perfect." She sobbed and blew her nose. Hakeem hugged her. It seemed as if the lights blinked faster in his dreadlocks. "Calm down, mom. It's all good."

Loraine pulled away from him. "Stop it. Can't I be a little sentimental on New Year's, damn it?"

Kristen looked at Hardy's lead piece. "I think it looks like an Oscar."

"True," Hakeem said. "It means that Hardy will win an Oscar."

Hardy took a sip of champagne. The stuff was way too sweet. He wasn't really keen on Hollywood, but that was hard to explain, so he kept it to himself.

The phone rang.

It was Tammy.

Loraine put her on speaker.
"Hi there. Just wanted to let you know that I'm still alive."
"Obviously," Loraine moaned. "Congratulations!"
"Thank you for your kind words, my dear sister. That's exactly what I need right now. Thank you."
"Okay," Loraine said. "What else is new?"
"Is Hardy there?"
"Yes, I'm here," Hardy said.
"I begged them to let me out, honey, but they won't let me go."
"Ah, what a pity ..." Loraine said.
"You can keep your venom to yourself," Tammy screamed. "It's not my fault that your life is a mess."
Loraine laughed. "Great. Thank you. Happy New Year to you too, and over." She hung up and unplugged the cord. "It's my phone and I just don't feel like talking to her, it's as simple as that."
Hardy felt bad for Tammy, but who knew what had been going on between the two over the years. Tammy wasn't easy to deal with but neither was Loraine.
 The countdown for New Year's started on television, and the Times Square ball slid down: *Five, four, three, two, one ...*

Loraine and Hardy hugged. "Sorry that I have called your Oscar a vibrator. It's an Oscar, and I wish you a happy New Year."

They held each other tight. Hardy could feel Loraine's big breasts on his chest. He was immediately turned on and felt an erection building up.

Hakeem stood beside them. "Where's daddy? Didn't he want to come?"

"Where should he be?" Loraine said gruffly. "In some whorehouse, of course."

Loraine and Hardy separated.

Kristen held out her glass. "Happy New Year!" She still wore the golden mask. Hardy and Kristen hugged. She was very skinny and could have fit into Loraine more than twice.

"Do you really think that my piece is a heart?"

Hardy nodded, and she gave him a gentle kiss on the cheek.

Shortly after midnight they were all in bed. Hardy lay on his couch, staring at the ceiling, unable to sleep. The room had no curtains, and street lights pierced through the windows. Hardy noticed that Loraine lay on her side, looking at him.

He was immediately rock hard again. Did she know that he had erotic fantasies about her? She almost certainly did. But why didn't she say anything, why didn't she give him a sign?

Hardy wondered if he should just climb into her bed and kiss her. Would she reject him, or would she willingly succumb? He already had one leg dangling out from the couch but couldn't drum up the courage and pulled it back. It was too risky and bound to be a disaster if they were discovered. Anything sexual between Hardy and Loraine was absolutely taboo. But that made it even more tempting. Loraine was the forbidden fruit, and he longed to release his tension between her big breasts. He was almost sure that she wanted it as well.

A police siren wailed in the distance.

"Good night," Loraine said and turned her back.

Hardy bit his lower lip. He had missed the right moment, and now it was too late. But maybe it was better this way.

"Good night," he mumbled and turned against the wall.

16.
BYRDSEED

The bell did not work, and Hardy knocked on Byrdseed's massive wooden door. No answer.
He already wanted to leave when the door opened: Carl — a skinny guy with glasses who resembled Lou Reed.

The loft was run-down. The gray paint on the bare concrete floor had chipped off in places, and the metal windowpanes, also painted in gray, were rusty. Musical instruments stood around: guitars, keyboards, an ancient zither, drums of various sizes, a saxophone, and a trumpet.

Chris sat at a huge mixing panel and fiddled with the buttons. He wore a plaid shirt and had his blond hair tucked behind his ears. It was odd: He resembled Kurt Cobain. He even had a cleft chin. Apparently, Byrdseed was a fusion of Lou Reed and Kurt Cobain. An interesting and explosive mix.
In a soundproof booth a guy played a conga drum, perspiring heavily. He was bare-chested and very hairy, with tufts of hair even sprouting from his shoulders.

The booth door burst open, and the guy stumbled out, wearing only a pair of underpants. "Is unbearable in this

85

here sauna," he said with a heavy accent. "Why must be so hot?"

"This is Mammoth," Chris said. "The best conga player of Azerbaijan."

The radiators in the loft could not be regulated and were boiling hot. Although it was bitterly cold outside, Byrdseed had left the windows slightly open to adjust the temperature. The soundproof booth obviously could have no open windows, so it heated up like a sauna.

"Why you not call plumber and cut heating behind booth?" Mammoth said. "I no understand."

"Because we like it this way," Chris said. "When we have the background girls here, they sing in bikinis, which is really good for the vibe. And Carl's guitar solos sound much crisper when he wears Speedos."

Mammoth shook his head. "You kidding, man, yes ...?"

Carl led Hardy into a small room with three windows.
"This is it."

Similar to the sound cabin, they had built an extra room with drywall at the other end of the loft. It was warm and drafty at once. The windows were sealed with clear plastic foil that was ripped open in places. A dingy mattress lay on the floor, and a Byrdseed poster adorned the wall. A corner of the poster had loosened and bobbed in the draft.

"And here's the best part," Carl said. "Come here!" He waved him over.

The room had a view on the Empire State Building. But only if you stood real close to the window.

"It's nobody's business that you also sleep here," Carl said. "You work with us, and that's it. But one thing's essential: Absolutely no visitors."

"No visitors? Why?"

"Several things have disappeared in the past, and we can't have that."

Hardy nodded. "Okay. No visitors. Could I stay here right away? It's kind of cramped where I'm crashing."

"Sure. Just put down the five hundred, and you're in."

Hardy counted out the money, and Carl slid the notes into his shirt pocket.

The loft was on the top floor of a commercial building. At 9:30 p.m. the super signed off, and officially, nobody was allowed to live there. A while ago, someone had tried to break in, and that's why Byrdseed wanted somebody to stay there at night.

Triggered by Carl's uncanny resemblance, Hardy heard the hook line of Lou Reed's hit in his inner ear: *Hey babe, take a walk on the wild side ..., she said, hey, honey, take a walk on the wild side ...*

It was amazing what you could achieve with only one song. Lou Reed was that one song, and it had made him world famous.

"You know you look like Lou Reed, right?"

"No, no," Carl said. "You got that wrong. He used to look like me when he was young, but that was way back in the seventies. He does not look like that any more. Let's put it this way: He would wish that he could still look like me but he doesn't."

Hardy nodded. "What about Chris? He looks like Kurt Cobain."

"That's a totally different story," Carl said. "Cobain is dead of course, and Chris never looked this way. He isn't even a natural blonde. He's just going for that look because chicks dig it. He tried it, it worked, and now he sticks with it. That's the deal."

"So you're a natural, and he's a fake?"

"Everybody's got to work with what he's got," Carl said. "And if you need to give it a little twist, give it a little twist. That's the way I see it."

Carl pulled a pillow and a blanket from a cluttered shelf. "You can use this," he said. "It can get quite cold in here at night."

Hardy spotted an outdated laptop on the shelf. "Does it work?"

"Well, the battery is gone, and it crashes sometimes. But if you save fast enough ..."

The laptop was quite heavy. "It smells a bit funny. It smells of cat."

"My girlfriend used it for a while, and I think her cat pissed on it, but it works."

"How much?"

"One hundred, and it's yours."

Hardy pulled out two fifties and Carl slid them in his shirt pocket.

Hardy improvised a table with plastic boxes and typed up scenes he had written by hand. Finally, he would get something done. It was impossible to work in Loraine's place. He had no privacy there, and the erotic tension threw him off track.

The smell of the laptop was annoying. Triggered by the stench, Hardy constantly had cats on his mind. He made a mental note: *Get Q-tips and chlorine.*

Hardy read through his new scenes. Some parts appeared shallow, and he deleted them. The text got better, but something was missing. He just didn't know what.

He stood up and stretched out. The loose corner of the Byrdseed poster bugged him. The pin had cut through the paper, so he pulled it from the wall and pressed it into another spot.

The poster was an image of the three wise monkeys, just that here, the monkeys had lifted their hands and were all eyes and ears. Caption: *See — Hear — Speak! — BYRDSEED!*

The fine print on the bottom revealed that Linda McMillan, Rainer's wife, had designed the poster.

The massive front door slammed shut. The musicians had left.

Hardy dozed off on the mattress but soon woke up since it had become very cold. The heating had been turned off. He went to the shelf, pulling out everything resembling a blanket.

The building narrowed upward, similar to a castle, and the wind violently blew around the edges. The entire house seemed to groan and crack, almost like a living being.

It was spooky.

Hardy turned on all the lights and blocked the entrance door with a large instrument case. He curled up in the fetal position and finally fell asleep again.

A dense and dark forest. Lightning and roaring thunder. Hardy drives an old Cadillac through the pouring rain. Suddenly, the car breaks down. Hardy tries to fix it but to no avail. He is drenched in rain and notices lights in the distance.

Hardy arrives at an old, dimly lit castle and knocks on the door which opens with a loud squeak. In the doorframe: Carl with outstretched arms, dressed as FRANK N. FURTER. Music sets in, and he starts singing: I'M JUST A SWEET TRANSVESTITE ...

Startled, Hardy wants to turn back, but right behind him stands Kurt Cobain, dressed as a cheerleader. Kurt pushes him, and Hardy falls onto the stone floor of the castle's entrance hall.

A huge big band is scattered around the room: all men, dressed as women. There's Bill, dressed as Whitney Houston, Earl as Tina Turner and a male salvation army choir wearing women's uniforms and heavy makeup. They all dance, singing: I'M JUST A SWEET TRANSVESTITE, FROM TRANSSEXUAL ..., TRANSYLVANIA ...

They pull Hardy from the floor, dance around him, and rip off his clothes, piece by piece. At once, he finds himself naked, tied to a wooden chair. While the cheerleader puts makeup on Hardy's face, Whitney Houston and Tina Turner weave his hair into pigtails.

Suddenly, FRANK N. FURTER tips the chair forward, so Hardy is now on all fours but still firmly tied up. To his horror, he realizes that his chair is cut out like a toilet seat, leaving his bare-naked butt sticking out. Looking back, he sees FRANK N. FURTER pulling his lace panties aside, revealing an enormous hard on. Smilingly, the transvestite bends over Hardy, ready to penetrate ...

Screaming in horror, Hardy woke up. He gasped for air and needed a moment to realize where he was. He checked his backside and was relieved to find, that everything seemed to be intact, and that nobody had actually penetrated him.
His vivid imagination was a blessing and a curse at the same time.

17.
CECI N'EST PAS UNE PIPE!

The bartender poured whiskey over the ice cubes in Hardy's glass. The lights were pleasantly dimmed in the bar of the Peninsula Hotel. The atmosphere was quiet and conservative. And that's exactly what Hardy needed right now.

He had bought a new outfit at a discount outlet. A dark blue dovetail suit and a quality shirt: snowy white, 800-thread count Egyptian cotton. He left three buttons undone to give a hint of his manly chest. His medium-length hair was cut in the style of the three musketeers, his beard trimmed to a subtle goatee. It was amazing what you got for ten bucks at the huge barber shop on Astor Place. Sure, you had to stand in line for a while, but it was well worth the wait.
Hardy's style was *Business Cool* and fit anywhere. In the office, at the Peninsula, on Madison Avenue. It was formally correct but still cool and on par with De Niro's style, just that De Niro paid a whole lot more for it.

The whiskey warmed Hardy pleasantly from the inside. The atmosphere in the bar was relaxed. Two guys with loosened ties chatted at a coffee table, and an older couple enjoyed some red wine in balloon glasses.

Dean Martin's "That's Amore" played in the background. Hardy liked the guy. He spread a good mood: *... tingelingeling, tingelingeling, and you sing vita bella, hearts will play, tippitippitay, tippitippitay, like a gay tarantella ...*

Hardy pulled out his notepad and wrote on his screenplay. Suddenly, he found himself in a chicken coop in Mexico, where the limo was hidden under a dusty tarpaulin. Maybe "That's Amore" could play in the scene. You wouldn't think of it right away, and it was a little crazy, but it fit somehow. The song was a counterpoint to the shitty chicken coop and therefore provided some comic relief, and it expressed Feinstein's almost erotic relationship with the limo. The song fit. Hardy made a note: *Check rights for "That's Amore."*

He noticed an elegant, mature lady on the other end of the bar, wearing a tight, short dress that showed her slender legs. Her glasses were tinted blue. Precious gems blinked on her earlobes.

"Chin, chin!" The lady drank to Hardy and pointed to the bar stool next to her.
He sat down beside her. She was clearly past forty, but that did not bother him. Her slender legs looked classy in her fine black nylons.
He noticed a handwritten sticker on her dress that read *Jackie*. Why would she wear a name tag?

"What did you scribble into your notebook? Are you a journalist?"
"It's a screenplay."

Jackie nodded slightly bored. "You just write, or also direct?"

"Both."

She took a sip of wine. "What's your name? Something I would know?"

"Hardy von Hachenstein. San Sandoval Newcomer Award."

Jackie pushed her glasses up her nose. "*Ceci n'est pas une pipe!*"

"Pardon?"

"*Ceci n'est pas une pipe!* You don't speak French?"

"Actually I do," Hardy said. "*... mais je ne comprends pas ...*"

She noticed the name tag on her dress and ripped it off. "A stupid salon. Salons are hip again. Totally boring. There is this part where everybody converses in French for half an hour, because it's kind of chic, but nobody can really talk." Jackie laughed. "And neither can I."

The glasses were empty, and the bartender stood before them. "One more round?"

Hardy nodded.

"What's your sign?" Jackie asked.

"My sign?"

"Your Zodiac. What's your sign?"

"Sagittarius."

Jackie listened up. "What date?"

"November 24."

She pulled out a small, tattered book and leafed through it. "November 24," she murmured. "With a little luck, this could still work, I think ... Do you know the time?"

"No."

"The time is important because of the ascendant. Was it in the morning, evening or at night."

Hardy shrugged. "In the morning, I think."

Jackie closed the book. "I need to go wash my hands." She grabbed her purse and went to the bathroom. She really had good legs.

"She's a regular," said the bartender. He was roughly Hardy's age. "Could've banged her by now, I guess, but I'm not really into old tarts. On top of that she's a nut case."

"She has great legs."

"Okay, the legs, but what else?"

"She's in her mid-forties, I guess."

"Not so sure, better pack on a couple more."

18.
WEST END AVENUE

"This is my husband Benny Drexler," Jackie said. "And this is ..." She smirked. "Hardy von Hachenstein, a filmmaker. Or at least, he pretends to be."

Jackie had mentioned nothing about Benny. Hardy had expected a possible sexual adventure, not an annoyed husband.

The apartment on West End Avenue was spacious and furnished in a conservative, baroque style. Above the couch hung an oil painting depicting cherubs dancing around a fountain.

Benny and Hardy shook hands. Drexler had a large bald patch surrounded by a gray tuft of hair. He was tall, thin, and looked frail.

They sat down on the couch. Jackie drank chardonnay and gave Hardy a whiskey. Benny nibbled on a grapefruit juice.

They were an odd couple. She was a *grande dame* with perfectly painted nails and first-class nylons. He was a pullover type with baggy corduroy pants and house slippers. Besides, he was at least seventy.

"Benny is a film and theater critic," Jackie said. "He writes for *The Times*."

Hardy listened up. A review in the *The Times* was like an accolade — it was the ultimate acceptance into the holy grail. It meant that you were an international player, somebody who really counted. And that's exactly what Hardy wanted to be.

Benny took a sip from his grapefruit juice. "Tell me the names of your films. Anything I should know?"
"*Cryptic X*. San Sandoval Newcomer Award."
"A feature?"
"Thirty-seven minutes."
"Ah, then it's only a short ..."
Drexler seemed relieved that Hardy was still at his humble beginnings.
"No, no, it's not a short. It's a short feature."
Hardy hated the word *short*. A short film was a mere joke, a finger exercise. *Cryptic X* on the other hand told a story with complex characters and dramatic twists and turns but without the usual feature length. A regular feature film had to be at least seventy-nine minutes. But the budget had been too small for the regular feature length, and besides that, the story needed exactly thirty-seven minutes to be told and not a minute longer. There was nothing worse than a stretched story.

"I'm working on a road movie," Hardy said. "This time regular feature length."
"Ah, really?" Benny looked skeptical. "Who's the producer?"
"Floyd Burns."
Benny nodded slightly annoyed. "Uh, Floyd Burns, Floyd Burns ..., everybody's talking about Floyd Burns. Okay,

he drew a few lucky numbers recently, but have you ever heard of *Milwaukee Express*?"

"Not really."

"You lucky son of a gun! Thank God this *œuvre* went directly to DVD. I really asked myself if Burns still has all his marbles. It could be possible that he produced this thing without reading the script, though. That would be the only excuse."

"But he also produced *Chicken Nuggets in Flatbush*, and that's a good one!"

"Agreed, young man. *Chicken Nuggets* is a good movie, even if it has weaknesses. At the end, Chicken Nuggets simply puts a gun to his head. And why? Because the screenwriter couldn't come up with a sensible conclusion. Bang, bang, Chicken Nuggets kills himself. No, my friend, this is just too easy. "

"Okay, but what could he have done? There was no way out."

"There's always a way. Why not an open end? Okay, we all know that Chicken Nuggets is in deep doo-doo, and that they will make mincemeat out of him if they catch him. Why don't we cut to a Franciscan monastery in the middle of nowhere? We see twelve monks with hoods from behind, singing. The camera slowly moves around the group, and one of the monks is the grinning Chicken Nuggets. Fadeout and credits."

Hardy laughed. "Not bad, really not bad."

Jackie seemed bored. She grabbed a worn notebook that looked like a diary and scribbled something into it.

"Who plays the lead in your film?" Benny asked.

"Avi Feinstein."

The critic raised his eyebrows. "Hah, Avi Feinstein ... It's really a small world. I just received an invitation from his PR department." He rummaged through a drawer. "Here are the tickets. *The Kalashnikov Concert*."

Hardy pulled his own ticket from his wallet and held it up.

Benny patted him on the shoulder. His mood seemed to have changed. "What was your name again?"

"Hardy."

"No, the last name."

"Von Hachenstein."

"You don't really look German. You don't even have an accent."

Jackie looked up from her diary. "The hair, the mustache ... His style is obviously inspired by the musketeers, which makes you think of France, naturally."

"Hair ...," Benny said. "In the seventies I still had plenty. It went all the way down here." He held his hand at chest level. "Unfortunately, all I have left now is a pigeon's nest."

Benny yawned and got up. "Have to get back to work."

He shuffled into his study, and an electric typewriter began clattering.

"Benny is old school," Jackie said. "At his age he no longer wants to mess with a computer."

She looked into Hardy's eyes through her blue-tinted glasses. It was an intense look that turned him on.

"Oh, damn, I just bought those!" Jackie had discovered a run in her nylons. "Twenty bucks, and I just bought them. Too bad ..."
Jackie slowly ran her hand over her thigh. Obviously, touching her legs aroused her.
"You can touch my legs if you like. Benny doesn't mind." She came closer and whispered, "He ..., we didn't do anything for a long time ... He has diabetes, and, uh ... we're friends."
Hardy let his eyes wander over her long, slender legs.

"Touch them, why don't you touch them?"

"What if Benny comes back?"

The typewriter continued clattering in the background. Jackie rolled her eyes. "I told you. It does not bother him." She dug her long fingernails in her nylons and smiled. "You're afraid of me, right? Most men are."

He put a hand on her knee and slowly slid up her thigh. The fine nylon felt good on her slender legs. He had an erection.

Jackie threw back her head, laughing. "All men are crazy about my legs."
She pushed his hand away. "Enough now. There'll be more next time. I want you to think a little bit about these legs."

19.
INTENSIVE CARE

"No flowers," the nurse said. "There could be insects or bacteria. Leave them here. We'll put them in the waiting area."

Tammy had been put up in a sterile single room. The only decoration was a calendar with a photo of traditional Asian dancers and the caption *Visit Singapore!*
Tammy had an IV line in her arm and looked pale. "It's about time," she said. "I thought you had abandoned me."
"Why are you in the ICU?"
"Don't know. I collapsed while walking in the yard. They say it was some kind of heart attack, but I think they just want to scare me."
She turned on a small transistor radio. "Someone forgot it here, and the nurse gave it to me." She listened to the oldie channel.

"I want to get out of here, Hardy, I can't take it any longer. One more week and I'll go mad. If I wouldn't constantly feel dizzy, I'd be long gone. — Did you bring me anything?"
"Flowers."

"Where are they?"

"In the waiting room. Not allowed in here."

"Did you bring something to drink by any chance?"

Hardy shook his head.

Tammy moaned. "Uh, freakin' flowers ... Screw the flowers, I need something to drink. Now that they put me up in a single room, it's difficult."

She pulled a Bible out of the nightstand and opened it. It was a dummy with a cavity and had a flask with vodka inside. She took a short sip and tucked the Bible back into the nightstand.

"You're still staying with Loraine?"

"Found something on my own. A small room in a loft."

"The question is still: Did you do her?"

"I didn't."

"Don't believe you."

"Why should I have moved, then?"

"That doesn't mean anything. If you had done it with her, that would kill everything in me. She always tries to steal my guys with her big tits."

Tammy slid her hand through his hair. "You look good with the new haircut. Almost like a musketeer ... Why don't you give me a kiss?"

They kissed. She smelled of disinfectant soap.

Hardy thought of Jackie. Had it been morally okay, playing around with her while Tammy was in the hospital? Probably not. Had he planned it? No. It had just happened, and in principle nothing serious had occurred. Moreover, Tammy was not a saint. When she hung out in bars, she flirted openly with men who bought her drinks.

A nurse stood in the doorway and tapped her watch. "Visiting hours are over."

20.
THE KALASHNIKOV CONCERT

Avi Feinstein, as Mario Cantagalo, called the waiter. "*Sambuca*, please!"

The curtain fell, and wild applause broke out. The play was a disappointment. After a few original scenes in the first act, the story fell apart, and the characters were no longer credible. Mario Cantagalo eliminated all his opponents one by one and drank, as soon as he got the news of a successful kill, a *sambuca*.

Hardy could not understand why the audience laughed at scenes that were not really funny. He suspected *claqueurs* in the audience.

Anyway, Avi Feinstein commanded a stage presence and looked younger in person. It helped that Hardy had seen him in the flesh.

The theater was larger than Hardy had expected. It seated more than five hundred people. He had looked out for Francisco, Benny and Jackie but had not seen them in the crowd trying to get in. A lot of pushing and shoving had occurred in the lobby. The PR department had given out too many complimentary tickets, which led to a small riot once all seats were taken. Hardy had been lucky to get in.

After the final curtain the masses trotted to the exit. Hardy pushed in the opposite direction to the green room.

A champagne party was being thrown backstage.

A security guard stopped Hardy at the door.
"Invitation?"
"I am a friend of Francisco Villanueva's."
"Who?"
"Francisco Villanueva."
The security guard was a muscular black guy with sunglasses and a walkie-talkie. Next to him stood a receptionist with a clipboard. "Villanueva is on the list but hasn't checked in yet. Can't let you in if he's not here."
Several people with invitations pushed Hardy to the side. He stood on tiptoe to find Francisco somewhere in the crowd. Maybe he had gotten in without being checked off the list.

Hardy spotted Benny and Jackie. She was drinking champagne, and he was sipping an orange juice. Hardy signaled at them, but they didn't notice him.

More and more people tried to get in with Hardy in the way.

"Look, you can't stay here, okay?"
"I know Benny Drexler over there," Hardy said. "The one with the gray tuft of hair."
"Drexler from *The Times*?"
Hardy felt that Benny's name carried weight.

"Wait a moment." The receptionist walked over to Benny, pointing to Hardy.

Hardy raised his arm.

Benny held a hand over his eyes and shrugged. It seemed he didn't recognize the filmmaker. Or maybe he didn't want to.
But Jackie had noticed Hardy. The security guard let him through.

Jackie left Drexler standing in the crowd.
"Why didn't you call?" she asked as she approached Hardy.
"I did. Always the machine."
"Why didn't you leave a message?"
"I did." He pulled a cell phone from his pocket. "I even left my number."
Hardy had bought the phone recently. When submitting his scenes to Feinstein he just needed to have a cell number. He got a bulky pre-paid device, the cheapest available.
"Funny, but there was no message ... The old man must have erased it. Certainly wouldn't be the first time."

Benny came up to them. Naturally, he was not thrilled to see Hardy and gave him an ice-cold "Hello!" while raising his juice.

A few steps away Avi Feinstein, sitting on an elevated throne-like chair, was being mobbed by fans. Hardy pulled out his script, but the throng blocked his path to the star.

A photographer, taking a few shots of Benny and Jackie arm in arm, motioned to Hardy to get out of the picture.

It was a shoot for a tabloid. Tomorrow they would probably show a photo with the caption: *Benny Drexler and Wife at The Kalashnikov Concert.*

A journalist from the tabloid asked Benny a few questions, and Jackie stood next to Hardy again. He held up his script. "How can I get this to Feinstein?"

Jackie pointed to a short, chubby woman with glasses who nibbled on a canapé. "That's his assistant. Mindy Goldfarb."

Hardy approached her and introduced himself as Francisco's friend. Mindy seemed exhausted, as she wiped her mouth. "Ah, Francisco," she said. "Yes, we invited him, but it seems he couldn't make it."

"We have a project for Avi." Hardy pointed to his manuscript. "The lead in a feature. I need to speak with him personally."

Two waiters offered drinks and canapés on silver trays. Mindy grabbed two canapés, and Hardy took a glass of champagne.

Avi was still surrounded by a trove of admirers signing autographs.

"Well, just look what's going on here," Mindy said, chewing. "It certainly will be difficult today."

21.
REUNION WITH AN OLD FRIEND

"Ah, this feels great." Benny leaned back in his armchair. "Standing around in this party bustle is not really my favorite sport."
They were sitting in a Cuban restaurant opposite the theater. Benny wanted to go straight home, but Jackie persuaded him to have a drink.

Hardy had Mindy's business card in his pocket. She had accepted the manuscript and promised to pass it on.

Benny massaged his temples. "Since you seem to be a writer," he said wearily turning to Hardy. "How did you like the play? An honest opinion, please."
It was clear that Drexler wanted to put him in a spot in front of Jackie.

The filmmaker took a sip of whiskey. "Some original ideas in the first act, but after that the plot falls apart. Cantagalo's killing spree is not enough to keep the story going."

Hardy shook his glass, so the ice cubes twirled around. He took another sip.

"Had his mother convinced him to abandon the drug trade since her best friend's son had died from an overdose, the story would have regained steam. Then Cantagalo himself would have landed on the hit list."

Benny listened up. "... not a bad idea." He quickly wrote something in his notebook.

Jackie drank chardonnay, as usual. She suddenly played footsie with Hardy under the table.

"There was too much laughter," Benny said. "Even in places that were not really that funny, do you agree?"
Hardy nodded.
"As a critic you feel like a fool if they hire a laugh track," Drexler said.

"I think it was stupid that Cantagalo did not marry his fiancée," Jackie said. "Instead of constantly cavorting with those party sluts, he should have done the right thing and marry her."
She kept on playing footsie with Hardy, making him slightly uneasy. Had Benny noticed it?

A strange guy was looking at Hardy through the window. He wore a shabby winter coat and a woolen cap. His eyes seemed to come out of their sockets, his face was emaciated, and he grew a long beard. His breath fogged the glass, which made him look like a ghost.
"You know this guy?" Jackie asked.
"No." Hardy emptied his glass. As he looked back toward the window, the man was gone.

Benny finished his ginger ale and slammed his notebook shut. "Done. Can we go now?"

"Why not stay a little longer, honey? It's nice in here."

Benny stood up. "I am leaving. Are you coming with me, or not?"

"I'll stay a little longer."

"Okay. Whatever. You have to know what you are doing." He turned and left without uttering another word.

Jackie ordered a new round of drinks.

"Let him be pissed off," she said. "He always wants to go straight home. It's really boring. I'm not dead yet, after all."

She raised her glass and they cheered.

"Listen," Jackie said. "Just to make it clear: Everybody thinks he's staff at *The Times*, but he's a measly freelancer. His writing pays hardly anything, and he is flat broke. We're old friends and got married for tax reasons after my first husband died. It's my apartment, and he lives there for free, got it?"

Hardy was astonished, having assumed quite the opposite. But maybe she wasn't telling the whole truth.

Jackie was wearing a short skirt again that revealed a lot of leg. Her high heels were tied with a small ribbon above the ankles, accentuating her calves. Hardy's eyes wandered over her slender legs.

"Touch them," she said smiling. "Go ahead, touch them."
"Here?"
"I know that you want it."
"Yes, but here?"

The restaurant was divided into two sections. In the rear they had dining tables and in the front lounge chairs. Hardy and Jackie were sitting side by side, slightly shielded from the other guests. He gently touched her thigh and was greatly aroused at once. Jackie casually grabbed his crotch and felt his erection.

Suddenly, she froze.

The man was staring through the window again.

It was Bill.

"He's pointing at you," Jackie said. "He wants you to come out. Do you know the guy?"
"I think so."
"What's he want?"
"I'll go out and talk to him."
"You better not," Jackie said. "Who knows what he's up to."

Hardy went outside.

"Sorry for the inconvenience, man," Bill said in a frail voice. "But I am not feeling well, really not feeling well. It's so freakin' cold, and I don't find anything I can peddle. And even if I would, in this weather it's impossible to sell stuff on the street. I have no place to crash, so I sometimes sleep in the shelter, but it's hell in there, man. Totally crowded, and sometimes you don't even get in. I've got terrible stomach pain, and if I eat something, it gets even worse. There's medication that helps, but they don't give it to you in the shelter. They give you a stinkin' aspirin, and that's it."

Hardy handed him a twenty.

Bill put the money into his coat pocket, his hand trembling. "Thanks, man. I won't forget this."
He gave Hardy a hug, sobbing. "Shit, I'm so damn embarrassed that I had to bother you, but I'm not feeling well, I'm really not."
He pulled away, put up the collar of his coat and disappeared into the night.

Hardy settled back into his chair.
"Who was this?" Jackie asked.
"An old friend who's hit hard times."
"He looks weird. Let's hope he's getting better soon."
She took a sip of wine. "Shall we go to your place?"
Hardy was taken by surprise. He couldn't possibly take her to the run-down loft.

"I just moved in. It's not even fully furnished yet."

Jackie threw him an angry look. "I knew something was wrong. Why can't we go to your place? Have something to hide?"
"It's a room in a musician's loft. They have stuff lying around and want no visitors."

Jackie let out a shrieking laugh. "That's a good one. Never heard that one before."

"But it's true."

"I want to see it. If you don't show it to me, I will leave you right here, right now."

She waved at the bartender. "The check!"

22.
TIMES SQUARE RETREAT

Jackie stood close to the window and looked at the Empire State Building. "The view is not bad, but there's a strange draft. Somehow, it's windy in your room."
She looked at the mattress, the only chair, and the improvised table with the clunky laptop. She laughed. "I think it's crazy here — I kind of like it. What can I say? It befits a budding filmmaker."

Carl was giving a guitar lesson. Through the drywall they could hear a student rehearse a riff many times over.

Jackie pushed her blue tinted glasses up her nose. "We sure can't stay here, but I just don't want to see Benny's house slippers now."

A few minutes later they were in a posh hotel room on Times Square. Jackie pulled back the curtains: flashing neon signs and an endless stream of traffic on Broadway and Seventh Avenue.
"Okay, now we can relax," Jackie said. "Are you relaxed?"
"Completely."

Jackie settled into a chair, kicked the high heels off her feet and stretched her legs on a divan. Her legs were really great.

They sipped drinks from the minibar and looked at each other.

"One thing needs to be clear from the start," Jackie said. "I will not sleep with you. If you are trying to sleep with me, you're out, got it?"
Hardy was surprised.
"Is that clear?"
"Okay."
"I want you to say it."
"What?"
"I want you to say: I will not sleep with you"
"Okay, I will not sleep with you."
"Thank you."

Hardy's mood was gone. What was that?

"Mind some music?"
Jackie threw him an angry look. "Why can't it just be quiet? What do you have against a bit of silence?"
"Nothing. Sure, silence can be a good thing, sometimes."
"Exactly."
Hardy downed his drink and poured another one.

Jackie turned on the radio. "Maybe you're right. Some music can't hurt." She fiddled with the dial but couldn't find anything she liked and switched the radio off again.

Leaning against the window, she stared down at Times Square. She seemed drunk already.

She turned around, tears in her eyes.

"Anything wrong?"
Jackie sobbed. "Nothing, it's nothing."
"For sure?"
"Yes, damn it."
She settled back into her chair and turned on the TV: a war report from the Middle East.

Hardy glanced at his watch: shortly after midnight.

"Am I boring you?"
"No, no, not at all."
"You looked at your watch."
"Just out of habit."
"Bullshit. People look at their watches when they're bored. I'm boring you because I do not want to sleep with you."

Jackie let herself fall onto the bed, face down.

The sound of machine gun fire on TV. A war commentator reported about casualties.

"Come here," Jackie said through the pillow. "Lie down beside me."
"Okay."
Hardy lay down beside her.

"Don't touch me, okay!"

She moved her hand slowly up and down his thigh but avoided the crotch area. Hardy was extremely aroused, but Jackie kept avoiding his erection. He almost trembled in anticipation.

"Do not touch me, all right?"

Jackie opened his pants and masturbated him. Her dark red fingernails were neatly manicured, and she wore several rings on her slender fingers.

"Say that you want to fuck me!"

Hardy was confused. What was that, now?
"Say it!"
Somehow, he could not get it out.
Jackie masturbated him stronger. "Come on, say it, say it!"
"I ... I .... want to fuck you."
"Loud, say it louder."
"I WANT TO FUCK YOU!"
Jackie moaned, and Hardy came so violently that he was shaking for a moment.

A cream cheese ad ran on TV.

Jackie smiled contentedly. "How do you feel right now?"
"Empty."
"Excellent."
She went into the bathroom, washed her hands and threw him a damp towel.

23.
THE JOB INTERVIEW

"Have a seat, Mr. Cornfield," the secretary said. "Someone will be with you shortly."
Hardy sat down on a white leather sofa. Harold Gallagher's office, on the 53rd floor, had a view of Central Park. The foyer was adorned with an antique wall carpet and a Modigliani sculpture.

Gallagher's muffled voice could be heard through his closed door. He was on a call.

Hardy had manicured his fingernails and wore a silk tie. He wondered if Eisenstein had ever worked outside the film industry. Probably. It was almost impossible that he immediately hit it big. How did he survive at a young age? And how had Truffaut and De Sica managed? Hardy made a mental note: *Study biographies of the greats!*

Tammy was still at the hospital. Admittedly, something morally wrong had occurred, but she would never know. Jackie was married and clearly a bit weird, and it was questionable if this thing would go anywhere. Probably not. Did he feel remorse? Not really. He would simply keep this little intimate encounter to himself, and nobody would ever know.

"Ah, there you are already. Mr. Cornfield. Harold is busy today, so you have to make do with me. Sorry." Colm Malone stood in the entrance of Gallagher's office, carrying a binder under his arm. He was casually dressed: light-blue shirt, black designer jeans, and a chrome-plated belt buckle in the form of the letter C. His thinning hair revealed a receding hairline.

They walked through the corridors. The 53rd floor, at the top of the building, was reserved for the most powerful partners. The fine carpeting muffled the steps, rendering the place quiet. Only the faint clicking of keyboards could be heard.

Colm's office, small but squeaky clean, was on the 17th floor. The view did not compare to Gallagher's but at least gave a glimpse of the East River through a gap between two high rises.
"Coke, water, ginger ale?"
Colm had a mini fridge in his office. A picture on the wall showed a neatly groomed Siamese cat.

Hardy sat on the guest chair and slid his resume across the table. Everything was made up, except for the job at Harper & Morris. He had simply searched the web, selected a few large law firms and fabricated references. He had put down the actual phone number for each firm but had altered one of the digits. If anybody would call, it would go nowhere, and he could claim it was a typo.

Colm examined the resume and picked up the phone. "Let's call one of the references ..."

Hardy held his breath. He hadn't thought that someone would actually call. He hoped that Colm would select Harper & Morris, the only entry that was valid.

Colm's finger wandered over the entries, stopping at a fake reference. Hardy had printed the numbers deliberately small.
Colm squinted. "Damn, I think I need glasses. Can hardly read the number." He dialed and tapped his pen on the desk.

He got a busy signal.

"Strange. How can it be busy? Nowadays everybody has call waiting." He dialed once more but got the busy signal again. "Okay, let's try another one." He threw Hardy a serious look. "The most recent one should work, I hope."
He reached Danny Moran's voice mail at Harper & Morris and left a message. Colm looked much more content now. "Let's see what Mr. Moran has to say about you when he calls back. Harper & Morris is a peer firm. One of the best, internationally."

He took a sip of his ginger ale.

"This is among us now, but you won't believe how many people show up in my office with a completely fabricated resume."
Hardy raised his eyebrows. "Ah, really?"

"It all looks good on paper, but when it comes to push and shove, there's no delivery, and we can't have that of course."

Hardy nodded. "Of course."

"That's why I am here. Leroux & Hempstead is a firm with the highest quality standards, and we strive to keep it that way."

Colm examined Hardy's resume again. "I don't see Concordance. What about Concordance?"

"Concordance?"

Colm made a note. His fingernails were painted with clear nail polish. "Trial Director ...?"

Hardy had no idea what Colm was talking about.

Colm shook his head. "We had expressly told your agency: Concordance, Trial Director, and languages. This is what we need."

Hardy secretly cursed the agency. Had they given him the right info, he could have prepared himself. Tutorials for almost anything were readily available on the web. But Bob Crevitz was attending a convention in Atlanta, so Hardy had received the info from Bob's assistant.

"Spanish, French, and German look good. That's exactly what we need. How good are you on a scale of five?"

"German five, Spanish and French four."

Colm slid a page across the table. "What's this about, roughly?"

Hardy looked over the text. It was a German email chain. Two physicians discussed the use of anticancer medication.

Colm nodded. "Not bad. I'm a total moron when it comes to languages, but I know what it says, of course."

He slid over a letter in Spanish. It was about building a toll road in Colombia.

Colm nodded. "Correct!"

He handed over a third page: Investment advice for customers of a French bank.

"Right again," Colm said. "Your languages are fine." He took a sip from his ginger ale, looking casually at Hardy's hands and shoes.

"Listen Mr. ... uh ...," Colm glanced at the resume again, "... Cornfield. You are the best in languages so far."

Hardy noticed that Colm's head seemed permanently bent to one side. He never held it upright.

"We have internal training courses for Trial Director and Concordance, so I don't see a big problem there, but what matters most to us is stage presence. After the test period, you will work with the highest level as linguistic support. We are talking about international tribunals in which you would be put on the spot." Colm snapped his fingers. "And you would have to click like this."

Hardy nodded. "Of course."

"Would you be willing — this is a hypothetical question, in the event that we should hire you — to make a commitment for one year?"

"Certainly."

Hardy knew that he would quit immediately if his script was given the green light.

"What do you do when you're not at work? Your hobbies? What do you do in your spare time?"
Hardy had no hobbies. His entire energy went into the script.
"Leroux is like a family," Colm said. "We see the employees as individuals with all their facets. "

Hobby, hobby, hobby ... what the hell was his hobby? Every regular person had some kind of hobby. What was his?

"Theater," Hardy said. "I'm a theater buff."
Colm raised his eyebrows. "What a coincidence. Harold is also a huge theater fan. He sponsors the Theater Company on 14th Street."
Colm made a note and rose up. "Don't want to promise too much, but you're on the short list."

They shook hands. Colm's deodorant smelled of jasmine.

Hardy walked toward the elevator, past the cubicles in the open plan office. Some of the staff threw him a quick glance.
Just before the exit to the elevator, Hardy turned around: Colm stood in his doorway. It seemed that he was checking out Hardy from behind.

Colm waved his fingers in a farewell, his head slightly bent.

24.
THE RECESSIVE GENE

Hardy stood in front of the firm's office building. A charcoal gray, monolithic block with opaque windows raising straight up to the sky

A beautiful, spring-like day. Hardy could have taken the subway but decided to walk. His new pad was not too far, and some fresh air would do him good.

Since it was strange that Francisco hadn't been at the premiere, Hardy had called the Lumière. From a substitute he heard that Jimmy and Francisco had been in a car accident and were hospitalized. He hoped that it was nothing serious.

Hardy strolled down Third Avenue. Heavy traffic was moving haltingly. The people around him walked incredibly fast while drinking coffee from paper cups or talking on their cell phones. The only guy taking it easy was a panhandler, sitting on a piece of cardboard. Facing the sun, eyes closed, he stuck out his shabby hat for change.

It felt like Hardy's cell phone was vibrating. He looked at the display, but there was no call. Until this moment absolutely nobody had called him. Could it be that the device was faulty? He threw a quarter into a pay phone and dialed his number. His cell rang and vibrated.

The default ring tone was annoying, and Hardy changed it to Caribbean steel drums.

He walked past the stone lions in front of the New York Public Library, taking in the architecture of the neoclassical building. Inside, they had archived a good chunk of mankind's achievements. Quite a bit was bullshit, though. Nonetheless, it had been archived. On the other hand, countless jewels of human creativity had sunk in the quagmire of history. Numerous geniuses whose talent was not recognized in their day had been all but forgotten. A terrible thought.
Eisenstein, De Sica, and Truffaut certainly had their rightful place in the holy halls. If Hardy would walk into the library now, he would no doubt encounter their work. Would he become their peer someday, or would he, like so many others, end up in the quagmire? Only time could tell. *Cryptic X* was a good start, but it was not enough. To be accepted in the holy halls, he still had a long way to go.

Hardy bought a cup of coffee from a street vendor and sat down on a bench in Bryant Park. The sun reflected in a high-rise window, blinding him. He shielded his eyes with his hand. The park was small but still a welcome oasis.

Hardy glanced at the paper cup. It was decorated with a Greek amphora and blue and white key patterns circling top and bottom. In the middle it read *We are happy to serve you* in an angular typeface resembling ancient Greek

It was not the first time that he drank from such a cup. They were ubiquitous. Almost every Deli and street vendor used them. What did this Greek design have to do with New York? Was it a general tendency toward Neoclassicism? Did New York see itself as a natural extension of ancient Athens and Rome? It seemed like it. A somewhat dubious connection, but it was evident in countless buildings and manifested itself even in a common paper cup.

Hardy took a sip of coffee, squinting against the sun.

He asked himself where his inner quest came from. Why did he feel the urgent need to tell a story? Why did he think that humankind needed to know about his take on the world? Actually, it was the deeper reason why he was sitting in Bryant Park right now. Without this inner drive, he might have married Trischa Warncke and become a sales manager at Farben Winkler in Bad Wildungen. And he might even have taken part in the annual flower parade and joined the local marching band. Hardy felt a cold shiver down his spine. The mere thought of Bad Wildungen terrified him.

Hardy's inner quest certainly did not come from his father, a senior teacher of Latin and math. Daddy had no artistic talent, and his sense of humor was close to zero. That's why they had never gotten along. It couldn't come from his mother, either, since she hailed from a petty bourgeois family of florists and gardeners. Sure, you could call a floral arrangement artistic, somehow, but was it art in the creative sense? Not really.

As a teenager, Hardy had thought that his mother perhaps had had an affair with a traveling gypsy, and that he was therefore different from the rest of the family. The gypsies camped on the city outskirts every summer, and Hardy felt magically drawn to them as a child. They lived in large camping trailers and sold fake Persian carpets door to door. And they hammered out mesmerizing music with all kinds of improvised instruments in front of a camp fire. None of them had formal education, and yet, their sound was just great. They were original because they had never followed any rules but set their own. Everything about them seemed fun and easy, and even their gold teeth looked cool. Hardy was fascinated by them and hoped that maybe he, too, had Gypsy blood running through his veins.

Unfortunately, adolescence made it clear that Hardy was not a gypsy child, since he partially resembled his father. He had inherited his father's nose and mouth, and his mother had given him his grayish-blue eyes.

Actually, there was only one possible explanation for Hardy's artistic drive.

A recessive gene!

For seven hundred years Hardy's family had produced nothing of lasting value. The sole outstanding figure had been Hartmut von Hachenstein, a 13th century minstrel. At the local history museum, they had a picture of him in which he stood on a medieval marketplace, holding a lute. Some of his sonnets had survived to this day. Even though the Middle High German lyrics were hard to digest, it was still obvious that Hartmut had been a great poet, skillfully telling the stories of his time.

Could it be that Hartmut's artistic gene had been dormant for seven hundred years and now manifested itself in a young filmmaker?

Hardy's phone rang. His very first call. He pulled the phone expectantly from his pocket. Who could it be?

It was Loraine.

"The hospital called me. Is Tammy with you?"
"Haven't seen her," Hardy said.
"She ran away. Very dangerous in her condition, but that's just who she is. If she shows up, tell her to better check herself back in. Her tests are not that good, that's all I know."

25.
R-E-S-P-E-C-T

Shortly after Hardy was back in the loft he heard a knock on the door. He peered through the peephole:

Tammy. Drunk.

She wore a shabby trench coat and a checkered hunting cap. Leaning against the wall, she breathed heavily.
He opened the door, and she threw her arms around him, reeking of alcohol. "Oh, baby, I've missed you so much."
Luckily, Byrdseed wasn't in. Certainly, they wouldn't appreciate Tammy in the loft. But how could he explain that to her? He needed to do it gradually. He just hoped that Byrdseed wouldn't show up. Losing his refuge was the last thing he needed right now.

"Damn, no sex all this time. I'm horny." Tammy kissed him and massaged his crotch. Because of her appearance, Hardy wasn't really turned on. Especially the checkered hunting cap looked weird. She kept working on his crotch anyway, and he started to respond.

Tammy ripped off her clothes but kept the hunting cap on. Hardy wanted to take it off, but she pushed his hand away. "Leave it. My hair looks terrible."

They made love. Sex with Tammy was always good, and when she was drunk it was even better since she lost all inhibitions. She liked to do the backdoor thing, sitting on top. While riding him, being bent slightly backwards, he could see her wet pussy, which turned him on enormously. Tammy, still wearing the hunting cap that seemed to be glued to her head, pushed against him ever harder. She screamed with pleasure, and when she came, she squirted warm liquid all over his stomach. Hardy came almost simultaneously in her backdoor and groaned. Sure, it was a slimy, animalistic affair, but it was extremely gratifying.

Tammy sank down on him and snoozed off, lying on his chest. Hardy also dozed off, and for a moment it felt like he and Tammy had become one with the universe.

When Hardy came to, Tammy stood at the window and looked at the Empire State Building. She was still naked except for the hunting cap. "The view is not bad," Tammy said. "How'd you get this place?"

"A weird arrangement," Hardy said, preparing for the moment when he had to explain why she couldn't stay with him.

Tammy fell into Hardy's chair and pulled her legs to her chest. "Got something to drink?"

The hunting cap started to grow on him. It looked cool on her. "Where did you get the hat?"

"Screw the hat," Tammy said. "I need something to drink. Besides: Where's the ladies' room?"

130

She got up and wanted to open the door that led into the recording studio, but Hardy held her back. "I have roommates. They're not here, but they can walk in any minute."

He wrapped a towel around his waist and threw the trench coat over Tammy's shoulders. They walked past the recording studio to the bathroom.

While Tammy relieved herself, Hardy stood guard and prayed that Byrdseed wouldn't come in. The bathroom was in a bad location since Hardy couldn't get there without passing Byrdseed's part of the loft. He spotted a bucket under the kitchen sink. He grabbed it and put it in his room.

When he came back, Tammy stood in front of the open fridge. "Two beers in here."

"They belong to Byrdseed."

"Byrdseed?"

"My roommates." Hardy pointed to the musical equipment. "The studio belongs to them."

Tammy grabbed one of the beers. "Can I take this one? You can put it back tomorrow, can't you?"

They sat in Hardy's room. Tammy on the only chair, Hardy on the upturned bucket.

"God, how I would like to record something again. I have ideas for a couple of songs. What's Byrdseed's game?"

"Jazz Rock."

Tammy finished the beer. "Ah, that was fast. I'll get the other one."

Hardy held her back. "Let me get it. Byrdseed doesn't want any visitors. If they come in and see you ..."

"No visitors? What the hell is that? You pay rent, don't you?"

Hardy grabbed the second beer from the fridge, took a swig himself and gave it to Tammy.

"Why did you quit the hospital? Apparently your tests are not all that good. You should have stayed put."

"Uh, screw the tests," Tammy said. "If this is life, I'd rather be dead."

She took a good swig from the beer. "I feel great, absolutely great. Now, that I'm out of that damn bunker, I feel like I could move mountains."

Hardy felt the urge to smoke a cigarette. He looked for his straw but could not find it. Instead he nibbled on the cap of a ballpoint pen.

Suddenly, Tammy's face went gray, and she grabbed her heart, breathing heavily.

"Are you okay?"

"Yes. Just a bit tired."

She fell on the bed, still wearing the hunting cap. Seconds later she was snoring.

The next morning, Hardy was awakened by a guitar riff. Carl practiced for a Broadway musical in which he had scored a job in the orchestra pit.

Hardy needed to pee and relieved himself into the bucket. He looked out the window. The Empire State Building glittered in the morning sun.

It was Saturday and still early, and he lay down again. Tammy's hunting cap had fallen off during the night. Her scruffy hair stood out in all directions.

She woke up and wiped her eyes. "Need to use the ladies' room."
Hardy motioned to her to be quiet and pointed to the bucket.

Tammy peed in the bucket.

She came back to bed and licked Hardy's nipple, knowing this turned him on. Hardy moaned, and she slipped under the covers, starting to work with his magic stick.

Carl knocked on the door. "Hey, man, are you in there?"
Tammy paused but remained under the covers, Hardy's magic stick in her mouth.
"Two beers are missing," Carl said through the door.
"Sorry, man. I'll put them back later today."
"I thought we had agreed that you wouldn't touch our stuff."
"It was late yesterday."
"That's not what we had agreed upon, man. That's exactly what we don't want, okay?"
"Okay."
"Good. Thank you."
Carl continued fiddling around on his guitar.

Hardy and Tammy had breakfast in the Bagel Maven on Seventh Avenue. They had quietly dressed and slipped out of the loft. Tammy wore the hunting cap again.
Hardy ate a cheese omelet and Tammy drank a can of beer. She could not keep down solid food in the morning.

It looked like the Bagel Maven hadn't changed its style since the fifties. Most guests seemed to be old immigrants. An old lady occasionally coughed and spit in a napkin.

"What the hell is this place?" Tammy whispered. "It feels like a cemetery."

"They have the best omelet around here," Hardy said. "And it's a good deal."

Tammy gulped down her beer and ordered another one. "Next week I have an appointment with welfare," she said. "Maybe they'll arrange another place for me."

Hardy nodded.

They kissed. The kiss tasted like beer.

Apart from the faint rattling of dishes in the kitchen, it was eerily quiet in the Bagel Maven. An old man at the next table had problems with his dentures. He took them out and put them in his pocket.

Carl walked past the window, carrying his guitar case. He threw Hardy and Tammy an angry look. He probably knew the two had stayed in the loft together.

They strolled along Broadway. A beautiful, sunny day. Tammy had folded up the stained trench coat and tucked it under her arm. She wore a black hoody with *Coney Island* printed on the chest and a pair of red leggings. Her leather boots were worn and bent up at the tips.

They bought a bottle of brandy, and each took a swig. Tammy stretched her arms, breathing deeply. "Ah, freedom ..."

In Union Square two buskers played "Sitting on the dock of the bay" in front of a small crowd. Tammy talked to them, and they nodded.

Taking position in front of the buskers, she spread out her arms: "Respect!"

The musicians played the intro, and Tammy sang:

Ooh, what you want, ooh, baby, I got ...,
Ooh, what you need, ooh, do you know I got it ...?

She pranced back and forth and choreographed the song with her arms. The crowd quickly became bigger, some people clapping along rhythmically. Tammy sang at the top of her lungs:

R-E-S-P-E-C-T, find out what it means to me ...,
R-E-S-P-E-C-T, take care, TCB ...

Tammy was in her element. She danced to and fro like a dervish, choreographing the music. But shortly before the end of the song she grabbed her heart and broke off. "Damn, I need to sit down." She dropped on a park bench, breathing deeply in and out.

The audience applauded and some people threw money into the buskers' hat.

"What happened?" Hardy asked.

"Damn, don't know, my heart is racing like crazy." She leaned back, breathing heavily.

Hardy massaged Tammy's temples, and she slowly got better.

She took a sip of brandy. "Ah, that feels good!"

She held her hand over her eyes to protect against the sun. "Am I mistaken, or is this Bill over there?"

Bill was sitting on the sidewalk of 14th Street on an upturned plastic crate, still looking emaciated and wearing a full beard. He had laid out old comics books, fashion magazines, and two videos with gay porn.

"I had nothing to do with the fire," Tammy said. "I really didn't. Must have been the Chinaman."
"Never mind," Bill said. "You're okay, and that's all that counts."
A few teenagers browsed through the comic books. "How much?"
"Fifty cents each."
Bill had opened his jacket. He was sitting directly in the sun, sweating slightly.

Noticing the videos, Tammy laughed. "Gay porn? When did you start liking boys?"

"I found them, man. Like everything else. They pay much better than the books."
Hardy discovered a copy of the screenplay for *Taxi Driver* among Bill's goods. The cover showed De Niro, sporting a Mohawk. It was not the first time that Hardy saw screenplays on the street. Apparently, there was a market for it. A considerable number of people were trying their hand at screenwriting and wanted to learn from the classics.
Hardy flipped through the script. It was a copy of a copy of a copy. A few of the words had faded and been traced with a pen.

Scorsese used a voiceover in the beginning. Hardy had not noticed this in the film, but he did not really watch it analytically at the time. The voiceover was good. It was an ideal tool to tighten the story and move it forward. Hardy made a mental note: *Try experimenting with a voiceover!*

"*Taxi Driver*, man," Bill said. "A classic. One of the best films ever."
"How much?"
"It's free for you!"
Hardy pulled out a ten, but Bill rejected the money with an outstretched hand. "Can't you accept a gift from an old friend?"
Hardy noticed that Bill wasn't wearing his talisman. "Where's your magical sphere?"
"Some scumbag stole it when I was asleep. If I ever find out who did it, I'll kill him."

Tammy looked bored. She took a swig of brandy.

"Come to think of it, I could use the ten bucks," Bill said. "My stomach's still acting up, and I need to get medication."
Hardy pulled out the ten, and Bill slid it into his pocket.

"Damn, I feel dizzy." Tammy tipped to one side, and Hardy secured her.
"Need to lay down," Tammy said with a meek voice.
Bill quickly put the books aside, and they placed Tammy on the cardboard that Bill used as a display. She gasped. "My heart, it's racing like crazy ..."

Onlookers gathered around them. "An ambulance," one of them shouted. "Call an ambulance."
"No," Tammy groaned. "No ambulance. I'll be fine ..."
She closed her eyes and tried to breathe evenly. Hardy held her hand, and Bill fanned some air toward her with a piece of cardboard.

Half an hour later they were at Loraine's place. Tammy lay on the couch with an ice pack on her forehead.
"Why can't she crash with you?" Loraine said. "It's already crowded enough here as it is."

Kristen came in, an envelope in her hand. "Here's the rent. A bit earlier this time."
She wore a baggy jogging suit at least one size too big. Her skin was pale and her ash blonde hair, which she had cut boyishly short, slightly greasy.
"Thank you, sweetie," Loraine said, putting the envelope in her pocket. "That's very kind of you."

Kristen disappeared, and Loraine turned back to Hardy. "Your new pad is only for one person? Why the hell is that?"
"Cool, my dear sister," Tammy said. "Cool, okay? Next week I'll be at welfare, and then they'll give me a new place or will remodel the old."
Loraine laughed. "My God, she's such a dreamer. Who do you think you are, honey?"
"You can't even accommodate your sister for a few days, can you? Not even for a few freakin' days?"
"Oh, stop that shit. You're already here, aren't you? Are you here or are you not?"

"I'm here. But I certainly don't feel a lot of sisterly love."

"Sisterly love, my ass. Since we were kids you constantly stabbed me in the back. Do you call that sisterly love?"

"Okay, is that why you fucked Steve?"

"I did not."

"You did."

"I did not. And if he were here, he would tell you that."

Hardy felt uncomfortable. The conversation developed in a direction he didn't particularly like.

"Funny..." Tammy said. "I saw you with him with my own eyes."

"It was a party at East River Park. We just danced, and you know that."

"Why did you dance with my guy? And let him fondle your tits. I saw it with my own eyes. If this is not totally wrong from the outset, I don't know what is. Did I once, only once dance with Earl?"

"No. But just because you don't particularly dig Earl, that's why."

Hardy's eyebrow started twitching.

"Since we're at it," Tammy said, pointing to Hardy. "What about this one here? You also did this one, right?"

"Thank you," Loraine said. "Thank you very much. This shows again what you think of me deep down. But that's not me. No, no, no. This is the image you have of yourself and project onto me."

"Okay, did you screw him or not? Tell it like it is."

"There was nothing," Hardy said. "I slept a few days on the couch, and that's it."

"Ha, ha, ha," Tammy exclaimed. "A skank with big tits and a guy with a hard cock in the same room, and nothing happens, right? You just prayed before you went to sleep, right?
"Exactly," Loraine said. "We prayed every night. Prayed to the dear Lord that you wouldn't come back!"

She left, slamming the door behind her.

26.
CODE OF CONDUCT

Colm put a heavy file folder on Hardy's desk. "All important info is in here. Any questions, call me, or turn confidently to Blanchette. She's been with us for more than ten years and is a valued colleague."

Blanchette nodded briefly, staying silent.

The office was a windowless storage room illuminated by harsh neon light. The walls were lined with boxes on metal shelves.
Hardy didn't know if he should be happy that they had chosen him. Sure, he needed the money, but the job represented everything he had never wanted to be. He immediately felt trapped. He hadn't even really started but already thought about how to get out.

Colm turned on the computer. "Your email is already set up. Just record your phone message, and you're good to go."
The phone resembled a large cube, cut diagonally in the middle. It had a beige-brown color scheme and the vibe of the seventies. Colm laughed, his head bent sideways. "Hah, you still have an old one — almost a collector's

item by now. Don't even know how they work any more, but Blanchette can surely teach you."

Blanchette was black, skinny, and very tall. She wore corduroy pants and a brown sweater. Her hair was braided into a wreath on top of her head.

Hardy wondered what the young Truffaut would have done in his situation. Would he have taken the job? Probably. He would have taken it while secretly working on his screenplay. And that's exactly what Hardy planned to do.

"Don't you want to know why you are the lucky one?" Colm asked.

"Sure," Hardy said. "Very curious."

"Well, believe it or not, but your hobby tipped the scales! Harold's love for the stage goes back to his school days. Unfortunately, he is very busy at the moment, but in due course he would like to meet you in person."

Hardy already dreaded the moment when he would have to face the boss. He feared that his time in the firm would be a constant walk on a tightrope. How could he pretend that he was the humble linguistic support Steven C. Cornfield when in fact he was none less than the budding filmmaker Hardy von Hachenstein, who had single-handedly conquered the Newcomer Award at San Sandoval and had been compared to the great Eisenstein?

Colm waved good-bye wiggling his fingers. "We'll talk." He left, and Hardy noticed that Colm's walk, just like his head, was also slightly bent to one side.

Suddenly, Colm came back.

"Sorry, but I forgot ..." He spread his arms. "Welcome to the Leroux family."
They hugged.
"I am sure that you will love it here." Colm said and padded Hardy on the shoulder. "Now you are one of us." He gave Hardy another hug and disappeared.

Hardy was a bit surprised and cast a questioning look to Blanchette: "What was that?"

"This is new. An idea of the marketing department. Leroux is not just a law firm, it's a loving family."

Hardy sat down at his desk and looked at the screen. He already had an email from Colm: *Welcome to the Leroux family. We are pleased to have you with us.*
It was probably a standard email they sent to each new employee. An electronic hug, so to speak. Probably also an idea of the marketing department. There was an addition: *We have loaded twenty dollars on your key card for the cafeteria. Your first lunch is on us! — Enjoy!*

Hardy felt like they had stuck him in a vice that was slowly tightening. He wondered why Colm had put him in this bunker. And why was the valued colleague Blanchette here? Had she chosen this place herself, or had she been put here for some reason?

Hardy had the flash drive with the screenplay in his pocket. He needed to complete the rewrite as soon as possible. If Avi liked the sample scenes, he would want to see the whole script.

Hardy glanced at Blanchette. Quite possibly she was a watchdog. Maybe Colm had put her here to spy on him. He left the flash drive in his pocket. Better to download the screenplay secretly. Blanchette was not to be trusted.

Hardy wondered if Mindy Goldfarb had passed on his script. He had sent her an email a few days ago and still waited for a reply. Could it be that his message had landed in her spam folder?

"Seventeen boxes for Steven C. Cornfield. Is that you?" The delivery boy wore the blue uniform of the mail room. He was black, short, and cross-eyed. Hardy signed the delivery list, and the guy stacked the boxes next to the desk.

On the first box there was a note from Colm. "All documents to be indexed, please."

Hardy opened box number one. The first page was a letter in Spanish with a stamped number at the bottom: TCA-000001. The second page had TCA-000002. Hardy shifted the boxes and opened the last one. Final page number: TCA-050365.

He turned to Blanchette. "Fifty thousand pages? Colm wants me to index fifty thousand pages? How long does this take?"

Blanchette shrugged. "Good people do it in two weeks, others take half a year."

Hardy went to the bathroom. He sat on the toilet lid and worked on the Christmas scene. It was one of the key scenes, and he had printed it and carried it in his jacket. Gangster Lugo, dressed as Santa Claus, distributed presents to the children of the village and sang with an angelic voice "Noche de Paz", while Feinstein, also dressed as Santa Claus, peered through the window. Ah, Christmas in Mexico was a blast, a visual delicacy.

Twenty minutes later, Hardy was back at his desk. He could not stay forever in the bathroom.
Blanchette now had a small radio on her table. Even though she wore button headphones, it was annoying since tiny bits of the music wavered over to Hardy.

Reluctantly, Hardy worked his way through the Spanish documents. They dealt with the construction and maintenance of a toll road in Colombia. An insanely dry topic. The documents had no chronological order which made them quite confusing. Occasionally pages were missing, some of which emerged later. And then there was a travel brochure for Disneyland. In English. It had the same control numbers as the other documents but made absolutely no sense in this context.

At lunchtime Blanchette disappeared. She had just dropped her headphones but kept the radio running, so the easy listening channel was now clearly audible. The tinny, high pitched sound of the headphones drove Hardy insane. He walked over to her table and muted the sound.

Finally alone, Hardy dialed Mindy Goldfarb's number. He had given her enough time to respond to his email.

Mindy's assistant answered the phone. Hardy was a bit surprised. Avi Feinstein's assistant obviously had herself an assistant.

"Mindy is currently in a meeting. Can I take a message?"
"When can I talk to her?"
"Hard to say. We are extremely swamped today. Just leave your number."
"I had given her a manuscript."
"We will call you back."
"I'd rather call again tomorrow."
"Sure thing. But tomorrow Mindy will be out of the office. Better call back on Monday."

Hardy silently cursed himself. Why hadn't he given Feinstein the manuscript directly?

"Just one question, is Mindy Avi's agent or his assistant?"
"Personal assistant. His agent is Fred Woodhouse, but he's sitting in L. A."
"Ah, okay. And Mindy only caters to Avi?"
"No, no, we provide service to a great number of artists. That's why we are so busy."

"I would possibly be interested. What's included?"
"Depends."
"In Avi's case, for example."

"Scheduling, tickets, hotels, wardrobe, cleaning, shopping. And then of course his dog. We also make sure that everything is kosher."

"Kosher?"

"For his mother's sake."
"The canapés at the premiere were kosher?"
"Certainly."
"And the champagne?"
"Yep."
"What do you charge? Let's say for a basic service?"
"You would have to talk to Marc Riviera. He's in charge of the service plans. Shall I connect you?"
"No. I will call back on Monday."

Hardy buried his face in his hands. He was still miles away from Avi Feinstein, and he didn't seem to come any closer.

Suddenly, Blanchette returned. She put her headphones on and threw Hardy an angry look. "Have you touched my radio?"
Hardy shook his head.
"Okay, I assume that it was NOT you, and that the volume has muted itself. For future reference: I do not find it cool if someone fondles my things. I hope, this is clear. Thank you."

Hardy got up and went to lunch.

The cafeteria of Leroux & Hempstead looked almost exactly like that of Harper & Morris: white furniture, a few terracotta pots with plants and a huge nature photo — not the bear with the salmon but some wild horses roaming the plains of the West. The view was not quite as good as at Harper & Morris, but you could see the East River.

Hardy wasn't really hungry and just got a cup of coffee and a New York cheese cake. The coffee was strong and aromatic and the sugar in the cake gave him an energy boost.

He sat in a remote corner of the cafeteria, pulled out his notepad and worked on his screenplay. It was nobody's business what he did in his lunch break, and probably nobody cared anyway.

27.
BAD TIDINGS

It was shortly after 5:30 as Hardy stood in the lobby of Leroux & Hempstead, staring out into the pouring rain. It was already dark, and the cars had turned on their headlights.

More and more people spilled out of the elevators. Very few carried an umbrella, and the lobby was getting crowded.

As always when it rained, a few street vendors had set up shop, but the cheap umbrellas where no match for the heavy winds and fell apart within seconds.

Blanchette squeezed past Hardy. She zipped through the sliding door, opened her giant umbrella and hurried to the subway. She was taller than anybody else on the street.

Finally, a vendor with better umbrellas appeared. Hardy bought one and rushed to the subway. In the middle of the packed platform played an African percussion band on pots and paint buckets. A Chinese woman sold chewing gum and batteries, and a disheveled guy held a homemade sign reading *Free Willy!*

The E train came in, and the crowd squeezed into the cars. Hardy stood no chance, he couldn't get in. New people kept coming down the escalators, and soon the station was packed to the brim again.

A woman with a woolen hat in Jamaican colors and thick horn-rimmed glasses danced to the African percussion music. The guy with the *Free Willy!* sign danced as well, trying to make contact with her, but she quickly shifted directions.

The next E train came in. Hardy pushed into the car, and the crowd behind shoved him further until he managed to secure himself to a handhold. He could hardly move, being wedged in. It smelled of mothballs and wet dog. He hated the smell of mothballs. It usually came from old women who put the stuff in their closets.

Hardy stared at Dr. Z's ad that promised silky clear skin by doing away with acne. The ad was all over the subway, and virtually everyone in New York knew it. Dr. Z had a baby face, and his gaze was somewhat cold. Hardy wondered who trusted this guy. Maybe it was just a PR idea, and Dr. Z did not really exist. It was probably a community clinic, and the marketing department had decided that Dr. Z should be its face.

At Penn Station Hardy stumbled out of the train. Hordes of commuters rushed past him to catch their connections to New Jersey and Long Island. It was noisy as hell.

He pushed his way through the crowds in the basement, passing bars, fast food joints, and newsstands. At 32nd Street he hopped up the stairs and opened his umbrella. It was still pouring, and thunder rumbled in the distance. His cell phone rang.

It was Loraine.

Hardy took cover under a ledge.
"It's all my fault," Loraine sobbed. "I shouldn't have kicked her out."
"She had a weak heart, mom," said Hakeem in the background. "She needed to cut out the booze, and she knew it."
Hardy pulled the cut straw from his pocket and sucked in some air.

Loraine blew her nose. "She collapsed on the street once again. But this time they came too late. When they arrived at the hospital, she was DOA."

Hardy stared into the rain. He bit his lower lip to make sure he wasn't dreaming.
Loraine sobbed. "I'm devastated. Please don't come over today, just come another day, okay?"

28.
A GHOSTLY PRESENCE

Hardy lay in bed, covering himself with blankets. The wind was howling, and the building seemed to moan and groan, trying to withstand the force of nature.
He couldn't believe that just a couple of days ago, Tammy was with him in that very same bed and very much alive. Could he have done something to save her? Probably not. Maybe he should have insisted that she'd go back to the hospital, but she would have surely escaped again.

Hardy blew his nose and started to sing: *Si-i-lent niiiight, ho-ho-ly niiight, all is calm ... all is bright ...*
He couldn't sing very well and hit some wrong notes but kept singing anyway. Somehow it helped. *Slee-eep in heavenly peeeace ..., sle-eep in heaaaavenly peaaaace ...*

A mighty thunder roared and the building trembled. Shortly after, lightning struck.

Hardy froze.

Outside the window hovered a misty outline of what seemed to be a woman. Could it be ... Tammy's ghost?

Hardy jumped up, turning on the lights. He was scared but also curious. He cautiously walked toward the window and that strange misty outline. But when he came close, the creature vanished.

Hardy was confused. Had he just witnessed a paranormal activity, or had it merely been a low hanging cloud?

Hardy was scared and felt that something was still there. He switched on the lights in all rooms and looked in every corner and behind the curtains. Suddenly, something jumped off a shelf and sent Hardy screaming. It was a mouse. The critter disappeared behind a stack of audio tapes.

Hardy sat down in the kitchen and drank from an open bottle of red wine that Byrdseed had left on the shelf.

The wine did him good.

He had not smoked for a quite a while now, always sticking to the straw, but all of a sudden he had an irrepressible urge for a cigarette. He rummaged through the trash bin, found a half-smoked butt and lit it. He drew in the smoke with pleasure, leaning back on his chair.

Hardy took another swig of wine and had a terrific idea. How about putting Tammy in the script? An African-American woman stranded in Mexico. Perhaps her character could be Feinstein's sidekick. The idea was good. It was even excellent. He would call the character *Tammy*, thus keeping her alive somehow.

Hardy fetched the laptop. He found a second bottle of wine in the closet and opened it. If Byrdseed did not understand this specific situation, they were monsters.

The idea with Tammy grew on him. A drinking, black singer and a delicate Jew, allergic to almost everything, was an interesting combination. He wrote a few scenes and laughed. Tammy was the missing element! With her cool *whatever* attitude, she was the perfect match for the control freak Feinstein.

Hardy wrote as if in a frenzy. Never had he come up with so many ideas, and, being engulfed in the creative process, the storm became insignificant background noise.

He fumbled another butt out of the trash bin and wrote down the wine brand. It was a Cabernet Sauvignon from Chile. The wine seemed to be a miracle elixir. In combination with the nicotine rush, it triggered an explosion of inspiration. Hardy did not necessarily want to start smoking again, but when it came to getting something on a page all means needed to be considered.
Usually, Hardy managed about three pages a day, but sometimes he had a hard time nailing down even one. On this very night he had already fleshed out more than fifteen pages, and he was far from done.

Hardy hammered away into the laptop until his vision blurred, falling asleep at the kitchen table in the middle of the night.

29.
WHEN THE SAINTS GO MARCHING IN

The urn stood on the kitchen table. Loraine, Earl, Hakeem, Kristen, and Hardy formed a circle, holding each other's hands. A proper burial would have been too expensive.
"She was who she was," Loraine said. "Despite everything, I will miss her. God rest her soul."

"Amen," Earl said.

They closed their eyes and held a minute's silence. Loraine sobbed, and Kristen blew her nose. Earl began singing: *Ah when the saints ..., ah when the saints ..., ah when the saints go marching in. Oh, Lord, let me be in that number, ah when the saints go marching in ...*

The others joined in. Earl drummed rhythmically on the table, and Hakeem slammed two pot lids together. Although they were only five, it sounded like a Baptist choir. Loraine stretched out her arms and sang at the top of her lungs: *Oh, Lord, let me be in that number, when the saints go marching iiiiiiin!*

Someone banged against the wall. "Quiet, you lowlifes!"

"Uh, screw yourself," Loraine yelled. "We are in mourning, damn it."

She wiped the tears from her eyes. "Okay guys, let's eat."

Loraine put the urn on the refrigerator. They had fish fingers, potato salad and discount beer.

After dinner, Hakeem lit a cigarette. "I'm supposed to meet up with my homies, mom. Can I go, now?"

"Okay, beat it."

Loraine brought a bottle of tequila and they all took a shot.

The phone rang. It was Bill. Loraine put him on speaker.

"Damn, it's surreal," Bill said. "When is the funeral? I would like to attend."

"Already over," Loraine said coldly.

"If I can help in any way ..."

"Not necessary. But thanks for the offer."

"Okay," Bill said. "Then again my sincere condolences."

"Sincere condolences, my ass" Loraine said after she hung up. She looked at Earl. "He did it. I just know it was him."

"I'm not saying that it was him, and I'm not saying that it wasn't him," Earl said. "I'm just saying that I saw him the next day with brand new clothing. How could he afford that?"

They drank another round of tequila, and Earl put on a CD — R. Kelly:

I believe I can fly, I believe I can touch the sky ...

Earl sang along, choreographing the song with outstretched arms and balancing on one leg, as if he were an eagle floating through the air.

Think about it every night and day, spread my wings and fly away ....

Kristen turned to Hardy. "I don't know," she said. "But sometimes this city seems like the loneliest place on earth."
She had put on a black skirt, a black blouse, and a tiny black neck scarf. It looked good on her and accentuated her lean figure. She had parted her ash blond hair on the side and framed her eyes with black eyeliner.
"I'm from Idaho. It's ultraconservative there but not as lonely as here."

Earl pulled Loraine out of her chair and danced with her. They started kissing.

I believe I can fly, I believe I can touch the sky ...

Kristen poured herself a shot of tequila and gulped it down. "Do you believe in reincarnation?"
"Depends on how you define it," Hardy said, gulping down a shot of tequila as well.
"I'm pretty sure that I was an untouchable in India in my past life. I constantly dream of it. The problem is that I am in love with a *Brahmin*. First and fourth caste! Absolutely impossible!"

Earl and Loraine disappeared into the bedroom. Shortly thereafter, the bed frame began banging rhythmically against the wall.

"Do you have any idea what you might have been before? It can also be an animal or a plant."
Kristen nervously tugged at her tiny black neck scarf. The stereo still played the R. Kelly song. Earl had put it on repeat.
"Maybe I was a minstrel." Hardy was slightly drunk already.
"Oh? How so?"
"A complicated story."

Kristen and Hardy danced. She smelled of *Patchouli*, just like Trischa Warncke at Hardy's very first kiss. The perfume had long gone out of fashion, and he was surprised Kristen still wore it. The Idaho native was skinny and lightweight. She wore no bra, and Hardy could feel her small, firm breasts. Their dance moves flowed with the rhythm of the music:

Think about it every night and day, spread my wings and fly away ...

Suddenly, the CD was stuck: ... *fly, fly, fly,* ...
They pulled apart, and Hardy tweaked the stereo. The buttons did not respond. ... *fly, fly, fly,* ...

Hardy pulled the plug, and it was finally quiet.

When he turned around, he saw Kristen sitting on the bed in her room. She waved him over.

30.
A LIVING LEGEND

Francisco sat in his office, sorting a few papers. He wore a huge orthopedic neck brace, which made all his movements look awkward.

"How did it happen?" Hardy asked.

"An accident on the way to the premiere. We were a little late."

Francisco took a sip of coke. "Seems like we did not really miss much. Avi was good as always, but in the second act the story fell apart. Drexler's razor sharp analysis in *The Times* says it all. And I agree with him. Had Cantagalo's mother convinced him to abandon the drug trade, then the story would have regained steam. Then Cantagalo himself would have landed on the hit list!"

"That was my idea!" Hardy exclaimed.

"Yours?"

"Yes, damn it! Drexler and I discussed the play after the premiere."

"Then you should feel honored. He is living legend as a critic. Rumor has it that he's working on a tell-all book about the media scene. Some people got damn cold feet already. How do you know him?"

"Through his wife."
Francisco muttered something in Spanish and crossed himself on the chest.

Hardy had called Jackie twice but only got the machine. He suspected that Drexler erased the messages before Jackie saw them. Even though their relation seemed impossible, he wanted to see her again. She had his cell number now, and he did not understand why she didn't call. Was it that old fashioned thing that the guy had to call first? But how could he get through to her, if Drexler controlled the phone? Hardy didn't know yet, but he would find a way, somehow.

Unfortunately, Hardy's flesh had been weak, and he had slept with Kristen. The tequila was to blame. Or maybe the *Patchouli*. Or both. The unassuming lady from Idaho was a sexual volcano. She had screamed in pleasure, clutching her nails into his chest and had fainted in the end. Nevertheless, there was no future for them. Hardy was attracted to flashy and flamboyant women, and Kristen was pale and bland. Shortly after the act he realized that he had made a fatal mistake. At dawn he had quietly disappeared.

"Jackie is the devil," Francisco said. "I don't know how many men she has driven to madness but certainly a lot. And it is rumored that she did away with her former husband. God bless him. Frankie was a good soul. A bit fat, yes. Some say he was impotent in his later years but a good soul."
Jimmy stood in the doorway. He had a gauze bandage around his forehead but still wore his rotated baseball

cap. "We're out of splicer tape, and the Talebi film needs a new head leader."

Francisco opened the safe and pulled out a twenty.

"Jimmy was with me in the car. We both live in Brooklyn, and he has a Chevette."

"Had," Jimmy said. "Had. A freakin' theater play ... I didn't want to go from the start."

He grabbed the twenty and vanished.

Francisco lit a cigarette. "Sure, Frankie's business was somewhat dubious. It was officially called *Cabaret*, but it was more than that. The lady in question was one of the dancers, only that he eventually made her honest."

Francisco blew smoke straight up in the air.

"Officially, they called it a heart attack, but who knows. It was an open secret she was cheating on Frankie with younger men, and he wanted a divorce."

Hardy didn't know if he could believe Francisco's story. It sounded a lot like hearsay. The truth was probably more complex.

Francisco put out his cigarette. "Well, let's get to the point. You gave Mindy the scenes for Avi, but she is not answering ..."

"How about we just call Avi directly?"

"He has no phone and no email. He communicates exclusively via fax to protect his privacy."

"Why don't we fax him the pages, then?"

"If he hates one thing, then it's long faxes using up his fax paper. You have no idea how busy he is. Let's stick to Mindy. She sees him almost daily."

He took out a notebook and flipped through the pages. "Mindy, Mindy, Mindy ... Here she is!"

He put her on speaker.

"I've heard about the accident," Mindy said. "On the way to the premiere of all things ..."
"Almost forgotten," Francisco said. "The neck brace will come off soon, and then I'll be as good as new. I have a young filmmaker here with me. He gave you a script ..."

There was a brief silence in the line.

"Damn, yes, but I have no idea where I put it. It was a hectic evening."
"No problem. The young man could reprint and leave it with your doorman. Would this work?"
Mindy sneezed heavily. She blew her nose. "Sorry, I think I'm coming down with something. Yes, of course he can leave it with the doorman."

"How's your dear father?"

"Doing much better," Mindy said. "He's in therapy getting used to the new hip."

31.
IN THE WRONG MOVIE

Hardy sat at a computer in the copy center on Second Avenue. Almost all workstations were occupied with people who seemed busy taking care of important projects.
At the copy machines a few guys produced homemade posters and flyers for a punk concert.
Iggy Pop's "Passenger" wavered over the sound system, and it smelled of hazelnut coffee.

Mindy's slipup was actually a blessing. Hardy now had the chance to submit the revised scenes with Tammy included.

To Hardy's left sat a guy who printed a screenplay for a horror movie, and to his right a woman worked on a dialogue scene for a romantic comedy. He could not believe it. Why did everyone write screenplays all of a sudden?
The woman had noticed Hardy's glance and turned her screen to the side so he couldn't see it. The horror film guy also turned his screen away. Even though those two worked on completely different genres, they seemed to harbor a certain fear that Hardy could steal their valuable material. To show his resolve, Hardy

wanted to turn away his screen as well, but he couldn't since he was sitting in the middle, so he simply pulled the monitor close to him, shielding it from view.

His cell phone rang. It was a number he did not recognize. Jackie perhaps? Hardy turned his screen to black to make sure his dear colleagues couldn't peak into his stuff.

It was Kristen.

"I thought, we could maybe catch a movie on the weekend."
"I've already made plans for the weekend."

The woman with the romantic comedy shot Hardy an angry look and pointed to his phone. He went into the corridor leading to the toilets.

"So what's doing?" Kristen asked.
"Busy at the office."
Hardy felt uncomfortable. How best could he get rid of her?
"When shall we meet again?" Kristen's voice sounded frail.
He couldn't tell her the truth straight away. It was too brutal. He had to do it gradually.
"Maybe next week for lunch?"
"Great." Her voice sounded cheerful, now. "What day?"
"Thursday?"
"Okay."

32.
CHEZ PIERRE

Mindy Goldfarb lived on the Upper East Side, not far from the welfare office Hardy had visited with Tammy but still in another world. The luxury building had its own driveway and a parking garage. A uniformed valet greeted people and parked their cars.
Above the massive sofa in the lobby hung an oil painting in Rembrandt style, and several issues of *Town and Country* were spread out on a coffee table.

Hardy pulled out the envelope addressed to Mindy.

"You're lucky," said the doorman. "There she is."
Mindy was stepping out of a cab. She looked tired, and her hair was slightly disheveled. She wore a rumpled trench coat and flat slippers without heels. Her feet were swollen.

"Sorry for the slipup. It was a busy evening. Crazy, crazy, crazy." She took a manuscript from her briefcase. "You won't believe it, but I found it: *Mayhem in Mexico*. Is that it?"
Hardy saw that Mindy's briefcase contained a bottle of wine.

"Take this version." He handed her the envelope and tore the old manuscript apart.

Mindy smiled. "The creative process. Always fascinating." She put the new envelope into her briefcase next to the bottle. "I have not eaten all day. How about Chez Pierre?"

The restaurant was on the opposite side of the street.

The waiter handed Mindy the menu, but she didn't look at it. "Anything kosher today?"

"*Coq au vin* and *cordon bleu*."

"Ah, *coq au vin*, wonderful. I'll take that. And a bottle of kosher chardonnay."

"And for the gentleman?"

"Kosher *cordon bleu*, please."

Mindy took the waiter's arm. "Just a quick question, Ricardo. I think I still have a voucher with Pierre because of the newspaper article. It would be valid today, wouldn't it?"

Pierre was sitting at a small table next to the bar. He was skinny and had a twirled, white mustache. He smiled at Mindy and stuck his thumb in the air.

"Wonderful," Mindy said. "Always good to know that one has friends."

Chez Pierre was a celebrity hotspot. The walls were adorned with gazillions of autographed photos. The only celebrity in the restaurant this evening, however, was Pierre himself.

"You keep kosher?" asked Mindy.

"Just out of curiosity. Wondering what's the difference, in taste."

Mindy came a bit closer and started to whisper. "You want to know the truth? Kosher is almost twice as expensive. Supposedly they have a special kosher section in the kitchen, but I doubt that they really follow proper procedure. Actually, it's all about the conscience. My father is deeply religious, and of course he knows that I am constantly attending receptions, so he hammered it into my brain: Make sure it's kosher! If it isn't, I am not supposed to touch it."

The waiter came with the wine. Mindy and Hardy cheered.

"Tastes just like ordinary chardonnay," Hardy said.

Mindy nodded. "My point exactly — the only difference is the price."

The label on the bottle had the seal of a rabbi.

"All of this borders on the absurd, of course," Mindy said. "Have you heard about the tap water controversy?"

Hardy shook his head.

"They discovered tiny microorganisms related to shrimp in the New York water supply. Drinking, cooking, for someone who is religious: no way! Even a shower is not okay."

"Shrimps?"

"Exactly. They can only be seen with an electron microscope but still. So they brought in water trucks from upstate, which was damn expensive."

The food arrived, and Mindy devoured her *coq au vin*. "Excellent. Pierre simply excels again and again. And it reassures the conscience."

Hardy tried his *cordon bleu*. The meat was tender and succulent.

"The thing with the tap water finally went to the highest rabbis in Jerusalem," Mindy said, chewing. "It took them several days to reach a verdict."

"So?"

"At the time of the Torah no electron microscopes existed. If you can't see the tiny buggers, they are not really shrimps, and the water is kosher. Case closed."

Hardy laughed.

He tapped his knife on the *cordon bleu*. "Just a question. As far as I know, a *cordon bleu* is a pork schnitzel with cheese and ham. How can that be kosher?"

Mindy spread her arms. "Well, that's Pierre, and that's why we love him. He's just an artist. He also plays the flute and writes bilingual poems."

Hardy glanced at Pierre. He was still sitting at the table next to the bar, scribbling something on a notepad. He probably just had a culinary inspiration or drafted a bilingual poem.

"With the *cordon bleu*, he has surpassed himself," Mindy said. "The schnitzel is a fine chicken fillet, the ham has been replaced with pastrami, and for the cheese they use homemade mayonnaise."

"But then it's not really a *cordon bleu* any more ..."

168

"It is, it is! It is a kosher chicken *cordon bleu!*"

Hardy thought about his screenplay. Wouldn't it be funny if Feinstein tried to keep kosher in Mexico for his mother's sake? The additional layer of difficulty could be a great comic element. In rural Mexico probably no one had ever heard about the concept. Feinstein would need to resort to surefire kosher fare like raw carrots — or go hungry. Keeping kosher in Mexico was a terrific idea. Just the mere thought of the frail Feinstein looking at a raw carrot was hilarious.

Mindy gazed toward the entrance. "Ruby Reitman!" she whispered.
The comedienne arrived in the company of an attractive young man. The two sat down at a table with a Reserved sign.

"She's been lifted five times," Mindy whispered. "In the past she didn't have almond eyes. And certainly no snub nose."
Ruby Reitman ordered the kosher *coq au vin* and a bottle of kosher chardonnay, just like Mindy, and the young man went for a salad.
Hardy scrutinized Ruby Reitman. Actually, she didn't look too bad. Almost like on TV. Sure, she had been lifted, but it looked fine in her case.
"Who is the young man?"
Mindy shrugged. "Maybe her personal assistant. Or some gay pal."
Hardy noticed that Mindy was a bit drunk already. She ordered another bottle of wine.

Pierre went over to Ruby. They exchanged kisses on the cheeks and made small talk.

"Jewish contribution to the arts obviously makes up a large share of world heritage," Mindy said. "Especially if one considers how few we are, compared to the world population."
Hardy nodded.
"Of course, one starts to wonder: Why? Where does it all come from?"

It was a good question.

Mindy took off her glasses. She had beautiful eyes. "Unfortunately, my eyes don't tolerate contact lenses. Glasses don't really suit me, but I can't live without them."
She took a sip of wine. "Where were we?"
"Why? Where does it all come from?"
"Yes, right! Where does it all come from?" Mindy already slurred a little. Hardy felt the alcohol as well. Could it be that kosher wine was stronger than the ordinary kind?

"A FEELING OF GUILT," Mindy said aloud. "A deeply rooted FEELING OF ETERNAL GUILT and an INSANE FEAR not to meet EXPECTATIONS."

Ruby Reitman looked at them. So did Pierre and the young man.
Mindy waved at Ruby. "I'm a fan," she exclaimed. "Very, very big fan."

The comedienne nodded slightly bored and continued to talk with Pierre.

"Early on she was quite funny," whispered Mindy. "But now all she does is gossip shows. And her voice is simply annoying, I find."
Mindy ordered a third bottle of wine. Hardy noticed that she had taken off her slippers. Her opaque panty hose had a hole, and her big toe looked out.

"Where were we ...? Ah, right, and there is of course the MYSTERY OF JEWISH SEX" Mindy said loudly and accentuated. "What do you FEEL when you have JEWISH SEX?"

Ruby Reitman and company looked at Mindy. The entire restaurant looked at her, now. Hardy held his breath.

"NOT THAT MUCH!" Mindy spluttered and giggled. "NOT THAT MUCH!"

Dead Silence. Clearly, the punch line was geared toward Ruby Reitman.

Pierre jumped up, pulling his flute from a shelf, but before he could play, Ruby started to splutter just like Mindy. "NOT THAT MUCH!" she shouted. "NOT THAT MUCH! This is fantastic. I will put it into my act."

They all laughed, and Pierre played a trill on his flute.

Hardy went to the bathroom and relieved himself. Suddenly, the hunk from Ruby Reitman's table stood at

171

the next urinal, which made Hardy slightly uncomfortable. The guy could have chosen the third urinal in the corner but instead stood directly next to Hardy.

"Ruby's pretty funny, isn't she?" the pretty boy said.

Hardy nodded. He had the feeling his private parts were being evaluated by his neighbor but didn't want to look him in the eye.
The pretty boy started whistling and relieved himself with a rather subtle trickle. Out of curiosity, Hardy cast a quick look to the side and contently observed that the hunk's manhood was rather puny and no match to his own.

While still in midstream Hardy's phone vibrated in his pocket. Startled, he almost wet himself as he fumbled out the phone.

It was Jackie.

33.
THE NAKED TRUTH

"Which floor?" asked the elevator operator.
"Twelve."
A soft gong sounded while the doors closed, and the elevator gently moved up.
Hardy was nervous, not knowing what to expect. Jackie had made a secret about why he should come by urgently.
The doors opened to the sound of the gong. The corridor was covered with a carpet like in a hotel, and the walls were adorned with etchings of 19th century New York.

Jackie stood in the open door, wearing a flowered morning gown and dark Jackie Onassis sunglasses. Her skin was pale, her lips without lipstick.
"Thank God you're here," she said, smelling of alcohol.

Hardy sat down on the living room couch. Why was she wearing shades?
Jackie poured two wine glasses almost to the brim, took a swig and settled into a chair. "I almost thought I'm going to go mad, honestly."
She lit one of her ladies' cigarettes, crossed one leg over the other and rocked her foot. Her open house

slippers had a few white feathers on the strap above the toes. Jackie's feet were sexy.

"Can I have a cigarette?"
"Sure." She slid the pack across the table. "I didn't know you smoked"
"Only occasionally."
"Yeah, it's out of fashion, but I just can't stop."

Hardy lit the cigarette. The nicotine immediately went into his brain and gave him a slight high.
"Nervous?" asked Jackie.
Hardy blew smoke rings into the air. "No."
"You can relax. We are alone. Benny is at a premiere in Chicago."

Hardy took a sip of wine.

"Don't you wonder why I am wearing dark glasses?"
"I do."
"Why don't you ask, then?"
"Okay, why are you wearing dark glasses?"

Jackie ripped them off. "That's why!"

She had an enormous black eye. It was swollen, and some parts shone blue, yellow and green. She put her glasses back on.
"It was much worse, but I still can't go out this way."
"Sure."
"Why don't you ask why I have a black eye. You don't care?"
"I do. Why do you have a black eye?"

174

"BECAUSE I DON'T LIKE SLUTS!" Jackie screamed, throwing her cigarette out the open window with an aggressive swing. "If I ever see that bitch again, I'll kill her."

Apparently Jackie had been in a catfight when attending a function with Benny, and the other woman had given her a good punch.

"Okay, but why did you fight?" Hardy asked.

"Why, why ... This bitch's been getting on my nerves for years. I just couldn't take it any more."

It was quiet for a moment. Jackie sobbed, and a tear ran down her cheek. "Sorry, I'm just so out of it because I've been stuck in here for almost two weeks." She slid over to the couch and fell into his arms. "Hold me tight."

Hardy hugged her and ran his hand through her hair. She wept, and her tears moistened his cheek.

"Sometimes I'm scared," Jackie said.

"Scared of what?"

"Everything. It's just all scary, don't you think?"

Hardy felt the warmth of her body. She sniffled, slowly sliding up her hand on his thigh.

Hardy felt paralyzed. He didn't know why, but his magic stick stayed limp.

"Nothing ...?" Jackie said.

She jumped up. "I don't turn you on, right? The way I am now, doesn't arouse you, is that it?"

Hardy kept quiet.

"But this is me," she said. "This is the real Jackie, the naked truth. Why don't you ask why I didn't want to sleep with you?"

Hardy's eyebrow started to twitch. The evening moved into a direction he did not like that much.

"Okay, why didn't you want to sleep with me?"

Jackie undid the belt of her robe, covered her breast with her hand and turned to the side. Shortly below the armpit was a red scar, about two inches long.

"That's why."

Jackie closed the robe again and tightened the belt. "They discovered a few knots several weeks ago, and I was terrified. Fortunately, it was benign. But it still hurts. Every touch hurts, you know?"

She wiped the tears from her eyes. "Wait a minute, okay?" She disappeared, and he heard her sing:

Nooooohhhh, rien de rien, noooooohhhh, je ne regrette rien ...

Shortly after, she came back, wearing the same outfit as in the Peninsula, the only difference being the dark sunglasses. "How's that? Does this work?"

Hardy nodded.

Jackie laughed. "All men are the same. It's sad, actually, but that's just the way it is."

She lay down on the couch and slowly opened her legs, showing him her nude pussy. The pornographic pose aroused him enormously.

"Come here. But don't touch my breasts, okay?"

176

Hardy penetrated her.

Jackie unbuttoned his shirt and ran her slender hands over his chest. He could not see her eyes as the sunglasses were just too dark, but somehow this added to the excitement. He kissed her finely cut lips, and they played around with their tongues. Jackie moaned and pressed against him ever tighter. Hardy felt that she was all his now, and that she entirely belonged to him. It was a magnificent feeling, and he didn't know if he had ever felt better. Probably not.
Hardy was close to climaxing but suddenly sensed an odd presence and looked back:

Behind him stood Drexler with a blinking ice pick.

Hardy screamed in horror and held his hands over his head.
Jackie shook him with both hands: "What the hell is wrong? Good Lord, it's only the curtain, honey ..."
Hardy looked at the window. The waving curtain reflected on the wall mirror behind him, and the blinking came from a silver curtain ring. His vivid imagination had once again played a trick on him.

Hardy was still on top of Jackie, his erection gone.

The shock had been worse than a bath in the arctic ocean.

34.
A SPECIAL DAY

Jackie took Hardy's hand. The love scene with Mastroianni and Sophia Loren had been masterfully directed, especially since Mastroianni was gay in the film.
They sat in the large auditorium of Lincoln Center. *Una giornata particulare* ran in the original Italian with English subtitles. Hardy knew the film. A classic of Italian cinema. Nonetheless, the screening was poorly attended.

Hardy and Jackie kissed. He stroked her legs, and she caressed his neck. It was romantic with her in the dark auditorium and almost felt like they were a freshly enamored teenage couple.

Fortunately, Jackie had built him up again after the utter horror with the curtain. Once on the couch and then again in bed.
He had spent the night with her but slept horribly. Benny's vibe was simply everywhere. His medication was lined up on the nightstand, and his house slippers were neatly arranged beside the bed.

"The movie was really sad," Jackie said. "I don't

understand why they didn't flee together. There was time to escape!"

Hardy and Jackie were sitting in an Italian restaurant, eating *ossobuco* and drinking red wine. Jackie was wearing the Jackie Onassis sunglasses again.

"He was gay," Hardy said. "There was no future for them."

"Gay, gay," Jackie said. "He slept with her. So maybe he wasn't *that* gay after all."

"He did it because he found her charming. He liked her."

"Nonsense. He had simply not yet found the right one, that's why. The two were a fantastic fit. They simply would have had to elope! To Capri for example!"

Hardy's phone rang. He suddenly remembered having arranged to meet with Kristen. He had completely forgotten about it and turned off the phone.

"Who was it, why didn't you pick up?"

"Don't recognize the number."

"Still, you could have picked up. Who knows, perhaps it was important."

"Probably a telemarketer."

"Or maybe a woman? Why don't we simply return the call?"

The waiter came to the table and poured wine into their glasses. In the background Adriano Celentano wavered over the sound system: *Azzurro ..., il pomeriggio è troppo azzurro e lungo ..., per me ...*

Hardy had agreed to meet with Kristen in a Café in the East Village. She had probably used a payphone from there.

"There is no other woman," Hardy said. "Only you."
"Give me your phone. Just a little test if you tell the truth."
"You're kidding, aren't you?"

"Give me the phone, or I will leave right now!"

Hardy had no choice but to give her the phone.
"Pretty heavy, that thing. Couldn't you get a better one?" Jackie peered from under her sunglasses, and part of her black eye was visible. She examined the phone.

Hardy held his breath. If Jackie managed to get a connection with Kristen, all hell would break loose.

Jackie pressed a few buttons, and the phone made an odd beeping sound. "Damn, I think I've done something wrong."
She shoved the phone back to Hardy. "I could have gotten one myself by now, but I don't want one because of Benny. No doubt he would constantly check up on me ..."
Hardy looked at the display. Jackie had landed on the page with the ringtones. "Hm, I think you've deleted the number."
"Jackie shrugged. "Okay, never mind. If it was just a telemarketer, it doesn't matter anyway."

Hardy put the phone away, casually turning it off.

"This thing has a camera, doesn't it" Jackie said.. "Why don't we take a picture? Today is a special day!"

"The camera is not that good, really."
"Nonsense, it's good enough for a snapshot." Jackie waved to the waiter. "A photo, please!"
Hardy pulled out the phone but deactivated the antenna.

The waiter took a photo.

"One more!" Jackie said. "This time with a kiss."
They kissed, and the waiter took a second photo. Jackie looked at the snapshots. "The sunglasses look completely stupid," she said. "But it's fine. The important thing is that we have immortalized this day, haven't we?"
She pulled a tattered notebook from her bag. "I collect worldly wisdom," she said. "When I hear something interesting, I write it down."
She leafed through her book. "Here, for example. An old fisherman in Ensenada told me this when I bought a necklace with a beautiful shell from him. "Touch your amulet, and pick a wave ...!"
Hardy didn't quite understand what she meant.
"Pick a wave, and take a wish, the fisherman told me. This wave will never come back ..."
Jackie took a sip of wine. "Understand?"

The stereo played: *Marina, Marina, Marina, ti voglio al più presto sposar ...*

"Do you think I look old?"
"No."
"We don't match. I'm too old for you, right?"
"Nonsense."

"How about we spend a weekend in Montreal? The food is excellent, and they have that certain *je ne sais quois*. We could check in as Mr. and Mrs. von Hachenstein and see if they buy it ..."

"And Benny?"

"Uh, forget Benny. He doesn't exist any more, okay?"

"Okay."

Jackie leafed through her notebook. "*Life is a tiny feather in a wild hurricane ...* Beautiful! I don't remember who said it, but it's beautiful."

She took Hardy's hand. "We'll always be honest with each other, okay? No lies, no cheating, no stupid games. Promise?"

Hardy nodded.

Jackie pulled him tight, and they kissed.

"Okay," she said. "But now comes the real important part. What's your worldly wisdom if you'd put it in one phrase? The most important thing!"

The waiter stood before them. "Another bottle of wine?"

Jackie shook her head. "Enough with the wine. It's time for *sambuca*."

"*Con la mosca?*"

"Of course."

The waiter disappeared.

"Okay," Jackie said. "So?"

Hardy knew that this was crucial. He could tell from the tattered book that Jackie cherished her collected wisdom more than anything. One wrong word could ruin it all.

Obviously, he could not come up with some lame, pithy Anglo-Saxon folk wisdom to the tune of *The early bird catches the worm* — it needed to be the opposite. Romantic, allegorical, and flowery.

Hardy had never asked Jackie about her roots. Drexler was Jewish, but Jackie was not. Why would she wear a fine golden cross around her neck if she were Jewish? Hardy suspected that she had Spanish or Portuguese ancestors, but this was not the right time to ask.

He remembered a Spanish poet, whose name had escaped him. He quoted from memory and tweaked it a bit to make it fit. He spoke slowly and accentuated, moving both hands in gentle waves:

Good is water and thirst;
Good is shade and sunlight;
... and the honey of rosemary flowers.

Jackie sat there, stunned. It had hit home like lightning. A tear ran down her cheek. "Wonderful," she whispered, scribbling the phrase in her book.

The waiter came back with the *sambuca*, putting out the flame with a small plate.

Hardy and Jackie savored the warm liquor and chewed the roasted coffee beans.

35.
PUT TO THE TEST

Upon Blanchette's request, office management had installed a room divider which was fine with Hardy since he now saw much less of her. Her presence was still to be felt, though, and that was bad enough.

Hardy stared at the pile of paper before him. He was on page TCA-009335. It was odd, but so far nobody had given the slightest comment on his work, and sometimes he felt that nobody ever would. He was working away without aim and purpose, and that made it even worse. Still, he needed to advance at least gradually. The chance that somebody would eventually check was remotely possible.

His office phone rang. Until this moment nobody had ever called, not even Colm. Hardy looked at the caller ID and froze:

It was Harold Gallagher.

What could the head honcho want? Was it about the TCA matter? It seemed strange that a partner would call a lowly linguistic support or legal assistant directly. He would always have somebody else call. Blanchette only received calls from Colm and never from a partner. Could it be that they found out that he wasn't really Steven C. Cornfield? Did Gallagher maybe have the FBI in his office?

Hardy did not pick up, and let Gallagher's call go straight to voice mail.

Shortly after, he checked the message. Gallagher sounded serious and firm. "Howdy, Steve. Call me back ASAP."

Hardy was extremely preoccupied by now. Why didn't Gallagher say what he wanted? This did not sound good at all.

Hardy had googled the boss out of curiosity. The firm's website showed the usual portrait with a bookshelf backdrop. Gallagher in suit and tie with a fatherly smile, exuding respectability. On the Theater Company's website he was pictured attending premiere parties and an award ceremony. In this artsy environment he seemed to be the king of casual, wearing shirts with sleeves rolled up, cheering with champagne, laughing and exposing his pointed teeth, making it obvious where his nickname came from. Behind his back he was called the *Barracuda*.

Hardy pondered if he should just take his things and run. But if it was really the FBI in Gallagher's office, they would have certainly placed some agents at the exits on the ground floor.

Hardy decided to face his destiny head on. Maybe he overreacted, maybe it was much simpler than he thought. But it was just so odd that the partner would call him directly. What the hell could he want?

185

Hardy picked up the phone and dialed Gallagher's number.

Unexpectedly, the Barracuda sounded quite friendly, now. "How's it going, Steve. Could you come by my office, I have a little question."
"Right now?"
"Yes." Gallagher sounded serious and firm again. "Or do you have anything else to do?"

Hardy took his toothbrush from the desk drawer and went to the bathroom. He brushed his teeth, splashed water on his face and looked into the mirror. He looked tired and a bit bloated. He had feared that a moment like this would come when he would be put on the spot without warning and without being able to prepare.
Hardy adjusted his tie. In his office he didn't wear it, but when he stepped out, he put it on. It was all about fitting in and flying low.

Hardy took the elevator to the 30th floor, then transferred to the second elevator tract leading to the 53rd floor. The lawyers had an express elevator that only stopped on floors 30 through 53. The other floors, assigned to service personnel, practically didn't exist for them.
From the start, Hardy had noticed that there was an invisible but extremely sharp dividing line between *attorneys* and *other people*. Certain areas or events were *attorneys only* and simply off limits for *other people*.
Hardy had heard that the firm threw a lavish outing for the lawyers each summer. It was usually held at some

186

exclusive golf course or a yacht club or something of the like. On the same day they also threw a party for staff, but it was a totally different affair. It was held in a ballroom in Brooklyn and consisted of musical entertainment and a dinner buffet with disposable table ware.

Hardy walked through the corridors of the 53rd floor. It was blissfully quiet, as the fine carpet suppressed the noise. Finally, he stood before Gallagher's office.
The secretary pushed her glasses up her nose and waved him in. "They're waiting for you."

Hardy took a deep breath and stepped in. Gallagher was chatting with two young men at the conference table. His six-year-old son was sitting on the executive chair at the desk, scribbling in a coloring book. Hardy started to relax a bit. At least this was not about identity fraud. Or so it seemed.

The view was spectacular. The sky over Central Park was blue with little white clouds sprinkled in. Birds circled majestically above the treetops. The most prominent spot of the office featured a large photo framed in gold:

Gallagher shaking hands with the PRESIDENT OF THE UNITED STATES.

The boss had noticed Hardy and waved him over with a smile, revealing his barracuda teeth.
"Sit down, Steve. Meet Ian McCloud and Jack Lee from our London office."

McCloud had a musketeer haircut and a reddish blond goatee. His style resembled Hardy's, except that McCloud was a redhead with freckles. Jack Lee looked like a young sumo wrestler, an impression intensified by his tight-fitting suit.

Hardy took a seat.

Gallagher had taken off his jacket and loosened his tie. His golden cufflinks resembled small golf balls.
"Okay, Steve," Gallagher said. "You probably ask yourself why you needed to stop by in my office, right?"
Hardy nodded.

"Well, it's rather easy," the Barracuda said with a sly smile. "We simply want to know if you would SELL US YOUR SOUL."

Noticing the photos by the bookshelf, showing a young Gallagher in the role of *Mephisto*, Hardy quickly realized what this was about. His brain worked on overdrive, scanning schooldays memories. He finally came up with the only line he remembered. Raising his arms in a theatrical gesture, he exclaimed:

Here now I stand, poor fool and see ...
I'm just as wise as formerly.

The Barracuda giggled and his young colleagues chuckled along. Gallagher's son looked up from his coloring book, mouth agape. Naturally, he didn't understand the context.

"Not bad, Steve," the Barracuda said. "It seems you really are a thespian at heart. But enough now — let's get down to business."

He slid a memo across the table.

"We just received this from a French expert. Unfortunately, he barely speaks English, and our French is a bit rusty. Can you help?"

"Where's mommy," shouted the little fellow, "She promised we'd to go to the movies today."

"She's on her way, Tyler. I've already told you so."

Hardy read the first few lines of the French memo. It was a complicated analysis of French-Swiss banking rules. He understood absolutely zilch.

"It's boring here!" Tyler jumped from the chair, trying to throw an autographed baseball into an umbrella stand.

"Stop it," Gallagher said. "Sit back and paint your book."

Tyler picked up the baseball and sat down at the table. He fiddled with the ball, threw it into the air, and caught it again.

"Sorry," said Gallagher. "The nanny is sick, and my wife had an urgent appointment."

Hardy's heart pounded in his temples. He had no inkling what the letter was about.

"How is it coming along, Steve? You got it?"

"Quite a lot of acronyms. Can I have some background?"

"Catch, daddy!" Tyler threw the baseball, but instead of reaching Gallagher, it hit the back of Hardy's head. The filmmaker groaned.

"Damn it, what's the matter with you?" Gallagher jumped up and grabbed Tyler by the ear.
"Okay, buddy." He took him to the corner of the room and let him face the wall. "You stay right here, now, until mommy arrives, and if I hear one damn thing from you, you'll get a set of hot ears you will never forget."

McCloud slid a note across the table: *ITE — illegal tax evasion; FCR — foreign customer recruitment.*
"Those are English acronyms, of course," McCloud said. "But they use them in French as well."

The text still didn't make much sense.

Gallagher sat down again. "We already know that they did it, obviously. The question is, is there anything in writing?"
"And then, of course, internal-external," Jack Lee said.
"And if the board knew about it," said McCloud.

Tyler sobbed in his corner but did not move.

Hardy was still fishing for meaning, sweating heavily. He quickly read the last paragraph again. There he had seen something with internal-external. He just had to deliver something, now.

"Internal, yes. External, no."

Gallagher nodded. "That's good, but we already pretty much knew that. The question is: What did they do internally?"

Hardy read the last paragraph again. Although he still did not understand the meaning he caught a few key words. "Something could be done with the hard drives," he said. "But then there's still the digital footprint."

The lawyers threw anxious looks at each other.

The door burst open: Gallagher's wife, a young, wiry blonde. "Sorry, honey, it's been a crazy day, and I almost totaled the Jaguar."

Gallagher looked petrified.

His wife laughed. "Just a little joke, honey. The Jaguar is fine."

Tyler threw himself into his mother's arms and sobbed. "What's going on, my darling, what is it? Your ear is red ..." She threw her husband an angry look. "Did you pull his ear again?"

Gallagher turned to Hardy. "Take the memo with you and translate the whole thing. We need to know the details."

"It's really mean that you always pull him by the ear, Harold. I thought we had discussed this ..."

Hardy sat at his workstation. Relieved that he had made it out of Gallagher's office, he closed his eyes and rested his head on his desk. Sure, he needed the money, but for how long would be able to endure this buffoonery?

Blanchette had tuned into the easy listening channel again. Since she sat behind the divider, now, she no longer used her headphones but played the music directly over the radio. Although the volume was low, it could still be heard. The music pierced Hardy's brain, and he could not concentrate. He felt the strong urge to kick down the divider and smash Blanchette's radio to pieces, but he held himself back. He would get to her one day but not now. He had to translate the damn letter.

Hardy spat on a paper towel, formed two small beads and plugged his ears.

36.
THE HEALTH LOAN

Bill stood at the firm's exit, next to the revolving door. He looked more emaciated than ever, with a thicker and longer beard.
Just like most of the other employees, Hardy had left the office at exactly 5:30, feeling exhausted.

"Three hundred bucks" said Bill. "What's three hundred bucks for you? And I just want it as a loan. You will get it back, man."

More and more employees poured out of the building. Some cast a curious look at the odd pair.
"How do you know where I work?"
Bill laughed. "I'm always on the street, man, and a few days ago I saw you walking by, all dressed up in suit and tie, so I followed you."
"You followed me?"
"Out of curiosity. You're obviously doing fine, quite unlike me. And since we're old friends, I thought it couldn't hurt if I ask you. Three hundred bucks, man, what's three hundred bucks for you?"

"I don't have three hundred, Bill. I can give you twenty."

"I need three hundred."

"Why three hundred?"

"Look at me. Something's wrong with me. My stomach is acting up. I have cramps and can't keep anything down. I need to see a doctor."

"What's with Medic Aid?"

"Won't work."

"Why?"

"A long story."

"Then go to the emergency room."

"I did. They gave me two freakin' pills that didn't do nothin'. I need three hundred bucks."

"But I don't have three hundred."

"So you want me to die in the gutter, is that it?" Bill had an insane look. It seemed like he would start screaming.

Suddenly, Colm stood next to them, his briefcase under his arm. "What's going on, everything okay?"

"Yes," Hardy said. "We're fine."

Colm took a short glance at Bill and padded Hardy's shoulder. "Okay, if everything's fine ... Have a nice evening." He left and disappeared at the entrance to the subway.

Bill held his stomach. He stood there, slightly bent forward, as if he had strong abdominal pain and would throw up any second.

Hardy dug into his pocket. "Here's forty bucks."

Bill did not accept the money.

"I need three hundred. A consultation with a doctor who can really help costs three hundred."

"Okay, if you don't want it." Hardy put the money away, ready to leave.

Bill grabbed his arm. His grip was surprisingly strong. "I want you to lend me the money, man. It's a loan, got it? You'll get it back in three weeks."

"Why me?"

Bill made a tired, circling gesture with his free hand. "Look around, man. No one's gonna freakin' help you in this freakin' city. Especially if you need it urgently."

"What about your book stand?"

"I am too weak to find new things."

"Why don't you go to welfare?"

Bill smiled wearily.

Blanchette hurried past them without casting the slightest look. She quickly disappeared in the subway entrance.

"I need three hundred, and I need them now!" Bill said determined.

"I offered you forty. It's all I've got."

Bill looked at Hardy with a piercing gaze. "Okay, I didn't want to go that far, but you force me to. You have a bank account, Mr. Steven C. Cornfield."

Hardy froze.

"How ... how do you know?"

"That's no great feat," said Bill. "You remember who brought up the idea in the first place, don't you? Who came up with it, tell me? A brief chat with the boys from your mail room was enough to find out that Steven C. Cornfield is alive and well. And how so? Only

195

because you put my idea into action! Did you tell me anything about it? I don't think so. Is that what you call gratitude? I don't think so. Do you think that's fair? No, it's freakin' unfair, my friend. You live like a king, and you owe it all to me. Without me you would still be an illegal sucker, just like when I met you."

"I'm sitting in a windowless bunker, Bill. It's like jail, man. And it doesn't even pay that well. The suit and tie mean absolutely nothing."

"I'm dying, man. You're letting me die because of lousy three hundred bucks? And it's just a loan, man. I want no damn alms. I will pay back every dime as soon as I get back on my feet."

Bill pulled a flyer from his pocket: The FBI's most wanted list. Top left there was a stapled business card: *Russell Linnard — FBI Identity Fraud Department.*

"I did not want to go this far, but you force me to," Bill said. "The FBI has an office at Federal Plaza. Russell is a real good guy who knows what he's doing. Nowadays, with the internet and all, identity fraud is one of their greatest problems, and they appreciate all the leads they can get. You're my friend, of course, and that's why I am asking you as a friend to help me out, man. It's a simple loan, that's all it is."

37.
LOOSE CHANGE

Hardy stood in the packed subway, seizing a handhold. The E train rumbled over the tracks and entered a curve, squealing. Hardy felt paralyzed, not perceiving anything around him. He cursed his fate. It was obvious that he was on Bill's mercy from now on, and he had grudgingly forked over the three hundred dollars. He hoped that Bill would get back on his feet and subsequently would leave him alone, but he feared otherwise.

The train stopped at Penn Station, and the filmmaker stumbled outside. As always the basement swarmed with commuters trying to catch their connections. Hardy accidentally bumped against a woman and apologized. His brain felt like cotton candy, and he could not think clearly. Moreover, his chest constricted, and he had trouble breathing. He stumbled up the stairs to the outside, leaning against a wall.

Traffic didn't move on Eighth Avenue, and numerous cars honked furiously. Hardy faced the huge post office across the street: a neoclassical building with Doric columns that resembled like a Greek temple. He stared at the phrase carved in above the entrance: *Neither snow nor rain nor heat nor gloom of night stays these couriers from the swift completion of their appointed rounds.*

Hardy felt exhausted. Somehow, he wished that he could get out of his skin. He wanted to flee and be somebody else. But he couldn't flee, and he couldn't be anybody else. He was who he was and had to stay the course, just like the good old U.S. mail carriers. He had seen the phrase before and, since it was incredibly poetic for the U.S. Postal Service, researched it. Far from having come up with it themselves they had plucked it from the work of Herodotus describing the ancient Persian system of mounted postal carriers.

Hardy went up to the loft. When he came out of the elevator, he was greeted by party noise: Byrdseed's release party. They had told him in advance, but he had forgotten about it.

He was tired, but he had to show his face at least for a minute.

The recording studio was full of people. They had drinks in hand and chatted in small groups. Chris explained the functions of a converted Rickenbacker guitar to a journalist, and Carl walked around offering guacamole and tortilla chips.

The sound system played Miles Davis.

Byrdseed could have put on their new album of course, but that would have been uncool. Byrdseed had style, and most of the selected guests knew the songs of *Loose Change* already anyway.

Rainer had come with his wife, Linda. She wore a fedora and an angler's vest, thus resembling the female version of Joseph Beuys. She had designed the cover of Byrdseed's new album: An open guitar case with some loose change in front of the arch at Washington Square Park.

Hardy shook hands with Linda and padded Rainer on the shoulder. They hadn't seen each other in quite a while.
Rainer held out a flyer. "Ever heard about The Quirks? They play in Basement 27 next week."
Hardy couldn't believe it. Of course, he knew them! The band was from Berlin, and their soundman was Kermit Drebbich who had formerly been the technician of Hardy's band, T.T. Embargo.
"Linda did the flyers, and we can put you on the guest list," Rainer said. "Are you coming?"
Hardy nodded and put the flyer in his pocket.

A short while later the filmmaker lay in his bed, staring at the ceiling. The drywall that separated his room from the recording studio was thin, and he could hear the party noise.

Hardy pulled the blanket over his head, assuming the fetal position. He slowly drifted away ...

Somewhere in the jungle. Hardy hears birds screeching and monkeys screaming, but not a single animal is in sight. The sun barely breaks through the dense undergrowth. It is hot and humid, and sweat runs down his body. Similar to Tarzan he is barefoot, wearing only a loincloth.

Suddenly, a feathered arrow zips past him, piercing a tree. Hardy hears a giggle and discovers a pygmy with a blowpipe. The little man wears war paint and resembles Bill. Another arrow zips past from a different direction, missing Hardy only by a hair's width. A second pygmy, who also looks like Bill, lurks behind a bush.

Hardy runs for his life, pursued by blowpipe arrows zipping around him. He stumbles through the dense undergrowth, branches slapping him in the face, rotten wood collapsing under his feet, sweat burning in his eyes. The cacophony of birds and monkeys gets louder, without a single animal in sight.

A Mini Bill, emitting a battle cry, jumps from a tree, clinging firmly to Hardy's back, biting him in the neck. Hardy screams and tries to shake off the monster but to no avail. The grip of the pygmy is like that of a vice.

In full running speed Hardy makes a quick half-turn, letting himself fall flat on his back. He hears a muffled sound resembling the bursting of a ripe tomato and a short groan. Relieved from the monster, Hardy jumps up and runs on, followed by a screaming mob of pygmies.

Suddenly, a deep abyss opens in front of him, the distance to the other side being at least twenty yards. Behind Hardy a horde of Mini Bills comes running and screaming.

He grabs a vine and swings, yodeling, across the abyss as he recognizes a familiar figure on the other side: Benny Drexler swinging a battle axe.

Hardy woke up, bathed in sweat. It was unbearably hot, since he had forgotten to turn off his recently purchased electrical heater.

He went to the bathroom. The loft was deserted now. Only a few glasses and dirty plates reminded of the party.

Hardy stared out the window looking down on Eighth Avenue. It was already three in the morning, but traffic never stopped.

38.
BREVITY IS THE SOUL OF WIT

Francisco moved his head back and forth, then circled it gently. "Today they removed the damn neck brace. I feel like a human being again."

Hardy was anxious to hear from Feinstein. It all dragged on for ages, and nothing ever advanced without him following up.

Francisco looked into his notebook. "Okay, here's Avi's fax number."

He scribbled something on a piece of paper and put it in the fax machine:

FRANCISCO HERE. READ MAYHEM IN MEXICO?

Hardy pressed his thumbs into his fists, hoping for the best. The fax machine communicated with Feinstein's machine and spat out a transmission report.

"Great," Francisco said. "At least his fax is turned on."

He lit a cigarette and flipped through a few bills.

It smelled of buttered popcorn. The documentary program from Iran had begun, and the lobby was filled with people who spoke Farsi.

Jimmy stood in the door, holding a mug of coffee. "Here's your java, Francy," he said. "Anything else?"

Jimmy and Francisco seemed oddly familiar, and Hardy wondered if there was something sexual going on between them.

A call came in, and the fax machine spat out Feinstein's response:

NO TIME YET.

Hardy felt a punch in the gut.

Francisco faxed back:

WHEN?

The answer came promptly:

FLIGHT TO LAS VEGAS NEXT WEEK.

Francisco faxed:

HOW'S MOM DOING?

Answer:

BETTER. THANKS FOR ASKING. OVER.

"Can I have a cigarette?"
Francisco smiled and slid over the pack. "I thought you had quit ..."
The filmmaker drew in the smoke and instantly felt better. "Do you think he will actually read it next week?"

"Nothing is certain," Francisco said. "But on the plane he sure would have time."

Hardy blew smoke rings into the air. "Kind of curious why Jackie married Drexler, of all people."
"Good Lord," Francisco turned his eyes skyward and made a cross in front of his chest. "Are you still seeing her?"
"They don't match. Not at all."
"If you look closely, they do."
"It seems that she's Spanish or Portuguese from her heritage."
"She's from good old Boston," Francisco said. "And her parents are Armenian immigrants. I heard that she was trained in classical ballet, but when she came to New York, she somehow ended up doing sleazy films."
"Pornographic?"
"Not quite but almost."

Hardy didn't have a mature female character in the script. A type like Jackie could be Lugo's sister and the mastermind behind it all. Jackie had the aura of a mean fairy tale queen, and Hardy had always liked the mean queen much better than the good one. The mean queen was dangerous and sexy, whereas the good queen was somewhat bland.

"Supposedly, Jackie and Drexler don't do anything anymore, but he's terribly jealous."
"And he has every reason to be, a fact you certainly know from your own experience, don't you?"
"I'm just a friend. Nothing else."
"Yes, sure," Francisco said, smirking. "Just a friend."

39.
THE QUIRKS

"Kiss me," Jackie said.
"Here? In front of everyone?"
She pulled Hardy close and gave him a passionate kiss, somewhat unusual for a lady her age.
They sat at a table in the gallery of Basement 27 with Rainer and Linda. Down at the stage The Quirks let it rip. It was a crazy avant-garde concert. Basement 27 was not particularly large and couldn't hold more than two hundred people. Downstairs, in front of the stage, it was standing room only, and in the gallery they had tables for special guests.

The kiss turned Hardy on, and he felt chipper. Ah, life was good, so good! He liked that Jackie acted so openly sexual, it was almost like a teenage romance. He simply felt good in her company. The only problem was Drexler. Sure, he wouldn't live forever, but nowadays you never knew. Modern medicine was quite advanced, and with a little bit of luck and freshly squeezed orange juice he might have twenty more years in him.

The Quirks wore red and white checkered overalls and matching pointed hats. They played a New Wave version of the folk tune "Hänschen Klein," which they had translated into English.

The band experimented with homemade instruments. Part of their arsenal were bagpipes fed by vacuum cleaners, a synthesizer based on Vietnamese car horns, and a xylophone fashioned from the bones of a Brandenburg bog body.

Until now, Hardy had no music act in the script. Actually, every feature film needed at least one live performance. It gave the audience time to breathe and provided local flavor. First, Hardy had thought of a *mariachi* band, but that was a cliché. Much better and more surprising was a Mexican version of The Quirks. Maybe they'd wear checkered cowboy hats and acutely pointed boots? Hardy made a mental note: *Research Mexican avant-garde.*

"Who's that?" Jackie said, pointing into the crowd in front of the stage. "That girl is staring at you. What does she want? I've noticed her for a while, now." Hardy looked down and froze.

It was Kristen.

Was this a coincidence, or had she guessed that he might show up at the gig of a Berlin band?

Suddenly, Kristen stood in front of their table, her usual pale complexion turned to red. "You cheated and you lied, you used and abused me," she screamed. "And you're a measly coward. Shame on you, you dirty bastard!" She spat on Hardy's face and ran away.

The Quirks switched to German in their song: *Stock und Hut, steht ihm gut, er ist wohlgemut ...*

"Lively young lady," Jackie said. "Unfortunately, she looks a bit like a ferret."

Hardy wiped the spittle from his forehead but felt it was still there: an invisible mark of Cain.
Rainer pushed his glasses up his nose. "What was that, Steve? The poor thing was completely blown away."
"Steve?" Jackie said, startled. "Why Steve? I thought your name is Hardy?"
"Hardy, Steve, all the same," Hardy said." Steve is my middle name. "
"Middle Name? Why do you use your middle name with him and not with me? And what did you do to the poor ferret?"

After the concert a party was thrown backstage. The press held interviews with the musicians. Drinks and snacks were arranged on a sideboard.

"It's pretty obvious that you slept with her," Jackie said gulping down a glass of wine. "The only question is: when?"
"It was a mistake. It just happened."
"Ha, ha ...," she imitated him. "It just happened ... The question is: Did you sleep with her, when we already knew each other?"

"It was before your time."

"Before my time ... really?"

"Man, Hucky, good to see you. Linda told me that you're here."

Before them stood Kermit, soundman of The Quirks and former technician of Hardy's Berlin band, T.T. Embargo. They hugged and padded each other on the shoulder.

"Where are the dreadlocks?" Hardy asked.

Kermit lifted his baseball cap, under which he concealed his baldness. He grinned.

"Wait a minute," said Jackie. "Hucky, why Hucky, now? I thought you were Hardy."

"A complicated story. In my early days I was Hucky, now I am Hardy."

"And sometimes Steve, right?"

Jackie lit one of her slim cigarettes and drew in the smoke vigorously. "Okay, then I just want to know under what name you fucked the ferret. Bozo the Clown?" She gave him a slap in the face and stormed into the ladies' room.

Kermit grinned. "You seem to be very well integrated already. Still doing music?"

Hardy shook his head. His time as a guitarist of T.T. Embargo seemed light years away. If he would have picked up a guitar now, he probably couldn't even play their songs straight.

Hardy was getting nervous. Where was Jackie? Linda looked into the ladies' room, but Jackie wasn't there.

Hardy walked around the backstage area, peering into the small adjoining rooms. Nothing. He went outside and checked the street, but she wasn't there either.

Hardy drifted through Greenwich Village, hoping to find Jackie somewhere in a bar. The streets were full of young revelers — a couple kissed, two guys shared a joint, a group of young women fiddled with their cell phones.

Jackie was nowhere to be found.

40.
A SMALL INVESTMENT

Hardy sat in the office and worked on the final scenes of his screenplay. Blanchette's spot was empty. She was on leave or sick.

Hardy felt extremely low because of Jackie, but what could he do? The best way to numb the pain was to immerse himself in his script. This way he was in another world, and the real problems faded away, at least for a while.

He wrote Jackie's character into the scenes with Lugo. The mean female element was great. Seeing Jackie as Lugo's sister in Mexico made him long for her even more. Why the hell had he gone to that damn concert? Without the Kristen incident everything would still be fine! — Hardy felt a strange presence and looked up:

Colm stood in the doorway, observing him.

The project manager had snuck up on Hardy without making the slightest sound. He looked serious. "How's it coming along, Steve? Everything okay?"

Hardy had feared that this moment would come one day. If Colm stepped around the desk, seeing the script on the screen, he would probably fire Hardy on the spot.

"They are getting a bit nervous upstairs," Colm said. "If you're not done soon, we will miss the deadline."

"Deadline ...?" Hardy said. "Nobody told me about a deadline ..."

"Well, I'm telling you now. I had hoped that you would have long finished. I had also hoped that you'd keep me in the loop about your progress."

"It's a challenging task," Hardy said apologetically. "It's all out of order, very confusing. And then there's that Disneyland thing. What am I supposed to do with that?" Hardy stretched out his arms and moaned, implying that he had been hard at work.

"Disneyland?"

Hardy put his arms down, thereby casually grabbing the mouse and clicking his script away. Now he had the TCA index on his screen.

"Yeah," Hardy said. "I separated it because I don't know what to do with it." Hardy slid the travel brochure across the table.

Colm looked at it and shook his head. "Fascinating," he said. "It has the TCA numbers, but it has absolutely nothing to do with the case."

"Exactly," Hardy said.

"I will investigate this," Colm said. "We have long suspected that we have some bad apples in the IT department. They drop a box of extremely sensitive docs on the floor and scan the material completely out of order. Apparently somebody in the IT department is planning a trip to Disneyland. I will make sure that this person gets to see Mickey Mouse soon. But on a one-way ticket."

Hardy's cell phone rang. Glancing at the display he saw it was Francisco. He turned the device off.

Colm checked his watch. "I'm on a way to a meeting, and I'm a bit late, so I'm going to be brief. As you've probably heard, we have a big problem with wasted time at company expense: web surfing, extensive private phone calls or simply squandering. No company can sustain this for long."
Hardy nodded. "Yes, sure, but Blanchette is totally clean, if that's what you are referring to. Don't know where she is today, though. Maybe on sick leave."
"Blanchette is beyond doubt," Colm said. "She is one of our best and most loyal employees, and she's helping me with reorganizing our archive."

Hardy suspected that Blanchette had snitched on him. She had noticed that he worked on his own stuff most of the time and passed it on. Why would Colm turn up unannounced, especially when she was away?

"Let me see where you stand," Colm said. "Let me see the index."
Hardy turned his screen around, and Colm studied the list. "You're not even halfway through. If you continue at this snail's pace you will finish next Christmas."
"As I said, it's a mess. ... All out of order. But I'm getting the knack of it. I think I can speed it up somewhat."

"I need a detailed status report by tomorrow," Colm said in a serious tone. "I need to know how many pages you can average per day. If you can't finish by the end of next week, we will need to rethink your assignment." He turned around and left, his gait slightly bent to one side again.

Hardy glanced out the door, making sure the coast was clear. He was anxious to know what Francisco wanted. If Feinstein had kept his word he must have read the sample scenes by now. Hardy nervously dialed Francisco's number. He pushed his thumb in his fist, hoping for good news.

"Good morning, my dear," Francisco said. "How are we feeling today?"
"Stop bullshitting, "Hardy said. "Did he read it?"
"Yes, he did."
Hardy's heart beat in his temples. He was incredibly nervous. "So?"
"We are one step further. He wants to see *Cryptic X*."

Hardy let out a sigh of relief.

"Did he say anything else?"
"No."
"Nothing at all?"
"He wants to see *Cryptic X*. Is that nothing?
Hardy was disappointed. He had expected a little more encouragement.
"That's just the way he is," Francisco said. "You have no idea how busy he is. That he has read it at all is fantastic."

213

"And now he wants to see *Cryptic X*?"

"Exactly."

"When?"

"He'll let me know."

"So there's no definite date?"

"His schedule is very hectic at the moment, but he'll squeeze it in, somehow."

Hardy didn't know whether to be happy. He had delivered the best and most impressive scenes. Did they lose their edge if taken out of context? In principle, no, but why didn't Avi say anything? The scene in the chicken coop was absolutely hilarious, and it had to trigger a reaction. Perhaps Hardy expected too much. Would Avi have wanted to see *Cryptic X* if he hadn't liked the scenes? Certainly not!

Blanchette came in, a binder under her arm. She ignored him, disappeared behind the room divider and turned the radio on. Hardy was sure that she had snitched on him. But why did she do it? Just out of pure meanness, or did she hope to advance in the firm? Probably both. She constantly brown-nosed Colm, which was simply disgusting. Hardy made a vow to himself: One day he would get even, one day, when she least expected it, he would set a neat little trip wire for her.

Hardy grabbed his things and left. It was almost 5:30, and he couldn't wait to leave the office. When he came out of the revolving door, he froze.

Bill stood next to the exit, smoking a cigarette.

"Just wanted to say thank you, man. You raised me from the dead!"

Bill looked much better. He had put on some weight, wore a crisp shirt and decent linen pants. He had shaved off the beard, leaving only a fine mustache on his upper lip, and the magical glass sphere dangled around his neck again. "I bought it back at the flea market. What could I do? After all, I don't know who the heck stole it. Can we briefly go to Roosevelt Park? Would love to have a word with you."

The park was a small oasis close to the office. The artificial waterfall drowned out the city noise.

"My favorite place," Bill said. "It's a pity that they close at 6:00 already."

A few birds chirped, and two pigeons drank water from the basin of the waterfall.

"Just wanted to say sorry, man. Sorry that I can't repay the three hundred yet. After all I just got back on my feet. But you'll get it all back. Guaranteed, plus interest."

Bill fumbled around with his magic sphere. "I can hardly find anything on the streets nowadays. Don't know if it's the economic crisis, or if there's a higher frequency of garbage trucks ... there's virtually nothing on the curb any more."

The park warden swept a few leaves together and looked at his watch. Bill and Hardy were the last visitors, and it was close to 6:00.

"But I have a solution, a surefire thing. The idea came to me here in the park ..." He pointed to the waterfall.

"Rain! Umbrellas! Sturdy umbrellas, quality umbrellas! It's damn windy here, and cheap umbrellas break almost instantly. In Chinatown I can buy some leftover stock of really good umbrellas. It's a slam dunk."

"And if it's not raining?"

Bill pulled a collapsible ventilator from his pocket. He switched it on and the rotors unfolded and started fanning. He moved the device in front of Hardy's face. "Let's say, it's really hot. Would you buy one for five bucks? Sure you would! And I will get them in Chinatown for two fifty."
The rotors stopped turning. Bill tinkered with the switch, but the ventilator did not work any more. "It's the batteries. Just put in new batteries, then it'll work again." He put the device back into his pocket.
"But that's not all..."

He dug into his other pocket and pulled out a pack of paper napkins. "Besides the obvious runny nose ... When it rains, you clean your shoes with them, and when it's hot, you wipe the sweat from your forehead. Absolutely everyone needs to have them. The third slam dunk, obviously. Of course, only if I can purchase at a reasonable price. Fortunately, I have a contact in Chinatown, where I get them for ten cents a pack. Even if I charge only fifty cents, the profit margin is excellent. But to make it all work I need a thousand bucks. Only then I will get wholesale prices."
"And you want those from me?"
"Yeah. As an investment. I will cut you in on the profit, of course."

"But I don't have one thousand."

"What about an overdraft? With your job that's no problem. It's an investment, man, and an almost instant payback is guaranteed. I'll give you twenty percent on the net profit. How does that sound?"

The warden stood next to them. "We're closing, now."

After Hardy and Bill had stepped out, the iron gate slid shut. The waterfall stopped, and the soundscape switched back to the noise of the city.

Hardy rode the E train clinging to a handhold, feeling paralyzed. As always the car was packed to the brim, and he could hardly breathe. And as always he saw the ad of Dr. Z, promising his patients wonderfully clear skin.

Hardy had agreed to fork over his last reserves in the slim hope that Bill's commercial enterprise would be a success, and this was the end of it. Bill had implied that the FBI gave out financial awards for informants and that he would probably make much more than a thousand bucks if he would give Hardy away.

Maybe Bill lied, but the filmmaker wasn't taking any chances. Not now, that Avi wanted to see *Cryptic X.* Feinstein was not just anyone and a much bigger fish than anticipated. Hardy had googled him. Through the TV series, Feinstein was a worldwide celebrity. *Carmine Medical Center* aired even in Germany, which meant that Hardy's mother — an avid fan of hospital series — had Feinstein in her living room on a weekly basis.

41.
BETWEEN MURNAU AND EISENSTEIN

The last scene of *Cryptic X* flickered over the Lumière's screen, the excellent projector producing a high-contrast picture. The print had a few scratches, though, as it had been shown at numerous festivals.

Otto Steinhagel knelt in the shadows of a huge headstone in his graveyard. It was foggy. He pulled a tarp from the headstone. Close-up of the inscription: *Otto Steinhagel, born: April 14, 1948; died: today.*
Steinhagel froze and turned around. Above him stood the grim reaper. The scary background music culminated in a final pizzicato bass. Fadeout and credits.

The lights came on, and it was quiet for a moment.

Hardy glanced at Feinstein who had put his feet on the seat row in front.
Avi nodded and slowly clapped. "It feels a bit like Murnau or maybe Eisenstein."

"Exactly," Francisco said. "And *Mayhem in Mexico* will have the exact same quality. Although one would expect that Mexico demands color, we'll do just the opposite and shoot in black and white."

"With ultrahigh contrast," Hardy said. "It will bring out the blazing sun."

Feinstein frowned. "Don't know if that's too good. Distribution will be limited, and we'll cut out a lot of channels right away. Besides, I always look totally emaciated in black and white. *Mayhem in Mexico* calls for color."

Francisco looked at Hardy. "Uh, what do you think? We could also do color, couldn't we?"

"I see the story in black and white," Hardy said. "It's classical, direct and down to the bones. From a cinematic point of view, it's a must for this existential epic. And I think every cameraman will agree."

"Sure," Avi said. "The only problem is that I look like a holocaust survivor in black and white. That's the problem."

Silence.

"I know a great cinematographer," Francisco said. "He is a color artist and closely works with the specialists from the lab. How about if we take out the gaudy jellybean tones and give it a more subdued sepia touch. It would then still be color but greatly refined. How about that?"

"I could live with that," Feinstein said. "It doesn't need to be jellybeans. As long as it's color, it's fine with me."

Hardy still saw the story in high-contrast black and white but knew he would not get away with it. Avi was the pivotal point of the project, and only with him on board there was hope.

They went into the office, and Francisco opened a bottle of champagne.

Feinstein grabbed a hat from the coat hook and put it on. He leaned close to Hardy and held his hand over his mouth. "We have no other chance," he whispered. "We need to steal the limo back."
Hardy imitated Tammy from the script. "Yeah, but how?"
"We'll beat them at their own game," said Feinstein. "We will lay out the bait, and once they bite, the trap snaps shut." He vigorously clapped his hands together.

Francisco chuckled.

Feinstein fell to the ground and held up his hand. "Give me the wrench!"
Hardy handed him a pair of scissors that lay on a shelf.
Feinstein crawled under the desk, as if it were a car.
"Damn it. It's all totally corroded," he moaned.
"And now what?" said Hardy, playing Tammy.
"My kingdom for a can of WD40 and a piece of duct tape," exclaimed Feinstein.

"Wow," Francisco said. "That's really deep. I mean, between the lines. The subtext is just fantastic."

The filmmaker was ecstatic. What a delight, to see his text come alive!

Feinstein rose back up and brushed the dust off his pants. "I'll gladly pass it on to Floyd, but he only makes decisions after seeing the finished script. Just one question ... It would not matter to me, but this is about my mother. I have the feeling, that something will happen between me and the black girl. Are there any explicit scenes? A black woman and me — it just wouldn't work for my mother."

Hardy pondered. There was a love scene, of course. And a steamy one at that. The antagonism between Feinstein and Tammy, and the resulting tension naturally screamed to be released in animalistic sex.
"There are only hints," Hardy said.
"What kinds of hints? Do they do it, or not?"
"It could have happened, or maybe it couldn't. We don't show it. It will remain open."
Hardy knew he had to rewrite the corresponding scenes. Feinstein's mother was not to be underestimated.

42.
THE DIE IS CAST

Hardy sat on the terrace of Riverside Café as he worked on the final version of the script. A beautiful Sunday afternoon. Joggers and bikers crowded the river walk. A boat floated across the Hudson.
The café's interior resembled the dungeon of a medieval castle, but it was actually the lower part of a bridge under West End Highway.

Hardy basked in the sun, drinking Chilean Cabernet Sauvignon and puffing on a cigarette. He edited all explicit scenes involving Feinstein and Tammy, leaving it at hints. It was even more elegant this way.
Hardy went over the final scene of the script. He had spent considerable time tweaking the conclusion, and it eventually worked.
Contently he blew smoke rings in the afternoon air. Looking over the promenade, he spotted a familiar figure:

Jackie.

She wore a white sweatshirt, white leggings and her blue tinted glasses, jogging along the river with a young man. They guy looked familiar, but Hardy just didn't know where to place him.

Jackie didn't live far, and maybe that's why Hardy subliminally had chosen the Riverside Café for the final draft. He wanted to meet her by chance. But certainly not like this!

Although Jackie had noticed him, she jogged past without a greeting and, after a few steps, took the hand of her companion.

Hardy felt a severe blow to the gut. But what could he do? Run after them and make a scene?

Hardy paid the bill and walked in the opposite direction to the subway. It was best to simply forget Jackie for now. He needed to finalize the script for Feinstein and still had to tweak a few scenes before the climax. That was all that counted at the moment.

After a few steps on the promenade, Hardy spotted Benny Drexler sitting on a park bench with a manuscript in his lap. The critic had seen him. "What a surprise, young man. You here?"

Drexler pointed at Hardy's screenplay. "Apparently you had the same idea. It's a wonderful place to get some writing done."

Hardy nodded.

"You must have seen Jackie. She thinks she has to do something for her body and has hired Ruby Reitman's personal trainer."

Hardy's eyebrow started to twitch. Now he remembered. The coach was the guy from Chez Pierre. Who the hell was he? He apparently "serviced" Ruby Reitman, and now he did Jackie as well?

Hardy took a glance at Drexler's cover. His tell-all book was entitled *At Times Like These*.

"I'm almost done," Benny said. "My only problem is the seventies. It was a wild time. Alcohol, drugs ... I just can't remember the details." He laughed.

Suddenly, Jackie and the personal trainer appeared. Jackie was limping. "Damn, I overdid it. I slipped, and now I can hardly walk." She waved briefly at Hardy without looking at him. "Ah, the filmmaker. What a surprise."
Jackie looked damn good. Hardy thought about how they had made love on the couch and how she pushed against him ever tighter. All of this seemed forgotten, now.
"We know each other," the coach said pointing his index finger to Hardy. "Chez Pierre, Ruby Reitman, and the Mystery of Jewish Sex!"
"Right," Hardy said.
"The Mystery of Jewish Sex?" Drexler looked slightly puzzled.
"Yeah," said the coach. "What do you FEEL when you have JEWISH SEX?"

He paused and looked at everybody.

"Okay," Jackie said. "What do you feel?"

224

"NOT THAT MUCH!" giggled the coach. "NOT THAT MUCH!"

Neither Benny nor Jackie laughed. The delivery hadn't been the best, and out of context the joke simply didn't work. It needed to be told by a Jewish woman, not a waspy personal trainer.

The coach wiped his eyes with his T-shirt. "Oh, how we laughed. Ruby is just too funny."

Hardy tucked the script under his arm and walked to the subway. He couldn't believe that Jackie had fallen for such a moron.

43.
A UNIQUE OPPORTUNITY

Hardy printed his screenplay at the office. He needed to save money wherever he could. Blanchette was back in the archive, and he had to make good use of his time alone. He printed in increments of ten pages and quickly placed them into his briefcase. Occasionally, he looked down the corridor to make sure nobody walked in.

The telephone rang. It was Bill. Hardy bit his lower lip. "Not again," he whispered to himself. "Please, please, not again." Hardy had googled Bill in the hope to find a skeleton in the closet, but he didn't have any luck. There were hundreds of William W. Williamsons, and none of them was Bill. It seemed that he didn't have a digital footprint at all. Or maybe it wasn't even his real name. Hardy had nothing to go by, and that made it extremely difficult to get a grip on Bill. The bloodsucker didn't seem to have a past.

"I'm calling since it's a bit urgent," Bill said. "A unique opportunity."
Hardy kept silent.
"Don't you want to know what it is?"
"Okay, what is it?"

"A stand at the flea market! You know what that means? Pure gold, that's what it means. But I would need two thousand bucks, that's how much it will cost."

"What's with the merchandise?"

"More than half of the umbrellas had defects. Bought as seen. The ones I checked were all fine."

"And the ventilators?"

"Don't know why, but they don't sell. Still have more than one hundred. I can give them to you, maybe you can sell them at the office."

Hardy knew that he was in serious trouble.

"The stand is a surefire gold mine," Bill continued. "I've lined up a supplier who'll give me secondhand clothes on consignment. Zero investment. He charges me five bucks for each item sold. If I sell a denim jacket for twenty, it's a whopping fifteen-dollar profit with just one piece. It's absolutely foolproof. It can't go wrong."

"I am broke, Bill."

"Nonsense. With a job like yours you have credit. I took the liberty to make a little research. Steven C. Cornfield has a credit card, now. Right or wrong?"

Bill was right.

"I beg you to give me a chance, man. With the stand at the flea market I am made. You'll get it all back with interest. What's the problem? I've always thought of you as a friend."

"I can't, Bill. I really can't."

"Okay, I did not want to go that far, but you force me to. One call to Russell Linnard from the FBI, and you're done. Guaranteed. And then, they will give me the money. I would be a fool to miss the opportunity of a lifetime. I need two thousand on Friday afternoon. We meet at 5:30 in Roosevelt Park. Roger and over."

Bill hung up.

44.
A CONSPIRATORIAL MEETING

Loraine and Hardy sat on a bench in East River Park. Occasionally a subway rumbled over the Williamsburg Bridge. A few teenagers zipped by on their skateboards, and a barge floated along the river.

"He stole three hundred bucks at my birthday party," Loraine said. "I didn't catch him doing it, but I know it was him."

"He has established a contact to the FBI," Hardy said. "One call, and I'm done."

Loraine raised her hands. "Relax," she said. "First and foremost, you need to relax. We are dealing with a measly worm. And we need to treat him like a worm, you understand?"

"Sure, okay, but what do you want to do?"

"I know exactly what will work for him. Leave this up to me. Where will you do the handover?"

"In Roosevelt Park. The small park with the waterfall."

"That's good," Loraine said. "It's actually very good. We'll get it settled, don't worry."

"Sure, but what's your plan?"

"Let me surprise you ..."

Hardy and Loraine shared a chewing gum. A barge hooted loudly.

"Earl moved back in," Loraine said. "We want to try again. He is getting older now and has problems with his stomach. I think that's the real reason. The problem is that he and Kristen can't stand each other. But I need her rent."

Hardy blew a bubble with his chewing gum.

"Just a small question," Loraine said. "Why did you nail this pale creature? What do you see in her?"
"It was the tequila."
Loraine laughed. "Yes, of course, the tequila. And Tammy's urn stood on the fridge in plain sight! Is nothing sacred to you?"
"It was a mistake, yes."
"You wanted to screw the grief away, is that it?"
"You slept with Earl, didn't you?"
"That's something completely different, my dear. Earl and I are practically married, but you have nailed a fragile elf instead, a virgin, so to speak."
"She was definitely not a virgin."
"Essentially, yes. She may have had one guy before you, if that. Maybe she even made it with a cucumber the first time. This is even more likely."
"Well, okay, so?"
"So? ... She tried to slit her wrists. And in my apartment. Everything full of blood. Do you think that's cool?"
Hardy spat out the chewing gum.
"If you penetrate an elf like her, then it's not just a fuck, it's the whole universe, get it? She has opened up to you ..."

230

Hardy had a severe headache. He massaged his temples.

"Okay, now that we're at it: Admit that you've fantasized about my tits. It's really just a rhetorical question, I know it anyway. I just want to hear it again from you."

Hardy nodded.

"Thanks. At least you're honest. Just so you know: My tits belong to Earl and to him alone. You and I are friends, and you'll never touch them, get it, never!"

"Okay."

"Well," Loraine said. "I'm glad we understand each other. I'll see you in Roosevelt Park."

45.
DINNER AT FEINSTEIN'S

"Not bad," Avi said. "I like it."
Hardy had prepared the cover of the screenplay himself, using images he had found on the Internet. All important elements were there: Feinstein with a Yogi bear hat, the limo in a ditch and the barren Sierra Madre — symbolized by a cactus and the skull of a horse.

Feinstein lived in a luxury building on the Upper West Side. His eleven-year old daughter, Miriam, sat at the piano in the living room and practiced "Für Elise." It was annoying because she kept hitting the wrong keys.
The living room was open to the kitchen, where a young man prepared dinner. He wore an apron, a white chef hat, and leggings.
"That's Wouter," Avi said. "My domestic assistant from Holland."
Wouter smiled and seasoned a fish fillet. Vegetables sizzled in a pan on the stove. It smelled of onions and garlic.

Feinstein looked at the cover again. "Well, there's one little thing, that I would change," he said. "Now, that

I'm looking at it closely, I would suggest we take out that horse skull."

"Take out the skull? Why?" Hardy asked.

"It's that holocaust thing," Avi said. "A skull just ... I don't know, I'd like to take it out. I think the cactus says it all, we don't need the skull. Do you mind ...?"

Hardy didn't agree. The skull represented the danger of the Sierra Madre and the danger of the entire enterprise. The skull was absolutely essential on the cover.

"Let me fix it," Avi said. "Just give me a second, and the cover is fine."

He opened the door to a side room with a large fax machine that was also a scanner, copier, and printer. Avi took a bottle of white-out and eliminated the skull from the cover.

The fax machine received a call and spat out a couple of pages. Avi took a quick glance and groaningly pulled out the phone jack. "No more bullshit today," he said.

Feinstein blew on the cover making sure the white out was dry and copied the page.

He showed it to Hardy. "Now it's perfect. What do you think?"

Hardy felt that the cover had completely lost its balance, but he was in no position to complain. "Beautiful," he said. "Absolutely perfect."

Hardy knew that he had to be smart. Once Floyd Burns green lighted the project, the cover that eventually would turn into a poster, would surely be discussed again. Maybe at that point he would have more pull and be able to wedge the skull in again.

Miriam still practiced "Für Elise" but constantly hit the wrong keys. "This piece is crap," she cursed. "I don't like it, daddy."
Avi rose and reached over her shoulder. "Here, this is how you do it." He played a few bars to show her. "Practice a little more until dinner, darling. You're almost there."
Miriam sighed and started again.

Avi flipped through the script. "Okay," he said. "Where is the love scene? I have to see it because of my mother."
"Page 103."
During their trip through Mexico, Feinstein and Tammy had constantly argued but needed to stick together because of their common goal. Finally, they sat exhausted in the middle of nowhere around a campfire and drank red wine from a leather pouch. Suddenly, all their quarrels seemed trifle. They looked into each other's eyes, and their lips grew closer. And at that very moment, Lugo started the limo and drove off with a howling engine and screeching tires.
"Hm, yes, that would work," Avi said. "And that's it. After that nothing happens?"
"We leave it open. The two are much too busy for sex. Sure, it might happen, but we don't show it."
"Not even as a hint?"
"No."

Wouter rang a bell. "Dinner is served."

Four gold rimmed plates were neatly arranged on the dining table: grilled cod with jasmine rice and bamboo sprats.

Miriam had slightly protruding ears just like Avi. Wouter took off his apron and sat down at the table. An impressive manhood loomed under his leggings.

Miriam frowned. "Why doesn't Wouter cook something tasty for a change? Something like hamburger and fries?"

Wouter blushed.

"It's quite simple, darling," Avi said. "We don't want to look like little pigs, do we?" Avi put his hand on Wouter's arm. "It is excellent, as always. Miriam has been brought up completely wrong by her mother, and this is the result."

Avi and Wouter were strangely familiar, and Hardy wondered if Wouter was perhaps more than a maid.

The intercom rang. Avi looked at his watch. "I can't believe it," he said. "Half an hour early, again."

Miriam jumped up and grabbed her bag.

"Tell your mother *vaffanculo*," Avi said. "Simply tell her *vaffanculo*."

"*Vaffanculo?*"

"Exactly. She knows what that means. And if she ever arrives early again, we won't pick up the intercom. Who the hell does she think she is?"

Feinstein had been divorced for two years. Hardy knew from Francisco that it had been a bitter battle.

Miriam disappeared, and they continued with their dinner. Wouter had an extremely strong homoerotic

235

aura. Hardy felt that the Dutchman was looking at him occasionally.

Avi took a swig of wine. "I will read the thing today in one go. I will see Floyd at a garden party tomorrow and will give it to him personally. He will be very surprised to see me on the cover."

Hardy felt damn good as he took a large gulp of wine. Never had he been closer to his big goal. The elegant apartment was illuminated by candlelight, and "Ave Maria" played softly in the background. Life could be quite pleasant at times.

Wouter licked his fork. "Is there possibly a teeny tiny part for lil' Wouter in the film?"

"The food was scrumptious, Wouter, but let's not get carried away, okay?"

Wouter laughed. "Ah, my dear Avi, it was just a joke. Why do you always have to be so serious?"

He cleared away the dishes.

"I have a small request," Hardy said. "My mother's birthday is coming up, and *Carmine Medical Center* airs in Germany. Could we take a picture together?"

Avi groaned loudly.

"I hate the role. I should have never accepted it. This crap is everywhere. I heard that the series starts next week in Cambodia."

"It's on in Holland as well," Wouter shouted from the kitchen.

Hardy took a sip of wine. "My mother likes doctor series."

Avi closed his eyes and rubbed his temples. "So does mine. That's the problem."

He lit a slim cigarette. It was the same brand Jackie smoked.

"It's all so predictable. I am the emergency doctor for the night shift, and of course I copulate with the night nurse, even though I'm married. And then there's the head physician whom I hate, since he constantly stabs my back. Every time I have to utter a word of this shitty dialogue, I'm ready to throw up. "

Hardy nodded sympathetically.

"That's why I love *Mayhem in Mexico*," Avi said. "One would think that it needs to be the young Jack Nicholson, who singlehandedly heaves the limo out of the ditch but no, it is the fragile, little Jew, Avi Feinstein. That's so much more interesting, isn't it?"

Hardy had tears in his eyes. Avi Feinstein was a genius.

"But I still need a photo for my mother. Mothers will be mothers."

"True," Avi said. "Mothers will be mothers."

Hardy pulled out a small digital camera, but Avi shook his head. "No way. Absolutely no snapshots. If we do it at all, we'll need to do it right." He waved to Wouter. "Get the new camera, please."

Avi turned to Hardy. "Wouter is actually also a decent photographer, so we are in good hands."

237

First they took a couple of shots at the piano: Avi playing and Hardy close by, listening intently. Then they cheered with their wine glasses at the dining table, and finally, Avi read a scene from the script while Hardy, sitting on the baroque sofa, applauded with his hands high in the air.

Wouter quickly checked the shots on the screen of the camera and nodded. "Very good, very beautiful, but lil' Wouter has one more idea. Something a bit more snappy."

"And that would be?" Avi asked.

"Why don't we put you two in the Jacuzzi? Bubble bath, Cuban cigars, and a cooler with champagne? That would just look great. What do you think?"

Avi blushed. "What's wrong with you today, Wouter? Did you forget to take your medication again?"

Wouter groaned. "I can't even make a joke. It was a joke, Avi. Where's your sense of humor?"

"Ha, ha," Avi said. "Very funny. Now give me the camera, and let me see the photos."

46.
SILENT WHISPERS IN THE PARK

Bill was sitting near the waterfall, reading *The New York Times*. He wore a white linen suit. Hardy sat down beside him. The sound of the waterfall, as always, drowned out the city din.
Bill looked at his watch. "Right on time. I love that. Thanks, man."
Since it was near closing time, the park was almost empty. Two older ladies were chatting in a remote corner. One of them knitted a sweater.
Hardy took an envelope from his jacket, and as Bill was reaching for it, Loraine rushed in from behind, sliding a steel noose over his head, pulling it tight around his neck. Bill grunted and sat there, petrified.

His eyes bulged.

Loraine sat in a chair right behind Bill, pulling the noose even tighter. From a distance it looked as if they were having a quiet conversation. "Listen, my little prince," Loraine whispered. "If you don't stop this crap from now on, I will finish you off, got that?"
Bill could hardly move. Loraine held the noose extremely tight. He stuck his thumb in the air.

"Great," Loraine said. "I am glad we understand each other. Just to make it clear: If you harass him one more time, only once, I will exterminate you. I don't care where you are, I'll find you and crush you like a worm, got that?"

Bill could not breathe. His eyes bulged out even further. He gave another thumbs-up.

"And since we're at it, you can also admit that you have stolen the three hundred dollars."

Bill gasped.

"I know it anyway," Loraine said. "I just wanted to hear it from you."

Bill was close to fainting. His skin seemed to turn blue.

"Admit it, or I'll finish you off right here and now!"

Bill stuck up his thumb once more.

"Two thumbs, to make it absolutely clear."

Bill held up the other thumb as well, and Loraine laughed. "Hah, I knew it."

She pulled the noose from his neck and Bill gasped for air. It was as if he had emerged from the depths of the ocean.

Loraine stood up. "Let's go. This piece of shit doesn't deserve another second of our time."

Bill kept sitting in his chair, putting his head back, gasping. A sudden gust of wind caught his newspaper and blew the pages into the bushes.

47.
OF DONUTS AND SEAGULLS

Floyd's office was in Brooklyn. A loft in Williamsburg was the new cool. Manhattan was out, Williamsburg hip. At least for the spearhead of the avant-garde.

Burns had read the script and invited Hardy to his office. Strangely enough, the big day fell on the birthday of Hardy's mother.

The filmmaker had arrived an hour early, strolling nervously along Bedford Avenue.

Hardy had emailed several photos with Avi to his sister but so far had not received a reply. Had his email been lost in cyberspace, maybe?

Once he had accidentally forgotten his mother's birthday, a fact that still haunted him. He went into an internet café, checked his messages and let out a sigh of relief. The awaited response had arrived. Subject line: *Mom wept with joy!*

Dear Holger,
You've made mom extremely happy. You and Dr. Darnell: that's simply sensational. We can hardly believe that you're going to make a film with him. As you know, mom gets confused when it comes to email and

technology, and she will also write a detailed letter, but here are a few quick lines I typed for her:

My dear Holger!
You have made us all very, very happy. You and Dr. Darnell, that's just incredible. I always knew that you would make something of yourself one day, although sometimes, I was worried about you, but that's all forgotten now. I am very proud of you and can't believe my luck.
But here's the best part — hold on tight — you surely remember Tim Martens who attended high school with Heidi. He now works at city hall and was here at my birthday party when we viewed your photos. Tim would like to immortalize you with the other greats of Bad Wildungen in the city hall lobby. They have a photo wall now, and he would like to include you and Dr. Darnell. I hope you don't mind.

Hardy was floored. The reach of *Carmine Medical Center* was simply mind-boggling. He continued reading.

Soon I'll write you a detailed letter and tell you all about your old friends. A lot has happened in Bad Wildungen, and you're surely curious who had a baby. Farben Winkler has opened a branch in Kassel, and Trischa Warncke has separated from her husband. That was a real shock for many and absolutely unexpected, since they had just built a new house. Well, more details later ... Anyway, we are very proud of you and curious how it all will work out. Maybe we'll see you in Hollywood soon. Who knows? — Your loving mother.

Hardy went back out on the street and looked at his watch. Still half an hour early. He sat at an outdoor café and drank an espresso.

Hardy wondered what Floyd Burns might be like. He had googled him. A few pictures showed him at film festivals with actors or directors on the red carpet or at a press conference. Burns looked surprisingly average. Narrow face, rimless glasses, short hair with side parting. The only thing that was unusual were his crooked teeth. The upper incisors tilted inward, and one canine was quite pointed, almost like in a vampire, just not quite as long and only on one side. A one-sided Dracula so to speak. Floyd's smile in the photos was cold, but that could be deceiving. It spoke for him that he stuck to his teeth. For a few thousand dollars he could have straightened them out, but Floyd was obviously not Hollywood. Floyd was Williamsburg.

Hardy looked at his watch. Another quarter of an hour. He didn't want to show up too early and took one more round.
What would Floyd ask him? Maybe to tell the story in a minute. Hardy had prepared for that, rehearsing before a mirror. In addition he was ready to act out the scene in the chicken coop and the scene where Feinstein heaved the limo out of a ditch.

Exactly at the appointed time, Hardy entered Floyd's office.
The receptionist looked up. "Mr. von Hachenstein?"
Hardy nodded.
"Sit down for a moment, I'll be right back."

He sat on the couch in the lobby. Trade magazines were laid out on a glass table, and tropical fish swam around in a massive aquarium.

The receptionist came back with an envelope. "Floyd apologizes, but he had to attend to an emergency."

Hardy, feeling extremely queasy, ripped open the envelope. Floyd had read the script but needed to fly to a problematic shoot in Canada. Conclusion: He found some scenes well crafted but felt the road movie genre was exhausted. Especially when set in Mexico, where legions of films had been shot already. He thought that a road movie could still be relevant but only if set somewhere in the vast Russian influence sphere, which, because of the geopolitical situation, was a place of interest and curiosity, thus facilitating a fresh cinematic angle.

Hardy wanted to scream. This could not be true!

The secretary looked at him worried. "You are very pale, Mr. von Hachenstein. Not feeling well?"

"The original is set in KYRGYZSTAN, damn it!"

The secretary looked at him perplexed. "Pardon?"
"Nothing. Forget it. When will Floyd be back?"
"We don't know yet. Problems on location. Would you like a donut?"
She pointed at a showcase with donuts. "It was Floyd's idea. We always have donuts. Sometimes we can be very busy here, with no time for lunch. And that's when you really appreciate a donut."

Hardy sat on a park bench on the East River bank and looked over to Manhattan. It was a beautiful day. The sky was blue with little white clouds sprinkled in. Barges floated past, seagulls shrieked.

He had read the letter at least five times, still wondering whether Floyd wanted to give him a chance or whether it was a friendly rejection. He forced himself to stay calm and evaluated the cold facts.
One: Avi Feinstein, an international celebrity, had liked the script.
Two: Burns found the scenes well crafted, a clear acknowledgement of Hardy's skill as a screenwriter.
And three: Floyd didn't even know that a Kyrgyzstan version existed. Maybe Burns could warm up to a merger of the scripts? Hardy could simply transfer the story from Mexico back to the vast reaches of the Russian influence sphere. Feinstein would still be allergic to almost anything, and it would be equally difficult to keep kosher in Kyrgyzstan!

Hardy transferred the scenes in his mind from one country to the other. Sure, it was difficult and a lot of work, but it was doable. Excitedly Hardy jumped up from the bench and paced back and forth. It seemed that had found the solution. He raised his hands to the sky and, as if talking to his maker, said: "Thank you, thank you ... THANK YOU!"

Hardy noticed a young couple with a toddler in a stroller, looking at him, concerned. They probably thought that he was a madman, turned around, and walked in the other direction.

245

It was lunchtime, and the filmmaker was hungry. Floyd's donut sat in a bag on the bench. He pulled it out and looked at it. It was a round one, without a hole. One of those with filling and sugar powder on top. Hardy took a bite and smiled contently: vanilla pudding — his favorite filling. The donut tasted great. Floyd knew how to pick donuts, and that was a very good sign!

Above Hardy, seagulls shrieked, begging for a share. Hardy ripped some pieces from the donut and threw them in the air. The seagulls caught the crumbs in midflight, shrieking excitedly.

Hardy's phone vibrated. He looked at the display, and his heart started beating violently.

It was Jackie.

"Benny had a stroke," she sobbed. "I am completely devastated."
"Where is he?"
"In the hospital. He wants to see you."
"Me?"
"Yes. Can you pick me up and go visit him?"

Hardy was stunned. What could Drexler want?

48.
THE LEGACY

Benny didn't look good in his hospital bed. Half of his face was paralyzed, and he couldn't talk. One arm and one leg were also paralyzed.

"Ten minutes max," the nurse said. "He's too weak for more."

Jackie didn't wear any makeup, and her nail polish was chipped. She took out a comb and straightened Benny's disheveled hair.
Drexler motioned with his functioning arm that he wanted to write something down. Jackie gave him a pen, and he laboriously scribbled a note on a piece of paper, handing it to Hardy.

Publish my book!

Hardy nodded. "Where is it?"
Drexler pointed to his jacket at the coat hook. Hardy pulled the manuscript from the side pocket. Even suffering a stroke, Drexler had still found the strength to grab it and take it with him.

The pages were neatly typed with Benny's electrical typewriter. Here and there a paragraph was crossed out, or an addition was scribbled into the margin.

"You want me to clean it up?" Hardy asked.

Drexler nodded, took the filmmaker's hand and squeezed it in gratitude.

Jackie and Hardy stood in front of the hospital. The nice day had turned cloudy, and it started to drizzle.

"I need something to drink," Jackie said. "Otherwise I'll go crazy."

They went to the same Italian restaurant they had visited after seeing *Una giornata particulare*. It felt like a déjà vu since Adriano Celentano wavered over the sound system again: *Azzurro ..., il pomeriggio è troppo azzurro e lungo ..., per me ...*

They drank a bottle of red wine. "I don't know," Jackie said. "But I feel safe in this place. I feel protected."

It started to rain heavily, and the people on the street were looking for shelter. The waiter put candles on the tables.

"The doctors said it's only a matter of time." Jackie blew her nose. "I don't know what to do. I want to help him, but I can't."

She pulled out a mirror from her purse and looked at herself. "Good Lord! — I'll be right back."

She disappeared into the ladies' room.

Hardy took out Drexler's script and read into it. It began in the 60's when Hardy was still a baby. Apparently Benny had been a buddy of Marvin Lockwood, a well-known activist at the time. Drexler's account of the late 60's and the protests against the Vietnam war were touching. He was a pacifist, trying to make the world a better place. But he was also a young man, looking for love, which wasn't easy since the girls went crazy for Lockwood while Drexler was reduced to look on from a distance. Somehow you wanted to know if Benny would be able to skim a girl from Lockwood, and that's what kept you reading. Hardy sincerely liked Drexler's writing. It had warmth and a human touch. You wanted to know more about him and be part of his world.

Jackie came back from the bathroom. She had put on makeup and lipstick and wore her blue tinted glasses.
"Sorry," she said. "The last couple of days were a handful. I just couldn't take care of myself."
She almost looked like on the day he had first seen her at the bar in the Peninsula hotel. She had even painted her fingernails in the bathroom and smelled of nail polish.

Hardy felt the urge to kiss her.

Jackie took a sip of wine and pushed her glasses up her nose. "You probably want to know what happened to my coach, do you?"
"Not really, but okay, what happened to him?"
"He's a good-looking guy, isn't he?"
"Yes."
"Ah, bullshit. Let's just forget about him. He's half gay, anyway."
"Half gay?"
"Haven't you noticed?"

"Well, now that you say so ..."

"I like brains," Jackie said. "That's what turns me on. I need a man who can talk."

She blew on her fingernails. "I was mad at you, very mad, but let's not talk about it any more, okay?"

The waiter came to the table and poured wine into the glasses. Jackie ordered another bottle.

She took a big gulp of wine. "It's a bit weird to talk about this, now, but you know what my biggest dream is and always was? From the poem you gave me I can tell that you'd like it."

She paused for a moment. It seemed that she was not sure if she should reveal herself.

"What is it?"

Jackie took off her glasses. Without them she seemed vulnerable, almost as if she had let down her guard. She looked Hardy straight in the eye.

"An Armenian church wedding."

Hardy was floored.

"Shocked?" Jackie asked.

"No, just surprised. Wouldn't it be a bit early?"
"Early? Do you know how old I am?"
"No, I mean for us. Wouldn't it be a bit early for us?"

Jackie frowned.

Hardy knew that he had made a terrible mistake and immediately attempted a U-turn. "No, yes, sure. I would love it, absolutely."

"Really?" Jackie's eyes brightened up and sparkled in the candlelight.

At once, Hardy understood that this was not about an actual commitment but rather about the *Honey of Rosemary Flowers*. It was all about this moment and the power of imagination. He played along and took Jackie's hand. "Close your eyes!"

They both closed their eyes.

"I can see it before me," Hardy whispered. "You all in white lace in front of the priest."
"Yes," Jackie said. "I have a tiara in my hair, and you wear a beautiful tuxedo with a light gray vest."
Hardy breathed in. "I can smell the strong aroma of incense in the air ..."
"Yes, yes," Jackie said excitedly. "And there's a choir singing. It absolutely needs to be *Amen, Hayr Surp*. It's a thousand years old. Unfortunately, I can't sing, but I'll play it to you."
"And then the church bells ring," Hardy said.
"Yes, yes, yes," Jackie squeezed Hardy's hand. "Oh, God, I am so excited."

Hardy had a stunning idea. Why not set the new script in Armenia? It had an ancient history and formed part of the Russian influence sphere. And it was the neighbor of Georgia, the birthplace of Stalin. It would

251

be extremely interesting if Stalin's limousine had ended up in Armenia, Georgia's arch enemy. It created all kinds of natural dramatic tensions and was just perfect. Much better than Kyrgyzstan. And on top of that, Jackie could be his advisor when it came to local flavor.

"What are you pondering about?" Jackie asked and yanked Hardy's hand. "Tell me, tell me ...!"
"Uh, I was just thinking that it would be beautiful if it rained white rose petals."
"Wonderful," Jackie whispered. "Absolutely wonderful."
She came closer. "You want to know a secret?"
Hardy nodded.
She squeezed his hand again, this time even tighter. "My panties are completely wet."

They locked their lips in a long and passionate kiss.

ABOUT THE AUTHOR

Matthias Drawe grew up in a DEFA[1] building at the border of Potsdam-Babelsberg and West Berlin. In 1970 he defected to West Berlin with his father, Hans Drawe, a former DEFA dramatist, in a spectacular escape. Risking their lives, they jumped over the Berlin Wall by using an unsecured film ladder.

At the beginning of the 1980's Drawe lived in a squatted house in Berlin-Kreuzberg which provides the backdrop for his novel *Wild Years in West Berlin*. In 1991 he founded Kellerkino, a small art-house cinema in Berlin-Kreuzberg.

After having shot three independent feature films in Berlin, Drawe moved to New York City and worked as a journalist for Deutschlandradio Kultur[2] the German equivalent of NPR. Drawe's radio features from around the world were brought to life by actor Christian

---

[1] Deutsche Film-Aktiengesellschaft, better known as DEFA, was the state-owned film studio in the German Democratic Republic (East Germany) throughout that country's history.

[2] Deutschlandradio Kultur (abbreviated to DLR Kultur or DKultur) is the culture-oriented radio station of the German national Deutschlandradio service. From 1994 to March 2005 the station was known as "DeutschlandRadio Berlin".

Brückner, who provides the official German voice for Robert De Niro, giving German listeners the impression that it was De Niro reporting.

Drawe divides his time between New York and Rio de Janeiro.

Matthias Drawe in New York, 2010

64204890R00141

Made in the USA
Charleston, SC
20 November 2016

SKIING

about the authors

All three authors bring long experience and interest in skiing to this book. They have been active ski instructors for many years.

Karl Tucker taught skiing for the Salt Lake County Recreation Department and for many years has taught at the Alf Engen Ski School. He has been director of the Brigham Young University Ski School since 1963. During this time the program has grown from 225 to 500 students per semester, and includes 37 instructors. A certified ski instructor, he has given numerous clinics and seminars for prospective ski teachers. Professor Tucker also serves as Head Golf Coach at Brigham Young University, a post in which he has been named Coach of the Year in District 7 five times. His 1981 golf team won the NCAA Golf Championship and he was named NCAA Coach of the Year. Professor Tucker received both his B.S. and M.S. degrees from Brigham Young University; he is currently active in the Professional Ski Instructor's of America— Intermountain Division.

Besides his current duties as Dean of the College of Physical Education and Athletics at Brigham Young University, Dr. Clayne R. Jensen has remained active in skiing. He has directed both Utah State University's ski school and the Beaver Mountain Ski School. Dr. Jensen has participated extensively in professional organizations, workshops, and conferences and has established himself as one of the prolific authors in the field, having authored or coauthored 15 textbooks currently in print and numerous professional articles. He has received several athletic and professional service awards and is included in such sources as "Who's Who in Education," "Who's Who in the West," "International Bibliographies," "Men of Achievement," and "Who's Who in America." Dr. Jensen holds B.S. and M.S. degrees from the University of Utah, and a Ph.D. from Indiana University.

Gary Howard began teaching in the BYU Ski School in 1965, and became the assistant director in 1969. In 1970 he assumed responsibilities as the varsity ski coach and continued until 1980. During that time the men's ski team won six consecutive league championships, and Gary Howard was named Coach of the Year each of those years. As a certified ski instructor, each year he trains about 40 new ski teachers for the BYU Ski School. In 1977 he was named head coach for the women's golf team and has developed the program to be a national contender. His teams have finished second in Region VII during 1980, 1981, and placed 11th at Nationals in 1979. Gary Howard received both his B.S. and M.R.Ed. degrees from Brigham Young University. He is currently active in the Professional Ski Instructors of America—Intermountain Division.

SKIING

Fourth Edition

Physical Education Activities Series

Karl Tucker
Brigham Young University

Clayne R. Jensen
Brigham Young University

Gary Howard
Brigham Young University

Wm C Brown Company Publishers
Dubuque, Iowa

Cover photo by Michael Kennedy, Aspen, Colorado

Consulting Editor

Aileene Lockhart
Texas Woman's University

Evaluation Materials Editor

Jane A. Mott
Texas Woman's University

contents

preface

Although skiing is relatively difficult, good instruction and adequate practice can make the typical individual a reasonably good skier in one season. Correct technique, well-designed, properly fitted equipment, and good physical condition are of prime importance for the good skier.

This book is especially written for the interested but nonexpert skier who wishes to develop skiing skills quickly. The use of this book along with good instruction will greatly enhance the learning process.

Self-evaluation questions pertaining to both knowledge and skill are distributed throughout the text. These questions give readers examples of the understanding and skill that should be acquired as they progress. The reader should respond to these questions thoroughly and competently, then devise additional ones to further stimulate learning.

The authors wish to express their appreciation to the Professional Ski Instructor's of America, Inc. and to Horst Abraham, Educational Vice President, for technical descriptions of the ATM (American Teaching Method), and for material used in preparing the illustrations.

origin and development of skiing

1

Somewhere in the past a primative man clad in bearskins found he could walk over snow without sinking if he had a long board under each foot. Successors of this man, the inventors of skiing, provided the ski with a binding of hide, which fastened the ski to the foot. Later, a stick was used to help the skier glide faster, and eventually, the stick was equipped with a disc to prevent it from sinking too deeply into the snow. These first ski poles may also have doubled as spears and javelins. With this new equipment, early man had found a better mode of travel.

Evidence of the skiing equipment just described, dating back four or five thousand years, has been found on rock carvings, and in peat bogs in Norway, Sweden, and Finland. Some of the skis that were found are short and broad, while others are long, slim, and almost perfect in form. These implements were as important to the people of the North as the wheel. Without them, people in snow- and ice-covered terrain could neither hunt nor travel effectively. Today the unknown man who invented skiing has been exalted to the rank of a deity, and is known as Ull, the forefather of all skiers.

In Norway a long piece of wood split from a log was called skida, the word from which ski evolved. Through endless generations since then the ski has been developed to near perfection. The modern ski is not simply a piece of wood. When placed on the ground it is far from flat. It rests on its two ends, creating a long, low arch called a camber. When the weight of the body is placed on the ski, it flattens and distributes the weight evenly. There is a groove on the bottom of the ski, exactly in the middle and on the long axis of the running surface. This groove provides steadiness by forming a rail of snow on which the ski runs. Without it the ski would not run true and would waver. The turned-up tip takes most of the strain on rough terrain. It breaks trail and keeps the ski on the surface. When the ski is edged, the tip digs deeper into the snow than the rest of the ski, since the resistance is stronger there. The edges of the ski are slightly curved, with the tip and tail broader than the center. Today the finest skis are made of steel, aluminum, and/or fiberglass with wood or foam cores. They are light but very strong and can be made with the desired flexibility and perfection that causes them to run true over the snow.

1

Development of the ski to its present state has been stimulated by its utility. It has been used as an implement of survival, as a tool of war in areas where rapid travel of troops over ice and snow was essential, as a weapon in contests of skill and courage, putting man against man and team against team; and finally, the ski has become equipment for winter recreation.

According to available information, the Russians were the first to use skis for warfare starting in the late 1400s. They were again used in the war between the Finns and the Russians in the late 1500s and by the troops of Sweden's King Vasa in 1555. French Alpine experts known as the Blue Devils clashed with German ski troops on the steep, rugged slopes of the Vosges Mountains during World War I. Austrian and Bavarian ski troops were also very active, and great battles were staged by ski troops in the Tyrol and the Dolomites. Finnish ski soldiers waged war against the attacking Soviets in the winter of 1939 and drove the Russians to one of the most bitter defeats in their history. In 1941 Russian troops on skis, aided by bitter cold and abundant snow, surprised the Germans and caused them to suffer one of their biggest setbacks of the war. Later, ski troops from other countries, including the United States, were active in various battles of World War II.

Except in the far northern countries of Europe and Asia, where Ull and Undurridis were known as the god and goddess of skiing and where every child grew up on skis, skiing developed at a rather slow rate. It was not until some Swedish explorer, Norwegian sailor, of Finnish diplomat introduced skis to the people of other countries that skiing really gained popularity elsewhere.

In 1681 one of these Scandinavian travelers reportedly arrived in the Austrian Alpine village of Krain and, sure enough, he was on skis. He so intrigued the Austrian villagers with his graceful slipping, twisting, and twirling down the mountains that the next winter it is reported most of the village members were skiing.

Skis were introduced in a similar manner to people in several other European countries. There are reports of an expedition making strange tracks over the snows of Greenland in 1722 and of a company of artistic performers on skis at an ice carnival in Canada in 1759. Then in 1856 John "Snowshoe" Thompson, an Alpine man, carried the mail over the Sierra Nevadas into California. A colorful figure, he boasted of his skiing skill and sneered at everyone who challenged him, so the skiing miners of Plumas and Sierra counties offered a cash prize for the winner of a ski race. John "Snowshoe" Thompson lost the race.

In the high Sierras where snow covers the mountains seven to eight months of the year, these men, like the people of Krain, Austria, became expert skiers. Many stories are told of competitions among the miners at such places as Rabbit Creek, Port Wine, Saw Pit Flat, Onion Valley, and Poker Flat. A few of the old timers of this hearty era still live to tell their tales.

The 1880s was a decade of progress for skiing. During this time in Davos, Switzerland, Colonel Napier, a slightly eccentric Britisher, boasted that his Norwegian butler was an expert skier. The whole village laughed as the two appeared on skis, for it was the butler's specialty to balance a tray with a teacup on it while he skied down the slopes. The old village carpenter, however, did not laugh. Instead he asked the Colonel to allow him to copy the skis. Not many years afterward, Davos sponsored its first ski competition.

Saint Moritz, Switzerland, could not remain behind for long. The chamber of commerce of that village built a hill for jumping, and its president, Ph. Marck, demonstrated the first jump in person. Not satisfied with jumping, the president climbed Piz Corvatsch and demonstrated his downhill ability. He became the first to make the famed downhill run over the notorious Isla Persa, a suicidal undertaking at that time. Today the Isla Persa has been skied by thousands of people.

A great impetus was given to skiing by Nansen, author of *On Skiis Through Greenland*, which was published in three languages in 1890. It inspired large numbers of people, especially in Germany and Austria, to take up the sport. Also it laid the groundwork for Mathias Zdarsky, who in 1896 published a system known as the Lilienfeld Skiing Technique. Zdarsky, a fantastic exponent of skiing, challenged the whole world and all the experts who preceded him. He was especially critical of the Norwegian technique and declared that the Christiania turn was a breakneck stunt that should never be used. In spite of his obnoxious personality and unorthodox technique, Zdarsky was very successful and left a colorful memory of himself.

George Bilgeri was an elegant nobleman who is still well known for his great contribution to the development of the sport. He instructed more than thirty thousand pupils without charge and is known as one of the real gentlemen of skiing. Among his innovations was the use of two poles instead of one. He was an excellent and exquisite colonel of Austria's famous Kaiserjaeger. In 1906 he wrote a book about mountain warfare and military skiing, and in World War I he commanded the Austrian Alpine troops on the Italian Front.

In 1909 a ski school was founded at Saint Anton in the Arlberg. Its founder became *the instructor* of the ski world. "Bend your knees! Shift your weight forward to the ski tips! More forward lean." The instructor was Hannes Schneider. This man of the famous crouch-ski position gave vitality to modern ski techniques.

Soon after 1910 Roald Amundsen, who was hailed as the last of the Vikings, in 99 days negotiated 1875 miles of frozen snow and ice from the Antarctic Circle to the South Pole and back again, crossing some peaks as high as 10,-000 feet. Although this man showed tenderness toward his fellow beings only on rare occasions, at the end of a long day's march he would take his skis into his tent instead of planting them in the snow as his comrades did. Amundsen's death was in keeping with his life; only a few men die victorious as he did in the cold polar region he seemed to love.

Skis climbed high in 1931 when Holdworth, an Englishman, ascended the ridge between Kemet and the Mead-Col in the Himalayas. From there he made the most daring downhill run ever undertaken—a dash to his lowest base camp, passing all intermediate points in a single run. Finch also used skis in his attempt to reach the top of Mount Everest, but he never reached the summit. Hannes Schneider and his comrades climbed phenomenal heights on skis during their Himalayan expedition.

In 1936 the great winter Olympics were held in southern Germany. The world's best skiers met: Niemi of Finland, Birger Ruud of Norway, Marusarz of Poland, Simunck of Czechoslovakia, Allias of France, Pfnur of Germany, and Lantschner of Austria. But the atmosphere of happy winter games turned cold when the competitors, as well as thousands of unknown skiers and spectators, saw signs of the oncoming war. Soon afterward the glittering resorts of Saint Moritz, Chamonix, Cortina d'Ampezzo, Innsbruck, Garmish, and other such jubilant ski places in southern Europe were empty and silent.

The next major championship was held in 1948, and skiing not only began to regain its prominence then but also moved forward phenomenally. Following the war skiing became more than a hobby for only the rich and more than a competitive sport for only the highly proficient. It became a social movement that has resulted in the development of many elaborate ski areas, greatly improved ski facilities and equipment, with increased emphasis on ski techniques and ski instruction. In the last two decades ski schools have developed rapidly. Ski clubs have cropped up everywhere. Certified ski instructors have become highly specialized. Ski competition has become popular and prominent on a local, national and international basis. Recently professional ski competition has proven popular.

International competition in skiing started again after World War II. During the 1950's the Austrian teams dominated the competition, followed by the French teams during the decade of the 60's. In the late 60's the concepts of World Cup and Nations Cup competition developed to honor individuals and teams that performed best during the entire year. During the 1970's many nations honored their world cup champions. Names like Nancy Greene—Canada, Karl Schranz, Annemarie Moser-Proell, Franz Klammer—Austria, Gustavo Thoeni—Italy, Marielle Goitschel, Jean Claude Killy—France, Hanni Wentzel—Lichtenstein, and Ingemar Stenmark—Norway, are familiar to the average skier.

After decades of development the United States teams are succeeding at the international level. Phil Mahre won two World Cup championships (1981, 1982) in Alpine skiing. Bill Koch won the 1982 cross country World Cup in a sport that had been totally dominated by the Scandinavians and Russians. The USA Women's Alpine Team brought home our first Nation Cup victory in 1982.

Not only has the United States gained recognition in the competitive events, but our teaching system is also gaining respect. Every two years instructional teams from the skiing nations meet at an Interski event to demonstrate and discuss their methods. The American Teaching Method has been very well received at recent Interskis, and other nations are now borrowing from it.

Skiing has grown from survival needs, through the adventure stage for the wealthy, into a social movement demanding improved technical equipment, elaborate ski resorts, and proficient ski instruction. It has become an industry in and of itself, but the adventure still remains and is open to all who wish to try.

fundamentals
and drills
2

There are certain preliminary exercises and maneuvers which must be learned before skiing on the slope can be successful. Because you want and should have the best possible opportunity to learn to ski in the least amount of time, it is imperative that you develop self-confidence and establish safe practices. Learning a few basics will help develop the confidence you need, reduce the fear of being injured, and acquaint you with most of the principles on which sound ski techniques are based. The following are some of the most important points to know and practice.

Carrying Equipment. Nothing so surely identifies you as a beginner than carrying your skis incorrectly. Place the bottom of your skis together, pick them up and place them on your shoulder, tips forward. To protect your skis, place them on your shoulder on their sides so that the skis will not scissor and damage the edges. The poles can be carried in the hand or over the other shoulder to help balance the weight of the skis. If you need to carry the equipment a long distance, a suitcase carry is recommended, provided your poles have straps. Several companies manufacture devices that enable skiers to carry their equipment like a suitcase.

Putting on Skis. This is extremely important because of the safety factor involved with the bindings. Ski shop experts should check the bindings before skis leave the shop, but you should know how to fasten them as well as how to release them. Your ski instructor will teach you how to use and adjust your equipment properly.

Walking and Stationary Drills. After your equipment is correctly fitted, you should experience the feeling of actually moving on the snow. In essence, your skis have become big feet, and you must now learn to handle them without stepping on your toes and heels. The following exercises should be practiced.

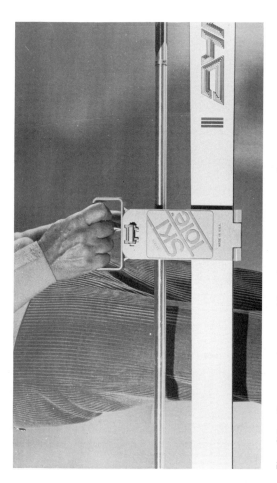

Fig. 2.1. Two ways to carry ski equipment: **a,** using pole straps to carry skis; **b,** a manufactured ski carrier

Wagon Wheel.   Stand on a flat area and without moving the tips of the skis, lift the tail of the right ski and displace it to the right. Bring the left ski alongside. Keep repeating until you've come back to your original position. Reverse direction by moving the left ski first.

Cutting the Pie.   This drill is done in the same manner as the wagon wheel, except that the tails are left in the original position and the tips are displaced alternately, thus simulating a pie being cut.

One Step Glide.   Using the poles for both balance and force, take one step, push with the poles, then follow with a gliding action.

Two-step Glide.   This calls for the same basic action as the one-step glide, except that two walking steps are taken before gliding. This results in more momentum and a longer glide.

Swing the Tails.   Lift the tail of one ski and, with the tip on the snow, swing the tail from side to side and lift it up and down. Do this alternately with the two skis. This teaches you to maintain balance on one ski while maneuvering the other one.

Swing the Tips.   Lift up one foot and then the other, moving the tip of the lifted ski up and down; this is followed by turning the lifted ski to the right and to the left.

Hop.   With weight supported by the poles, jump with both feet, shifting the tails of the skis alternately to the right and to the left.

Step Sideways.   Step to the side, then back, alternating to the right and left and gradually increasing the tempo. This adds to your balance and agility on skis and teaches you to handle them with ease.

From the description of Sequential Leg Rotation (SELR) and Simultaneous Leg Rotation (SILR) (p. 10) do the legs move sequentially or simultaneously in the following walking and stationary drills: Wagon Wheel, One Step Glide, Hop?

Falling and Getting Up.   The inevitable will happen—you will fall. At first it will occur rather suddenly and without any control. After several falls, you will find that you have a little time to control how you land. Every effort should be made to try to land on your hip with your knees up and your body uphill from your skis.

   To get up, put the skis below you and straight across the fall line, tuck the legs, then turn your knees and ankles toward the slope to help set the edges firmly. Remove the pole straps from the wrists and plant both poles slightly behind the shoulder (fig. 2.2). Grasp the handles with the upper hand and

Fig. 2.2. Getting up

Fig. 2.3. Ski tracks illustrating climbing techniques (herringbone, side step, and diagonal side step)

place the other hand near the basket. Then apply force, pushing yourself to a standing position. If the snow is deep and its surface soft, a crisscross pattern should be made with the poles, thus forming a platform so that you can push yourself to a standing position without your hands and poles sinking too far into the snow. If you fall downhill, rotate the body 180° so the skis are below you before you try to get up.

Sidestepping.   This drill provides preparation for climbing hills. With the skis directly across the fall line, set the edges by rolling the ankles and knees toward the hill. Use the lower ski as a platform from which to push and step up with the upper ski; set the upper ski firmly, then close the lower ski to it.

Diagonal Sidestepping.   This is done in the same way as the side step, except that the skier moves diagonally up the slope as each step carries him forward and upward.

Herringbone.   This is another way of traveling up a slope on skis. First practice the technique on a flat area without using the poles. The position of the skis is with the heels close together and the tips separated as in Cutting the Pie. The action is similar to walking with the toes pointed outward. Emphasize transferring the weight alternately from one ski to the other, then stepping forward with the unweighted ski. After this has been practiced many times, it becomes rather simple and begins to feel quite natural. After the basic technique has been mastered, the poles may be used to increase the tempo and the force, both of which are necessary for faster and steeper climbing.

When sidestepping skis are perpendicular to the fall line with edges set. What action sets the edges of the skis? What trace pattern is left on the snow when sidestepping is executed successfully? Unsuccessfully?

---

american teaching
method
3

Following World War II the interest in skiing began to increase throughout the United States. However, different methods of teaching skiing were used in various regions. Skiers traveling from one ski area to another would find it difficult to continue a particular method of instruction. In the 1950's the French and Austrian ski techniques were most frequently used, but not everyone was qualified to teach these systems.

DEVELOPMENT OF THE AMERICAN SKI TECHNIQUE

Recognizing the need for a standardized system of teaching which could be used throughout the United States, interested professionals met at Alta, Utah, in 1958. Representatives from the Professional Ski Instructor's Association, National Ski Association, National Certification Committee, and other groups concerned with skiing and ski teaching were in attendance. Their combined efforts resulted in formulating the American Ski Technique. However, this initial effort did not seem to live up to expectations. Consequently, the American Ski Technique was not so widely accepted as had been hoped.

Since that beginning the American Ski Technique has undergone several revisions, each attempting to define skiing skills and maneuvers more adequately. During this same period new materials and technology resulted in notable improvements in ski equipment. As the equipment improved, ski technique likewise changed. The American Teaching Method (ATM) is the latest effort to integrate knowledge gained from research within the areas of motor learning and biomechanics to form a coherent system of teaching. Although the ATM is continually being updated, it has acquired considerable respect both at home and abroad.

THE AMERICAN TEACHING METHOD

The primary goal of the ATM is to develop a christie and refine it as the basis for safe and efficient skiing. The ATM recommends the Graduated Length Method (GLM) which incorporates the progression to longer ski lengths. By way of clarification, this means that beginning students would use a shorter ski to increase their learning rate and also to reduce the likelihood of injuries. Students are then equipped progressively with longer skis as their abilities improve and their performance warrants. Some students, however, are encouraged to stay with shorter length skis simply because this is more compatible with their mental and physical capabilities. While the GLM is desirable, the cost of buying longer skis sometimes makes this system impractical for the average skier.

The ATM has made several significant contributions to our understanding of ski technique and its application to teaching situations. While it is not necessary to discuss all of these contributions, two should be brought to the skiers attention. From the earliest days of the American Ski Technique, constant effort has been made to describe skiing in its simplest form. The first effort resulted in seven principles of skiing. The ATM has succeeded in incorporating those seven principles into three basic skills which are relatively easy to identify. These skills are *turning, edging,* and *pressure control.* All maneuvers in skiing can be described using these three skills within the framework of a balanced position upon the skis. For further discussion of these skills and the definitions of unfamiliar terms used herein, the reader is referred to Chapter 10, Mechanical Analysis and Definitions.

The second contribution is the distinction made between Sequential Leg Rotating (SELR) and Simultaneous Leg Rotating (SILR) movements made during the various turning maneuvers experienced while skiing. SELR refers to a one-two motion of the legs similar to normal walking, whereas SILR refers to a one-movement where both legs move in the same way at the same time, like jumping on a trampoline. It should be noted that for years the ability to ski parallel was considered the tool of the most proficient skiers. But when the top racers were observed in action it was noted that they were often using stepping (SELR) movements rather than parallel (SILR) maneuvers. The situation dictated the leg action; thus, the ATM has established learning progressions in both stepping and parallel maneuvers to help the skier adapt to various snow and terrain conditions. One is not considered superior to the other, but both are necessary to broaden the skier's development.

SPECIFIC MANEUVERS AND EXERCISES

The following section identifies a progression of maneuvers in which the skier should become proficient. These maneuvers are cumulative, assisting the skier to become a master of all skiing situations. Methods and exercises which have proved successful in helping to develop the maneuvers or turns are here listed. Each exercise is designed to aid the skier improve one or more of the basic skills listed earlier—*turning, edging,* and *pressure control.* It should be noted that the skier becomes proficient at a maneuver only as the skills are refined. The maneuver or turn is described in general terms so as not to impose personal style; it is not necessary to become proficient at a maneuver before working on the exercises in the next maneuver. Indeed, many of the exercises used in lower level turns are helpful in refining the basic skills necessary for advanced turns, and should often be repeated.

Straight Running

Selection of terrain for this maneuver is highly important because the slope must be long, smooth, free of traffic, and have a natural runout. Body position should take into account the following points: (1) hands within the field of vision, (2) all joints slightly flexed, (3) body weight on the entire foot, and (4) skis approximately 12 to 14 inches apart (wide-track position). The body is perpendicular to the skis at all times, and the skier should feel that it is a natural position (see fig. 3.1).

Specific Methods and Exercises

1. Rock fore and aft, causing the ankle joint to bend and extend while standing.
2. Balance on one foot, then on the other.
3. The first run should be on a gentle incline. Have the skis in wide-track position during the running. Step into parallel track and back during runout.
4. Repeat exercises #1 and #2 while sliding.
5. Step into a parallel track, step turn to a stop.

Basic Wedge

In order to move into the basic wedge position the student should push the heels out at the same time that the toes are being pointed together (see fig. 3.2). Repeat this pivot until the transition into the V, or wedge, position feels smooth and easy. If pushing the skis out into the wedge position is too difficult, it can be accomplished by unweighting one ski, pushing the tail of that ski out, and then repeating with the other ski. Weight is equally distributed on both

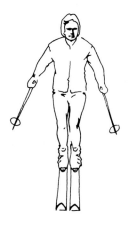

Fig. 3.1. Straight running

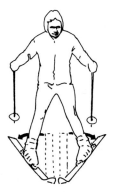

Fig. 3.2. Basic wedge

skis. Tails are equally displaced from the body. The wedge is a braking maneuver, and the braking effect will be little or great depending on the width of the heel displacement. The following exercises should be repeated, varying the width of the wedge from a narrow (gliding) to a wide (braking).

Specific Methods and Exercises

1. Body should be semirelaxed and in a natural position.
2. Standing at a wide-track position, push tails out into a wedge. Do this automatically by up-unweighting and down-unweighting.
3. Let the wedge glide to the runout. In other words, do not overwedge or stop the skis.
4. Try gliding and then blocking the speed of the runout by unweighting and forcing the heels out.
5. Alternate the straight running position and the wedge position.
6. Improve edge awareness, roll knees in and out, and check the results. Students should feel skis slow down when knees are rolled in and an increase in speed when skis are rolled out.
7. Look forward and stay relaxed.
8. Visualize the wedge as a basic straight-run position with double stemming, or with both skis steered at the same time.

Edge control is very important in skiing at all levels. How does adjusting the inner edges affect progress in the wedge position? Check your own trace pattern left in the snow to see how it changes when edging is increased? Decreased?

The Wedge Turn

This is the first experience the student will have in getting the feel of turning the skis with a skidding action. Actually, the skis will be turned by steering and/or shifting the weight from one ski to another.

Specific Methods and Exercises

1. While moving along in a gliding wedge, steer into small deviations to the left and to the right.
2. Encourage a more pronounced knee bend.
3. Start downhill in a wide-track position, then push the outer ski into a wedge position and steer a gentle turn by turning the foot toward the direction of the turn.
4. Alternate the amount of knee bend to complete the turn.
5. Move weight toward the ball, middle, and heel of the foot while the turning effect of that leg continues.
6. Do wedge turns through slalom gates (ski poles, gloves, and other items may be substituted for racing poles).

Fig. 3.3.   Basic wedge turn

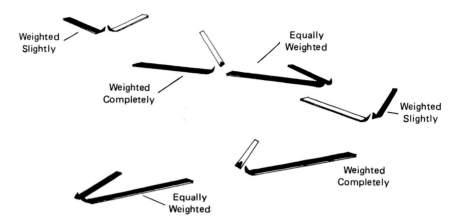

Fig. 3.4.   Diagram showing phases of wedge turn (note: darker skis show weight distribution.)

Fig. 3.5.   Traverse position

7. Gradually emphasize the turning of the inside leg in the direction of the turn until the edges match and a skid is achieved.
8. Try to strengthen balance and acquire the skill of being able to move from one edge to another.

Traverse Position

As the skis cross the slope (fall line), they should be parallel and the weight should be more on the downhill ski than on the uphill. The body is in a natural, semirelaxed position (see fig. 3.7).

Specific Methods and Exercises

1. Keep the ski edges equally toward the slope.
2. Keep more weight on the lower ski than on the upper one.
3. Have the uphill hip slightly projected or protruded.
4. The uphill shoulder should be higher than the downhill shoulder.
5. Knees, ankles, and hips should be angulated or inclined toward the slope.

Fig. 3.6.   Sideslipping

Learning to Skid the Turn

At this point it is important for the skier to gain a variety of experiences with the gliding wedge. Emphasis should be placed upon skiing many miles over terrain that gradually becomes more challenging. The experience of skiing many miles over regular terrain should raise the skier's confidence level significantly. As the confidence level rises, so should the speed of the skier increase. The combination of speed, terrain, and steering should result in turns with a skidded finish.

Specific Methods and Exercises

1. Alternate sharp short turns with round longer turns.
2. Link turns while skiing quite fast.
3. Make non-stop runs.
4. Bob up and down turning the turn.
5. As turn finishes, match the inside ski with the outside ski.
6. All of the exercises should be done from a very narrow wedge.

Side Slipping

Side slipping exercises will aid the skier in developing a skid at the end of the turn. From a traverse position, the edges of the skis are released and the skis are allowed to slide sideways down the hill.

In both the traverse and the wide track position the skis are parallel. Describe the different relationships these two techniques have with regard to the fall line; use of edging; distribution of weight.

Specific Methods and Exercises
1. Weight stays more on the downhill ski.
2. Use the knees to release and set the edges.
3. Make continuous side slips for longer distances.
4. Apply leverage forward and back while slipping, and observe how the skis respond.

Fig. 3.7.   Wide track christie with a pole plant

Pole Plant

The introduction of the pole plant always seems to be a frustrating experience for skiers entering the intermediate phase. Up to this point they have used the pole as a balancing factor or as a crutch to keep from falling into the hill. Consequently, the pole seems to drag in the snow. By now the skier should be experiencing some form of weight transfer to the outside ski during the turn. The pole plant can serve two purposes: (1) as a timing device to indicate when to shift the weight; and (2) as an aid in the shifting of the weight to the outside ski. The pole should be planted lightly on the inside of the turn and quickly removed from the snow so as to keep the hands in front of you while skiing.

Wide Track Turns

The experiences gained in the gliding wedge and in the side slipping exercises should establish a basis for wide track turns. From a wide track position the skier should increase the leg action, coming to a complete stop as would a hockey player on ice. By initiating the turn with single leg action and finishing with double leg action, the skier turns against the fall line. This maneuver is referred to as hockey stop, and is clearly illustrated in Figure 3.8. The hockey stop illu-

Fig. 3.8.   Hockey stop

strates the main goals of wide track turning: increased use of weight transfer from ski to ski, and accelerated play of edges and pressure to make greater use of the ski shape.

As proficiency in these wide track christies increases, the skier carves the turn better and is able to negotiate steeper slopes at higher speeds. This is because the skier can check speed and make turns using double leg action. These wide track christies are really parallel christies and give the skier the sensation of turning on both skis at the same time. There is also a feeling of anticipation and coordination for the pole plant so that the skier not only anticipates the next turn but is ready to make parallel turns from a balanced position. As confidence increases the skier will be able to ski steeper terrain, bigger bumps, and moguls.

Identify the important features of turning which can be learned by mastering the hockey stop.

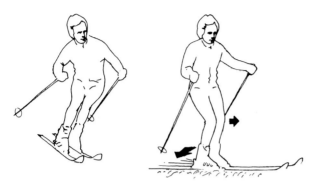

Fig. 3.9.   Christie uphill

Specific Methods and Exercises

1. Ski long distances.
2. Uphill christies from a steep traverse.
3. Uphill christies from the fall line.
4. Begin the turn off a small bump.
5. Use up unweighting movements to start turn.
6. Vary the radius of the turns.
7. Vary the speed of the turns.
8. Link turns together in a comfortable rhythm. You may want to hum to yourself to establish such a rhythm.
9. End some of the turns with a hockey stop.

Rebound Turns

As a skier becomes more proficient in wide track turns, he or she will observe that the distance between the two skis becomes narrower. Also, the skier will feel greater pressure upon the skis toward the end of the turn. This pressure will result in a rebounding action causing the skis to become unweighted. This rebounding action can be used to its fullest or it can be absorbed to some degree. The next turn is initiated during this rebound phase.

In the actual performance of a rebound turn, the skier will turn with force into the hill and set the edge as the pole is planted. A pivoted push off or rebound propels the skier toward the fall line. The skier changes edges and with the torso facing downhill, experiences a feeling of anticipation. The arc of the turn is controlled by the amount of steering and pressure applied as a skier increases the amount of edge set. (Chapter 10 discusses anticipation in greater depth.)

It should be noted that when a ski is placed on its edge and pressure is applied to the ski, the design of the ski will cause the ski to carve rather than to skid. As the skier becomes proficient at rebound turns, he will notice that his skis are carving more and skidding less.

Fig. 3.10.   Rebound turn (parallel christie with check)

Specific Methods and Exercises

1. Uphill christies with emphasis on more edging. In a wide track make un-hurried turns in gentle terrain. Start each turn by trying to lay the outside knee onto the inside boot.
2. Repeat the same exercise and apply pressure to the outside ski.
4. Make hockey stops with increased carving and less pivotal action.
5. Use hard edge sets at the end of a turn to create a platform to push off from.
6. Soften edge set at the end of the turn to smooth out the rebound action.

Short Swing

The short swing is an enjoyable way of skiing where the terrain is not too diffi-cult. It is also a very effective way to ski steep terrain where the skier must be aggressive. The best explanation of a short swing is that it is a maneuver used by experts usually on steep hills for the purpose of controlling their speed with short turns. By definition it would be short linked parallel christies in the fall

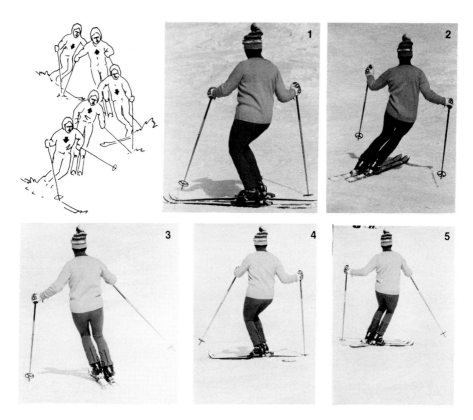

Fig. 3.11.　Short swing

line that have very little or no traverse between turns and use a carved or skidded arc to finish the turn.

Certain things must be done in order to accomplish the short swing. There must be a definite edge set and the pole plant must be coordinated with the edge set. Also, there must be a rebound action or pivot push-off, anticipation, angulation, and leg rotation to control and maintain the arc of the turn. There is a definite sinking toward the edge set and the pole plant as the skier turns out of the fall line. The upper body faces downhill. As the lower body moves into the next turn the skier will draw into alignment with the blocked upper body. There is a definite sinking and steering and an increase in angulation and anticipation (see fig. 3.11).

Specific Methods and Exercises

1. Practice the short swing in shallow terrain.
2. Practice the short swing in medium terrain.
3. Practice the short swing in steep terrain.
4. Work on edge control.

5. Work on pole plant.
6. Improve carving by sidestep wedge turns with leverage.
7. Do short swings in soft and hard snow conditions.
8. Practice slalom turns with wide gates.

Step Turns

As mentioned earlier in the chapter the ATM has developed a separate progression for step turn maneuvers. SELR movements deal with stemming and stepping and are basically a one-two action where one ski moves then the other follows. The first ski can be moved into a convergent or stemmed position, a parallel position, or a divergent or scissor position. Should the skier decide to follow the step turn progression he may comfortably do so after the side slip exercises.

What are the function and involvement of the upper body when executing a series of short swing turns?

Stemming

Either ski may be stemmed to initiate a turn. The use of a downstem helps to check speed, create a platform from which to rebound, and sets up strong rotary motions in the turn. The uphill stem allows the skier to make an easy edge change and to be more tentative in the initiation of the turn. As a skier's confidence increases, the uphill stem will become aggressive. In either stemming action the width of the stem and the degree of the edge will dictate the radius and speed of the turn. Both stemming actions require a pushoff from the downhill ski to transfer the weight to the uphill ski and begin steering into the turn. The skis are matched and steering continues with both legs. Both turns are effective on steep terrain with bumps.

Specific Methods and Exercises
1. Use a wide stem for short radius turns.
2. Use narrow stem for long radius turns.
3. Vary the amount of edging on the stemmed ski.
4. Vary the speed of the turn.
5. Vary the strength of the push-off from the downhill ski.
6. Move the weight to the toes, the middle, and the heels during the turn—which ever feels best.
7. After some practice the uphill stem can be made with a step and go action.

Identify the different advantages of the uphill stem and the downhill stem turns. How does the size of the stem relate to the radius of the turn?

Fig. 3.12.   Downstem christie

Fig. 3.13.   Upstem christie

Parallel Step Christie

Gradually the skier will diminish the amount of stemming at the beginning
of a turn and will develop the ability to step from a downhill ski to a parallel
uphill ski. This sets up a carving action and is considered the simplest form
of turning parallel. As shown in the accompanying figure (Fig. 3.14) the single
leg action, or stepping up to the outside turning ski, now becomes a double
leg action which involves both skis in turning. The figure also shows how the
stem-step has diminished from a stem-step to a parallel-step.

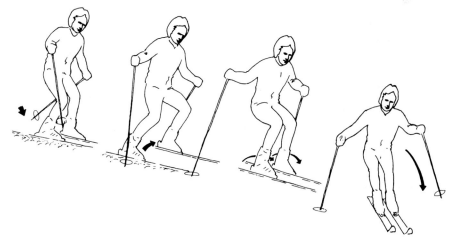

Fig. 3.14.   Parallel-step christie

In order to accomplish this parallel step christie from a previous turn or traverse, the uphill ski is stepped out and placed flat or on the inside edge. Simultaneous sinking aids preparation for a push-off from the downhill ski. Momentum is created by matching the downhill ski alongside the other, and steering, edging, leverage, and leg rotation control the arc of the turn.

The pole plant in the parallel-step christie is done in conjunction with the push-off from the inside ski. When stepping parallel to the outside edge, the pole plant is delayed and coincides with the matching of the skis as they are brought together. In order to time the pole plant properly it must be remembered that the whole action is a smooth and flowing one.

In this particular maneuver the pole must be carried in a relaxed manner. Otherwise the skier will stiffen up and find that even the initiation of a small turn will be jerky and difficult and will have a tendency to throw the body off balance (see fig. 3.14).

Specific Methods and Exercises

1. Start from a wide track and move to a narrow track.
2. Try to improve the fluidity and smoothness of the stepping action.
3. Practice stepping to inside edge, flat ski, and outside edge of the step ski.
4. Vary the amount of leg separation when starting the turn.
5. Ski over moderate bumps and gentle terrain during straight runs and christies.
6. Improve carving ability by doing uphill christies, christies to a stop, varying the degree of slope, and also using wide and narrow tracks intermittently.

Scissor Step

This stepping action is characterized by the diverging action of the stepping ski similar to skating. During the turn, as the downhill ski is turned through the fall line, the skier skates off onto the new outside ski. The outside edge is engaged and the weight is projected forward onto that ski. This is followed by a change in body inclination, a lowering of the ski onto its inside edge, and strong turning impulses added. The skier's ability to carve should be strongly advanced in this turn.

In changing from a traverse or turn into a parallel step christie, what are the first actions the skier takes?

Specific Methods and Exercises

1. Skate on level terrain.
2. Scissor step from a steep to a shallow traverse.
3. Wedge in the fall line and alternately lock one, then the other edge.
4. From a steep traverse, take two skating steps into the hill then skate and link a turn across the fall line.

Fig. 3.15.   Scissor step turn

HOW TO BECOME AN EXPERT SKIER

The expert skier approaches all snow conditions and each different terrain problem with confidence. This is one of the many factors that distinguishes the expert from the rest of the skiers on the mountain. This seemingly effortless movement through difficult terrain and/or "impossible" snow conditions leaves all other skiers with the desire to imitate. Most often these efforts to imitate fail because the individual is not properly grounded in the fundamentals discussed earlier.

Even after the acquisition of the basic skills of skiing, the skier still must learn more to become an expert. Now it is necessary to learn to adapt all that is known to the special problems created by the different snow conditions: ice, powder, deep snow, and heavy snow. Also, the skier must learn to handle speed and to ski big bumps and steep slopes. The ability to maintain control while skiing in the above conditions distinguishes the expert from all other skiers.

How to Handle Speed

A skier will start to ski faster after acquiring a feeling of control over the skis in the beginning maneuvers. This feeling of control and speed is what skiing is all about. It is a most exciting feeling to know that if an unusual situation should arise, such as another skier moving in an unexpected direction, it is possible to move to one side or to stop if necessary.

The sensation of speed itself is a great experience. The skier quickly learns that the skis respond better with less effort at high speeds, but only up to a point. More skill in the fundamentals is required to advance beyond that.

The skier first must learn how to ski rather slowly on gentle terrain and then increase his speed as his confidence and ability to handle the terrain increase. It goes without saying that the skier should look over the entire area to be skied in order to plan what to do. Some may want to ski fast where there are few bumps and then slow down, controlling their speed through narrow areas where turns have to be made rather quickly. The one thing a skier should not do is look at the feet, thus limiting the range of vision to only a short distance in front of the skis. One must be able to "feel" his way down the mountain, looking at least 25 to 30 yards ahead in order to see what path to take. Looking ahead is also important in developing one's ability to adjust to changing conditions or congested areas.

The fun and joy of skiing consist in being able to control speed while making a descent down the mountain. There is probably nothing more satisfying than to look back up a steep area that you have skied in control with confidence. Probably more important is knowing that the speed has been at a level you could control.

Handling Bumps

Whether you like it or not, the short choppy bumps are here to stay. Skiers have to learn how to do things differently when skiing through bumps and on steeper slopes. While it used to be possible to ski around the bumps with the longer skis, now the bumps sometimes have to be hit head on and skied over the top and down the side. This is because the short skis have made the bumps very steep, close together, and, in some areas, rather treacherous.

A term the skier needs to become acquainted with in skiing these bumps and moguls is *reploiment*. This has significance when bumps are absorbed by the legs and the knees (see fig. 3.16).

Reploiment has to do with the relaxation of the extensor muscles while absorbing the bumps. This means that the legs yield to the bump as the skier approaches it so that the body will pass over the bump without much of a jolt. Otherwise, the skier's descent of the mountain will be characterized by jerky turns, lack of balance, and a great deal of struggling to stay upright.

In order to ski faster and still maintain control on bigger bumps, the skier must learn still another movement. This is referred to as *avalement*. *Avalement* is the retraction and extension of the stomach muscles, pulling the knees up to the chest and then extending them down again. This has to do with actually retracting the legs toward the stomach. In order to do this the skier must control the stomach muscles in an action similar to a diver doing a jackknife.

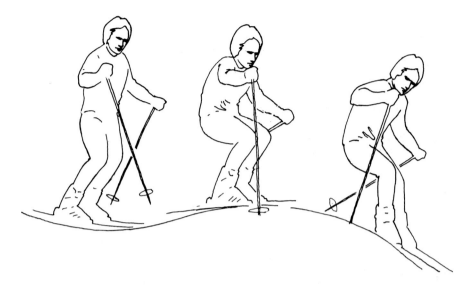

Fig. 3.16.   Skiing bumps—avalement

The jackknife action takes place as the skier moves into the bump, followed by an immediate leg extension on the other side of the bump. The object here is to keep one's skis on the snow at all times. Timing becomes a most important factor now. The feet have to be projected and extended down the bumps or moguls and then be twisted in the direction of the new turn. With the proper pole plant, reploiment, and avalement the skier can move down steeper terrain with sharp bumps, absorbing the action with the legs and stomach muscles and maintaining balance and speed under control.

Tips for Skiing the Bumps.

1. Do christies with avalement on gentle terrain.
2. Read the type of surface you are skiing and keep a proper angle to the fall line. Do not let the angle become too steep.
3. Do not sit back too far, but stay in more of a relaxed position so that the legs and knees can help in the bumps.
4. Keep practicing on steeper slopes, bigger bumps, and sharper moguls.
5. Check speed on the flat part on the top of the bump.

How to Ski Deep Snow

Of all the experiences in skiing, deep snow probably is the most intriguing. To the expert skier, being able to ski and handle deep snow is the ultimate. There is no other feeling like it, experienced only when a skier becomes proficient in skiing the deep snow with confidence and proper technique. However, the skier certainly needs to become very good on hard surfaces before expecting to be a very good deep powder skier.

Fig. 3.17. Powder sequence

There are many types of deep snow, and the skier's ability to tell the difference may be the key to skiing that type of snow well. The heavier the snow, the more difficult it is to make good turns and ski in control. The lighter and fluffier the powder snow, the easier it is to handle.

When should the techniques **reploiment** and **avalement** be used and which is the more dynamic technique?

Tips for Skiing Deep Snow.
1. Keep the skis fairly close together—avoid crossing the tips.
2. Keep the weight equally balanced on both skis.
3. Bank the turns with both skis, rather than leaning heavily on one ski.
4. Keep the back straight—simulate sitting on a low chair.
5. Knees should be flexible and move easily in either direction.
6. The pole plant becomes only a timing device; do not lean on it.
7. Turns become easier when the skier has confidence to ski near the fall line on steeper slopes.

8. Keep the upper body fairly still and let the lower legs and feet do the turning. Point knees in direction of turn.
9. If the snow is deep, retract the skis out of the snow, turn, and then extend the skis back into the snow.

There are many techniques that can be employed while skiing deep snow. However, confidence is the ingredient that makes them successful. As skiers become more confident, they will want to challenge steeper slopes and deeper snow. They should use any and every available skill they can employ to increase their enjoyment.

A general reminder for all skiers, especially those entering the expert stage, is that skiing is meant to be fun. Accept new challenges and ski the hill. Do not let the hill ski you!

conditioning
for skiers
4

Effective muscle conditioning will improve your skiing, help you to enjoy longer ski sessions, and reduce your chance of injury. Conditioning is well worth the effort; in fact, it is essential to good skiing. The four characteristics of conditioning that are fundamental to skiing excellence can all be improved through the following program, which is especially designed for skiers.

1. *Strength* is the ability to contract the muscles with great force. Strength is important because the muscles must be able to support the body and effectively maneuver it through the vigorous actions required in skiing. Without adequate strength, maneuverability is greatly restricted. Also, the possession of strength is important in the prevention of injuries, since strong muscles help to stabilize points and resist undesired and hazardous movements.
2. *Muscular Endurance* is the ability of the muscles to resist fatigue. Endurance is important in skiing because the muscles must perform sustained and repeated contractions. Lack of endurance results in early fatigue and loss of skiing pleasure. As the muscles fatigue, both the ability to react quickly and the ability to maneuver effectively are drastically reduced. This lessens skill and also makes you more prone to injury.
3. *Flexibility* is the ability of the muscles and connective tissue to stretch. Flexibility is important because it not only improves your ability to assume the various body positions essential to good skiing but also causes the muscles and connective tissues to be less prone to injuries from overstretching.
4. *Cardiovascular Endurance* is the ability of the cardiovascular system to effectively supply oxygen and nutrients to the working muscles and to keep the muscles free of waste products, mainly carbon dioxide and lactic acid.

HOW TO DEVELOP STRENGTH

Strength can be increased best by applying the two principles of strength overload and progressive resistance. *Strength overload* simply means that when muscles are contracted regularly against resistance that is heavier than they are accustomed to (this is overload), they will respond by increasing in strength. If they are not loaded beyond their usual levels they will not gain additional strength (except that attributable to normal growth in a growing person). *Progressive resistance* means that as the muscles become stronger, the loads against which they contract must be progressively increased in order to continue to apply overload. An effective strength-building program is one that applies these two principles regularly to the muscle groups needing strengthening.

HOW TO INCREASE MUSCULAR ENDURANCE

Increased strength causes some increase in endurance because strong muscles contract against a given resistance with greater ease than weaker muscles and therefore will experience fatigue less readily. In order to develop additional muscular endurance, the principle of *endurance overload* must be applied. This is done by exercising repeatedly against relatively light resistance for many repetitions. While strength development requires heavy resistance with a low number of repetitions, endurance can be developed with lighter resistance and many repetitions.

HOW TO INCREASE FLEXIBILITY

To increase flexibility the muscles should be stretched gradually and slowly until the stretch pain is felt, then held in the stretched position for several seconds during each repetition. The exercise should be repeated several times in succession. Jerky movements causing sudden overstretching will cause mild muscle injuries and should be avoided. Stretch slowly and smoothly.

HOW TO INCREASE CARDIOVASCULAR ENDURANCE

In order to increase this form of endurance, the muscular system must be worked to the extent of vigorously taxing the cardiovascular system. This results in overloading the cardiovascular system, meaning that it is worked at levels higher than it is accustomed to. Regular overloading stimulates the system to become better developed and more efficient, thus causing it to resist fatigue longer. Running is the best activity for developing this form of endurance among skiers because running and skiing involve many of the same muscles.

MUSCLE INVOLVEMENT IN SKIING

Practically every muscle in the body is used to some extent in skiing. However, since a great majority of the muscular work is done by only the following muscle groups, the conditioning program should emphasize the following:
Ankle extensor muscles—located in the back of the lower leg (calf)
Knee extensor muscles—located in the front of the upper leg (thigh)
Hip extensor muscles—located in the buttocks and the backs of the upper
    legs
Back extensor muscles—located along the back, close to the spine

Hip rotary muscles—located all about the pelvic region
Trunk rotator muscles—located all about the waist

The Muscle Exercise Program

Each exercise in this program is designed to increase muscular strength, endurance, or flexibility in the specific muscle groups where these traits are needed.

Exercise 1 increases flexibility of back and leg extensor muscles. From a standing position with the arms extended over the head, bend slowly forward at the hips. Continue moving downward, placing the hands on the floor near the toes, with the head hanging low between the arms. Hold this position for six seconds. Return to starting position and repeat the exercise five times. Add one repetition every two days up to ten repetitions.

Exercise 2 increases the flexibility, strength, and endurance of the hip and waist regions. Lie on the back with the legs straight and the arms outstretched and flat on the floor. Bring both legs upward, then sideward to a position near the left hand. Return to the starting position and repeat to the right side. Repeat the exercise five times to each side and add one to each side daily until fifteen repetitions are done on each side.

Exercise 3 increases the strength, endurance, and flexibility of the lower leg and foot muscles. Stand facing a wall with the feet together. Lean against the wall with the body inclined as far forward as possible without raising the heels from the floor, rise high on to the toes, and hold the position for six seconds, then return the heels to the floor and hold that position for six seconds. Repeat ten times and increase by one repetition each day to twenty repetitions.

Exercise 4 increases the strength and endurance of the foot and the leg extensor muscles and increases coordination of hip and leg rotation movements during unweighting (upward) action. From a semicrouched position jump

---

Evaluate personal weaknesses such as your physical condition. Are there lacks of strength, endurance, or flexibility? If so, select and practice appropriate exercises to improve your physical condition and which will contribute to your efficiency and enjoyment when skiing.

---

upward; rotate the hips, legs, and feet to the left; and land in that position. Rotate the shoulders only slightly in the opposite direction. Jump again immediately and rotate the legs to the right. Jump successively and repeat the rotations twenty times to each side. Increase the number by two jumps each day. The feet should clear the floor by 2 inches on each jump.

Exercise 5 adds strength and endurance to the extensor and rotary muscles of the back. From the prone position with the hands clasped behind the back, raise the chest from the floor, rotate the shoulders to the left as far as possible, and hold the position for six seconds. Return to the starting

Fig. 4.1.   Exercise 1   Fig. 4.2.   Exercise 1

Fig. 4.3.   Exercise 2   Fig. 4.4.   Exercise 2

Fig. 4.5.   Exercise 3

Fig. 4.6.   Exercise 4

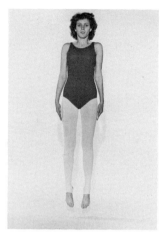

Fig. 4.7.   Exercise 4

Fig. 4.8.   Exercise 5

Fig. 4.9.   Exercise 6

Fig. 4.10.   Exercise 7

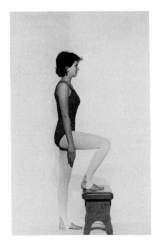 

Fig. 4.11. Exercise 8   Fig. 4.12. Exercise 8

position and repeat the exercise to the right. Repeat the exercise ten times, rotating alternately to the left and right. Increase the repetitions by two each day.

Exercise 6 increases strength and endurance of the knee extensor muscles. With the back to a wall, gradually lower the body and move the feet away from the wall until the upper legs are horizontal and the angle at the knees is 90°. Hold this position until the muscles of the thigh ache. Repeat the exercise three times. Progressively increase the time the position is held each day.

Exercise 7 increases strength and endurance of abdominal muscles (trunk flexors and rotators) and improves rotary flexibility of the hips and lower back. From the supine position with the hands on the chest and the knees elevated, sit up, shift the knees to the left and shoulders to the right, and touch the hands to the floor beside the right foot. Repeat the exercise twenty times, touching the hands to alternate sides. Add two repetitions each day.

Exercise 8 increases endurance of the leg extensor muscles. Stand in front of a bench or similar item. Step onto the bench with one foot then bring the other foot up beside the first. Step down in the same manner. Repeat with the opposite foot. Continue the exercise, alternating the feet, until the thigh muscles feel fatigued.

Skiers should be aware that running, running in place (bringing the knees high), and running up and down stairs are all excellent methods of conditioning the muscles of the lower extremities and for increasing the endurance of the total body. Vigorous participation in sports that require much starting and stopping and changing of direction is also desirable. Among such activities are soccer, basketball, and tennis.

REMEMBER, THERE IS NO SUBSTITUTE FOR GOOD MUS-
CLE CONDITION, IT WILL HELP YOU SKI BETTER AND MAKE
YOU LESS PRONE TO INJURY.

CARDIOVASCULAR DEVELOPMENT PROGRAM

Vigorous running is the best activity for developing cardiovascular endurance.
The running might be done up and down hills, on a track, on a soccer field, or
on a basketball court. Regardless of where it is done or whether in a game or
nongame situation, it will have a similar result. In other words, if the running is
vigorous enough and long enough in duration, it will provide a stimulus for
increased cardiovascular development.

The most efficient method of developing this form of endurance is a systematic program of interval training, meaning that you run at a fairly fast rate
for a given distance, then after a short rest repeat the work bout. You should
continue this procedure through several repetitions. It has been found that the
most effective procedure is to work vigorously for 4 to 5 minutes at a rate that
will keep the heart rate above 160 beats per minute and to rest only a few minutes between work bouts. However, it is possible to gain a good amount of
cardiovascular endurance by doing shorter work bouts, such as wind sprints. Also, cardiovascular endurance can be increased significantly by exercising at a
slower pace for a longer distance, such as in cross-country running or cross-country skiing.

STRETCHING BEFORE SKIING

It is a good practice to start your day of skiing with a few stretching exercises.
When you get to the top of the hill before the first run, do the following four
stretches.

Stretch 1: Slide one ski forward and put your weight on it. Keep the other leg
straight and extended behind you. Stretch the calf muscles.

Stretch 2: Kick one ski in front of you and rest it on its tail. Keeping the knee
as straight as possible, flex forward at the hips. Stretch the back muscles
of the thigh.

Stretch 3: Swing the ski slowly behind you and rest it on its tip with the tail
of the ski by your shoulder. By pulling the tail forward the front muscles of
the thigh will be stretched.

Stretch 4: After repeating one, two, and three with the other leg, spread your
skis apart, flex at the waist, and slowly shift the body toward one ski and
then the other. Stretch the muscles of the inner thigh. Your leg should
now feel relaxed, warm, and ready to respond to the challenge of skiing.
Repeat these stretches after lunch or any time you feel you need a quick
warm up.

Fig. 4.13.   Stretch 1

Fig. 4.14.   Stretch 2

Fig. 4.15.   Stretch 3

Fig. 4.16.   Stretch 4

rules of etiquette and safety

5

Observing correct rules of safety and etiquette will not make you a champion, but it will make skiing safer and contribute both to your skiing pleasure and to that of others. Following are some rules that should be observed at every ski area.

1. Take lessons from a well-qualified instructor. A sound foundation provides the most direct route to successful skiing. Good instruction will help to improve technique rapidly and reduce the chance of injury.
2. Develop and maintain a satisfactory level of physical fitness *prior* to the beginning of each ski season. Information on how to do this is covered in chapter 4.
3. Prior to the beginning of each day of skiing do some loosening and slow stretching exercises to prepare your muscles. Then during the first run, practice drills that will sharpen your skills and make you ready for regular skiing.
4. Always ski in control. There are few things more aggravating than a dangerous, out-of-control skier crashing down the mountain, unable to turn or stop and knocking down skiers like bowling pins. For your own safety and the safety of others, always stay in control.
5. Be alert to other skiers. When you plan to pass another skier call to him "track right" or "track left," indicating on which side you plan to pass. If you are the front skier, take the warning and ski straight ahead or move in the opposite direction.
6. Make periodic checks of equipment to be sure it is functioning properly. This is especially true for safety bindings. A binding that is set too tight or one that is clogged with ice and snow forfeits any advantage that it was designed to give.
7. Observe all trail designations. Uniform markers are used by major ski areas to indicate the degree of difficulty of the various ski runs. The markers are as follows:

a. green square—easier run
b. yellow triangle—more difficult run
c. blue circle—most difficult run
d. red diamond—use extra caution
e. fluorescent orange octagon—avalanche danger

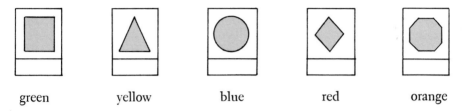

green   yellow   blue   red   orange

8. Avoid skiing when you are fatigued. Fatigue slows reaction time and general alertness and thus contributes to injury proneness.
9. Do not stop in the middle of the run. Always move to the side where you will be out of the way of other skiers.
10. Cover your sitzmarks. Leaving a pit in the snow from your fall is like deliberately preparing a trap for another skier. Sitzmarks are the causes of many accidents.
11. Do not break the lift line. Ski area managers usually try to keep chiselers in place, but it is the responsibility of the individual skier to show this courtesy to other skiers.
12. While in line, avoid stepping on the skis or poles of other skiers. Although it is important to keep the line closed, also show respect for the other skier's equipment.
13. If you are a single in a busy line, double up with someone, preferably a person near your own size. Equal size is especially important on double T-bar lifts.
14. Treat the lift as you would your own equipment. Swinging, bouncing, and other unnecessary movements are hard on the equipment and present a safety hazard. On T-bars and Poma lifts, stay in the track.
15. Upon debarking from the lift, immediately move out of the way. Although the view is breathtaking and your equipment needs adjusting, study the view and adjust your equipment away from the debarking point.
16. Respect slalom flags set up by clubs or racing groups. With permission, you may use the course, but if you knock down the flags you should replace them immediately.
17. During rest periods and after skiing put your equipment in the equipment racks. Do not leave it around for others to trip over or to clutter up the area or where it will likely be stolen.
18. Remember that loose clothing and extra-long hair are hazards on rope tows.
19. Use sunburn cream and nonbreakable sunglasses.
20. Drive safely to and from the ski area.

HEALTH HAZARDS

In addition to the rules of courteous and safe skiing, there are certain health hazards that the winter recreationist must be especially concerned about.

Frostbite

Frostbite results from the freezing of a part of the body. The frozen area is usually small and is frequently on the nose, ears, cheeks, fingers, or toes, since these are the areas where blood circulation is least adequate. Just before frostbite occurs, the surface area will be slightly flushed. As the condition develops, the skin color changes to white or grayish white. Pain is sometimes felt early, but subsides later as the area becomes numb. Sometimes the victims are not aware of frostbite until someone tells them about their pale, glossy skin.

Frostbite can usually be prevented if a person is alert to the symptoms. The cold body part can be warmed with additional clothing or by placing it against a warm area of the body. The hands can be placed between the thighs or under the arms. The nose can be covered in the bend of the elbow or with the hand, and the ears and cheeks can be covered for short periods with the hands. Exercising of the fingers and toes will help to maintain better circulation in those areas.

The first-aid treatment for frostbite includes the following:

1. Apply firm pressure against the frozen part with a warm hand or other body part.
2. Cover the frozen part with a sufficient amount of soft, warm clothing.
3. Be sure the victim's total body is well insulated with coats, blankets, and so on to maintain normal body temperature.

Mild exercise of the frozen part will help to restore normal blood circulation more quickly. It is important to avoid rubbing the area because the skin can readily be damaged. Avoid heat that is greater than body temperature, as the skin will burn readily due to lack of circulation.

Snow Blindness

When the eyes are subjected to the reflection of sunlight from the snow, partial or total temporary loss of sight might result. This can occur on cloudy days as well as clear days. The reflected rays cause the following three conditions:

1. The ultraviolet light may sunburn the eye.
2. The dazzling visual rays cause squinting and eventually spasms of the muscles surrounding the eye.
3. The infrared rays may coagulate the protein of the structure of the eye.

The symptoms are the following:

1. Burning or smarting underneath the eyelids
2. Spasms in the muscles surrounding the eyes
3. Bloodshot eyes
4. Watering of the eyes

Prevention and treatment involve protecting the eyes from the sun's rays. This is best done by the use of quality sunglasses or goggles. If further treatment is required, the person should be blindfolded, with the eyes closed, or placed in a dark room. Aspirin will help reduce the pain. Also cold packs applied directly over the eyes will help. The application of pure oil, such as mineral oil, will reduce the irritation under the eyelids. Similar results may be obtained by washing the eyes with a *very mild* boric acid or salt solution.

Sunburn

Participants in outdoor winter activities are very subject to sunburn on the face because the sun's rays not only hit the face directly but also reflect from the snow. The application of almost any kind of oil on the skin will help reduce sunburn, but certain chemical preparations (suntan lotions) are more effective than pure oil. The best treatment for sunburn is the application of cold packs, calamine lotion, pure oil, or a combination of all of these.

Mountain Sickness

A person who ascends rapidly from a low to a high elevation sometimes experiences a condition known as mountain sickness. The symptoms of the sickness are lack of energy, brief periods of dizziness, loss of appetite, and a general feeling of weakness and nausea. Prevention and treatment involve a more gradual change in altitude, deep breathing, rest, and nourishment from quick energy foods.

Hypothermia (Prolonged exposure)

A person excessively exposed to the cold first chills profusely, then the surface areas gradually become numb. Subsequently the skier begins to get drowsy and movement becomes difficult. Eventually unconsciousness and death will occur. Obviously, this condition is prevented by doing whatever is necessary to keep the body temperature at normal.

If hypothermia does develop, the treatment involves warming the body to normal temperature as quickly as possible by moving the person into a warm shelter and applying blankets or other wraps or by placing the person in a tub of warm (78° to 82° F), but not hot, water.

Fractures

Unfortunately, leg fractures occur frequently among skiers. The best way to prevent a fracture is always to ski in control and be sure your safety bindings are properly adjusted and functioning correctly. When a fracture occurs, the victim should be made comfortable, but remain as motionless as possible, and the ski patrol should be notified immediately. If ski patrols are not available, as in the case of ski touring, someone else will have to perform that role. The fractured area should be immobilized by splinting the body part with the best material available. Then, while keeping the victim as motionless as possible, transport to where help can be obtained. If the person is seriously injured, it might be advisable to keep the victim warm and comfortable and bring help instead.

Skiers should be aware that they are enjoying an outdoor sport and that the wintery environment can have certain effects on one's physical condition. How would you recognize the following conditions in yourself or fellow skiers: frostbite, snow blindness, sunburn, mountain sickness, hypothermia?

selection and care
of equipment
6

Next to acquiring skiing skill and developing excellent physical condition, good equipment is of prime importance in helping you ski better. Equipment alone will not make you an expert, but it will add to your skill, safety, comfort, and pleasure.

WHICH SKIS?

How can you tell which is the right ski for you when there are more than 100 different brands of wood, metal, and fiberglass skis, all currently sold in the U. S.? Only you can make the choice, but you should do so on the basis of certain facts. The three most important functions a ski is designed to perform are *track*, *edge*, and *turn*. *Tracking* means the ski will run a straight course down the fall line without weaving and wobbling. Ability to *edge* means the ski is able to hold a straight course while moving diagonally across the slope. Ability to *turn* means it will slide smoothly when desired and carve the turn when edged. In order for skis to *track* effectively, the following characteristics are essential:

1. The tips are pointed and turned up in a gradual slope so the skis will move over obstacles and uneven terrain without changing direction. Also, tips of this kind help prevent skis from crossing each other and from diving under soft snow.
2. The bottoms are flat and perfectly flush, with the steel edges, except for the center groove, which increases tracking ability.
3. The skis must be without warp or twist, and the groove must run straight down the middle.
4. The bottom must be smooth and slick.
5. Good camber is necessary to distribute the body weight evenly over the surface of the skis.
6. The forward portion must be flexible, with the flexibility steadily reduced toward the center portion. The tail portion is slightly less flexible than the forward portion.

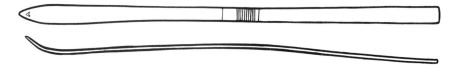

Fig. 6.1.   Top and side views of a ski illustrating shape and camber

7. The side camber resembles a gradual hourglass shape. The skis are widest at the shovel near the tip, narrowest at the waist, and somewhat wider at the heel.

Effective edging requires all the above design characteristics plus one other feature—sharp edges. For best results, the edges should be flush with the bottom of the ski and protrude slightly beyond the ski's edge. Edges must be of hard steel, sharp, and firmly attached to the ski.

Some of the characteristics essential to tracking and edging have an adverse effect on a ski's ability to turn. Camber, sharp edges, middle groove, and long skis all hinder easy turning; therefore, ski designers strive to achieve a compromise between characteristics contributing to tracking and edging and those contributing to turning. In soft snow, somewhat longer and more flexible skis are best because they will not sink into the snow as much. On hard snow, shorter skis have the advantage of responding to turning pressure more quickly than do longer skis.

Metal Skis

Because of their durability, metal skis took over the quality market about 20 years ago, and now they are widely accepted for both recreational and competitive purposes. Metal skis obtain their strength primarily from aluminum sheets that are light in weight, but very strong. The cores are made of wood or foam, with plastic side blocks to prevent water from entering the structure of the skis. The wood cores are of three types: (1) fir plywood, (2) particle board made of compressed wood chips, and (3) laminated hardwood. Steel edges are used in metal skis both to obtain the necessary biting action and to contribute to the structure of the ski. The edges are usually bonded into the edges of the structure in full-length ribbons. This makes the edges stronger and they stay sharp longer. The bonding process between the different layers composing the ski is the vital factor in creating strength. Most of the real improvements in metal-ski design have resulted from internal alterations aimed at increasing the bonding strength between the layers. A key advantage of metal skis is that they can be rebuilt or refinished. So long as bonding remains intact, only the effects of extreme wear and tear limit the life of the skis, and since it is possible to replace the edges, plastic surface, and even the structural membranes themselves, metal skis have strong appeal to the skier who is investing in a pair of quality skis. Important features to look for in metal skis are the correct amount of flexibility for your weight and skiing ability, and bonded full-length edges.

FRP (Fiberglass) Skis

Today, fiber reinforced plastic (FRP) skis have become more popular than the metal skis. Recent improvement in the processes of combining plastic and fibers of different types in various combinations has produced skis that are both strong and lightweight. This material derives its great strength from the combined strength of millions of glass fibers interwoven and locked into the plastic substance. The three basic elements of FRP construction are: (1) the plastic material, resin; (2) the glass fibers themselves; and (3) the composite reinforcing layers, which are combined, curved, and shaped. A variation of any of these three elements affects the characteristics of the end product, which may range from poor to superior. These three variations may be conveniently controlled to: (1) obtain desired flexibility at any point along the ski, (2) control the tortional effects of the ski, and (3) prevent excessive vibration of the ski.

One of the problems facing the manufacturers of the FRP ski is how to service and rebuild them. Even though it is true that you cannot heat an FRP ski, melt the glue, reseal, rewood, and reconstruct as easily as you can a metal ski, progress has been made in these directions. You should look for the same design features in FRP skis as in metals and woods. However, it is extremely difficult to determine the quality of FRP skis by the appearance alone.

Ski Length

After a model is chosen, the final consideration should be to determine the appropriate length. The length should be consonant with the height, the ability, and the weight of the skier, keeping in mind that shorter skis are easier to maneuver while longer skis give a smoother ride. Currently the thinking of most of the experts is that the skis should be slightly longer than the skier is tall.

WHICH BINDINGS?

There are numerous brands of ski bindings on the market, so that it is difficult to decide which is best for you. But you are more likely to select the best one if you know what to look for. Selection should be based on consideration of the individual factors of weight, strength, and ability of the skier. The desirability of any particular binding is determined primarily by how well it serves the following two purposes:

1. It must hold the boot firmly while you perform ski exercises and maneuvers. In other words, you must be able to apply sufficient force in every direction without releasing the boot.
2. This same binding, however, should release your boot when you make a mistake or fall, thus helping prevent injury.

Practically all the bindings now sold are the safety type, that is, they are designed to release the boot when a given amount of force is applied. Some bindings release only in the lateral directions, some release in the lateral and

Fig. 6.2.   Three different styles of alpine ski bindings

vertical directions, and a few bindings release in several intermediate directions. Experimentation with releasing action of different bindings has shown that the safety of bindings depends primarily on these four factors: (1) the binding must be designed soundly and with great precision, (2) it must be mounted and adjusted carefully and correctly, (3) the boot must be compatible with the bindings, and (4) the skier must follow through with adequate maintenance and periodic readjustments. Neglect of any of these factors will greatly increase the chances of injury.

In recent years, many conscientious ski-shop operators have moved toward increasing the safety of bindings by the following methods:

1. Selling only merchandise that is of top quality and has maximum safety features.
2. Providing competent shop operators who mount each binding exactly as it should be mounted.
3. Thorough testing of each binding after mounting for correct adjustment and alignment.

There are always three parts to a binding: toe piece, heel attachment, and safety strap or ski brake. Every binding should have a toe unit that at least allows release of the boot from lateral twisting, with release in other directions being highly desirable. Heel attachments consist of a step-in or latch-in arrangement that fastens the boot to the heel plate, thus securing the boot in place.

The ski brakes have almost completely replaced safety straps on new equipment. Both serve the purpose of keeping the released ski from sliding down the hill and hitting other skiers. Straps are made of leather or nylon and are of several different styles. They usually are attached in some way to the binding and to the ankle. Ski brakes are levers attached to the binding and held parallel to the ski by the boot. When the boot is out of the binding, the spring loaded lever assumes a 90 degree angle to the ski and extends below the running surface. The level either digs into the snow or flips the ski over so it will not slide. The ski brake provides the added safety of allowing the skier to get away from his own equipment during a fall.

Development of safety bindings has greatly improved skiing safety, resulting in many would-be nonskiers becoming ski enthusiasts. But it is important to note that simply because a binding has some safety aspects, it is not necessarily safe. Only those bindings that have passed the test of time and practical use should be trusted. Compared to the cost of a serious sprain or a broken bone plus the accompanying misery and inconvenience, the cost of a good safety binding is negligible. But regardless of how good the binding is, it will not reduce the chance of injury to zero. Correct mounting and adjustment, as well as good conditioning, skillful skiing, and correct safety practices while on the slope, are just as important to safety as your bindings.

Once good bindings have been correctly mounted and adjusted, what must the skier do to insure maximum safety?

HOW TO SELECT BOOTS

Many experts acclaim boots as the most important piece of ski equipment and say that modern ski performance would be virtually impossible if it were not for the great advances made in boot design.

Boots, which are your vital linkage to your skis, must prevent the foot from slipping, twisting, or lifting. Also, they must restrict movement of the ankle. The boots must be strong enough and durable enough to withstand the strains of pull against the bindings, and they must keep your feet dry and warm.

Fitting the boots to provide the necessary comfort, support, and control of the skis is very important. Following are important guides to help determine a good fit.

1. The boot should be snug from the ball of the foot to the heel and upward to the ankle without having to tighten the buckles excessively.
2. The heel cup should hold the heel firmly in place.

Fig. 6.3.   Three different styles of alpine ski boots

3. The toes should have ample room so that circulation, which is important to warmth, is not restricted.
4. The boot should provide strong and rigid support, especially in the lateral directions.
5. You will be wise to find someone who is an expert in fitting boots to help you select the best fit for you.

WHICH POLES TO BUY?

You can buy a pair of ski poles for less than ten dollars or you may spend as much as fifty dollars. Even though price is not the important factor, it is highly correlated with good design and quality. Following are important points to consider in selecting poles.

The length of a pole should be approximately 75 percent of the skier's height.

The weight of a 54-inch pole is from 10 to 16 ounces. Steel poles are usually heavier than aluminum poles, but weight is less important than balance or swinging weight. Rather than weighing a pole, swing it to get the feel of its balance. If more of the weight is near the handle, the pole will be easier to manipulate than if the weight is concentrated near the basket.

One of the ways pole designers achieve good balance and strength is by swagging the shaft of the pole into a gradual taper. Swagging is a process of tapering a pole and hammering the tube to a smaller circumference. This results in a thicker layer of metal toward the bottom, which in turn means added strength. Taper is very important to good design.

Handles are made of various grades of plastic, vinyl, rubber, or leather; the better materials are more resistant to cold and moisture. Top-quality poles have vinyl handles. The exact shape and size of the handle is a matter of individual preference.

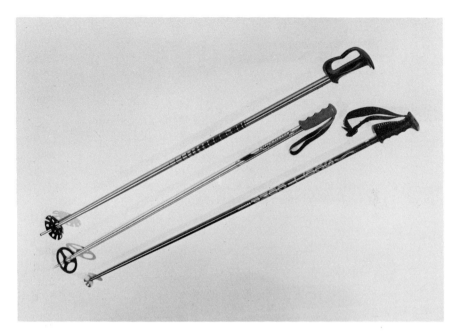

Fig. 6.4.   Three different styles of alpine pole grips and baskets

Pole straps, when they are used, are usually made of leather and may be either straight or shaped to fit more comfortably about the wrists. They may be adjustable or nonadjustable. A strap that is too short does not allow a correct grip and one that is too long gives inadequate support. Some straps are releasable, so that with a sudden jerk they will release from the pole. This is a good safety feature which may prevent serious arm and shoulder injury if the pole catches on a tree or some other object.

The basket should be well constructed of durable plastic, leather, or hard rubber. The spokes should be flexible and the basket should be at least three inches from the pole tip to insure that it will not loop over the tip.

It is essential that the tip be sharp enough to penetrate crusted snow. It should be made of hard metal that can be sharpened when necessary.

WHAT CLOTHING TO BUY?

The first function of ski clothing is to keep you warm. If it is attractive and fashionable at the same time, so much the better. The theory of keeping warm calls for keeping body heat in and cold air out. This is most effectively accomplished with layers of highly insulated clothing, which trap the body heat. For a skier the layers usually consist of underwear (shirt and long johns), turtleneck shirt, stretch pants, sweater, and parka or Windbreaker. The extremities are protected by socks, gloves, and headband or hat. Quality in ski clothing is usually about proportional to cost.

Following are some guides for selecting and wearing ski clothes.

1. For the most warmth the fit should be snug but not tight and should allow for free flow of blood to all parts of the body.
2. Clothing should be soft, light, and warm for its weight.
3. The outer layer should be water- and wind-repellent.
4. Clothing should be durable, especially at the seams.
5. Heavy-duty zippers and fasteners should be used.
6. Clothing should be fitted around ankles, wrists, and neck to reduce heat loss.

The kind of material determines the warmth of clothes. Thermo tests have provided evidence that down is warmer per unit of weight than any other material. Comparative warmth ratings are as follows:

Down	100%
Dacron	50%
Feathers (finely processed)	46%
Quilted batting (2/3 wool, 1/3 rayon)	23%
Sheepskin (standard sheerling used in clothing)	16%
Alpaca pile	7%

A *parka* should be warm but not heavy, loose but not hanging, and, the fashion designers say, slim rather than bulky. The classic parka is usually made of three heat-trapping layers of fabric, a water- and wind-resistant outer layer (shell), an insulating filler, and a liner.

Today when people talk of *ski pants* they mean pants made of stretch fabric. Stretch fabrics are available in assorted qualities with different characteristics. Most stretch fabrics combine a stretchable nylon or spandex fiber with wool or a synthetic, such as rayon or acrylic. The biggest problem in buying ski pants is to find the correct fit. The fit should be taut but not tight. Pants should be smooth but not strained across the buttocks and lower abdomen and thighs, and should not cup under the buttocks. The line from hip to ankle should be straight and tapered.

Many people now prefer a *bib ski pant* that is a little more roomy and comfortable to wear.

Turtleneck shirts and ski sweaters should be made of a highly insulated fabric with a weave tight enough to insure good fit and to maintain proper shape. The fit should be snug around the bottom, wrists, and neck.

Underwear should be full-length and made of soft, absorbent material. It should have high-thermo quality. *Socks* should be light in weight but thick enough to provide adequate warmth and padding. *Sunglasses and/or goggles* are absolutely essential. Hands are among the first parts of the body to suffer from cold, therefore warm and water-repellent *gloves* are very important. A mitten of equal weight is warmer than a glove because mittens have less surface area through which heat is lost. You will find a knit hat or headband highly useful on cold and moderately cold days.

CARE OF EQUIPMENT

Skis should be handled so that they are not chipped and scratched by being knocked against each other or against other objects. Between skiing sessions and during the off-season, skis should be placed in a vertical position to prevent warping.

Boots should be kept as dry as possible. This is accomplished by preventing water from getting to the inside and by keeping the outside well conditioned with a waterproof substance. Between ski sessions and during off-seasons, boots should be mounted on ski boot trees or placed in the ski bindings to prevent the soles of the boots from warping. Boots should be stored in a cool place.

Bindings should be kept clean of dirt and grime and should be periodically checked to be sure they are firmly attached and correctly adjusted.

During the off season the springs in the bindings should have all the tension removed from them.

Skis should be tuned periodically to insure proper and consistent performance. Most ski shops offer this service for a small fee, however, many experienced skiers prefer to do the job themselves. To do the job, you will need the following tools and supplies: matches, P-tex candles, metal scraper, plastic

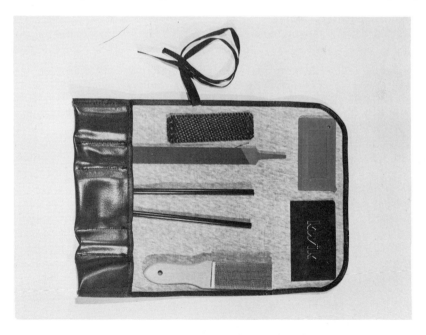

Fig. 6.5.   Items used in tuning skis: **top left to right,** plastic scraper, metal scraper; **bottom left to right,** sureform file, 12′ file, P-Tex candles, file card

scraper, a 12″ milbastard file, rags, cork, sharpening stone, wax, flat iron, wax remover, and file card. Now follow these steps:

1. Remove all the old wax from the bottom of the skis.
2. Light the P-tex candle and while holding it close to the bottom of the ski, allow the P-tex to drip into the scratches on the running surface.
3. Use the metal scraper to remove all excess P-tex from the running surface.
4. Place the file flat on the ski at about a 30 degree angle to the length of the ski and file from tip to tail. As the grooves of the file fill with P-tex, they will need to be cleaned with a file card. Continue filing until the running surface is smooth and flat and the nicks have been removed from the edges.
5. Place the ski on its side and file the edges, removing all nicks. Try to bring the edge to a 90 degree angle.
6. Use the sharpening stone to bring both bottom and side edges to sharpness. Dull the edges from the tip to about 8-10 inches back from the tip.
7. Wipe edges and running surface with a rag to remove all foreign substances.
8. Heat your iron and while holding the wax against the bottom of the iron, run a thin line of wax along both sides of the groove on the bottom of your skis. Place the iron on the bottom and iron the wax out flat. Caution should be taken so that the iron is not too hot, as it can damage the ski. If the wax starts to smoke, it's too hot.
9. Using the plastic scraper remove excess wax from the groove and the bottom surface. Polish wax slightly with a cork.

Skiers who enjoy the performance of good equipment will keep their skis tuned and waxed on an almost daily basis. When so doing, many of the above steps can be eliminated, thus requiring only about 10 minutes to accomplish. At the end of the season, tune your skis and wax them, making sure the edges are covered with wax before putting them away for the summer.

All modern ski bases are made of plastic and will usually slide over the snow without wax. However, all manufacturers recommend waxing the skis because this will help preserve the plastic and keep it from hardening. Waxing is an art among racers who are waxing for all the speed they can get; but for the average skier, several wide temperature range waxing systems exist. No one system is particularly better than another. Most skiers are well served by any system if they will take a little time to learn how it works. Often, beginners are afraid to wax because they don't want to go faster. But a waxed ski runs more smoothly than an unwaxed ski, and a smoothly running ski is easier to maintain balance on than one that is inconsistent in its sliding.

competitive skiing

7

Competitive skiing has become a very popular winter sport, but until recently it was little known to spectators because most people were not able or willing to climb halfway up a ski slope to see a race and were not willing to brave the weather. With the development of television, however, ski racing has gained much in popularity among noncompetitors. It is now possible for the public to enjoy exciting ski competition on both national and international levels.

For years the Europeans dominated the international competition in major ski events, but gradually and steadily the United States is beginning to compete on a par with the great European skiers.

Traditionally the two categories of ski racing events were *Alpine* and *Nordic*. The *Alpine events—downhill, slalom, and giant slalom—*have been dominated by the Austrian, French, and Swiss racers, while *the Nordic events— jumping and cross-country—*have been the traditional domain of the Scandinavians. All these events are under the international control of the Federation Internationale de Ski (FIS), whose business it is to seed racers by awarding FIS points. In recent years a new form of competitive skiing has emerged known as *freestyle*. It is not yet well standardized and is not regulated by the FIS.

The acquiring of FIS points is very important to a topflight competitive skier. The winner of a race is awarded 0.00 points and for each second slower than the winner a racer may pick up from 1.5 to 10.9 points. This is not a straight mathematical calculation, but is based on tables made up by the FIS. Because course conditions are worse later in races than at the beginning, adjustments are made to compensate for racers who run the course late in the race session. Another adjustment is made to account for the total time of a race, since it is more of an accomplishment to finish one second behind the winner in a two-minute race than in a one-minute race. One more complication appears when FIS tries to equalize competition on an international scale. This takes into account the FIS rankings of the racers involved in the race. If only top racers are in the race there is no penalty involved, but with only lesser racers, penalty points are awarded to the race. This means that even the first-place winner is penalized (receives less than a perfect score) since the competition is considered too weak to warrant a perfect score. The formula for determining penalty points is complex and beyond the scope of this chapter.

The seeding of the racers comes after the field is closed. The racers are ranked according to their FIS-point standing from least to most points. Then the racers are divided into groups of fifteen. The lowest FIS-point group races first. After the groups are determined, the racers draw for starting position within their group. Early positions are considered most desirable.

Two of the problems that lead to controversy are the location of the races and the seeding positions. Most FIS-sponsored races are held in Europe, so it is hard for skiers of non-European countries to compete in them. Yet unless a racer is able to compete consistently in FIS meets, it is difficult to establish a high FIS seeding. Thus after entering one of these races, the racer is in a low FIS-point group and races under poor ski conditions. This makes it very difficult for non-Europeans to work their way up.

ALPINE EVENTS

The *Alpine events* are probably the most exciting to watch. They are like the sprints in a track meet. The *downhill* is primarily a test of speed and courage. The *giant slalom*, originally intended to be a toned-down downhill, has become a unique event that requires the racer to maneuver as fast as possible among approximately 60 gates. The *slalom* is designed to test the skier's agility, quickness, technique, and balance while racing through a series of closely linked gates. The one rule common to all these events is that both feet must pass through the gate. It does not matter whether the skier goes through forward or backward as long as both feet pass between the poles. In only the downhill is the skier allowed to practice the course before the race. The giant slalom and

Fig. 7.1. Downhill racer in action

the slalom require that the racer walk up the course and memorize the gate sequence.

The *downhill* is probably the most highly regarded of the Alpine events. The terrain for the race is carefully selected to include various conditions, such as gullies, bumps, rolls, schusses, and sudden changes in steepness. The course is generally laid out to follow the fall line and to avoid any sudden change of general direction. As in all skiing events, safety is a prime concern. Gates are used to guide racers away from dangerous areas and to keep their speed under control.

Major international downhill races for men must have a vertical drop of 2,600 to 3,300 feet over a course of two to three miles in length. For women the vertical drop is between 1,300 to 2,300 feet with the course length between one and one and a half miles. The races below this international level are scaled down according to the class of racers involved. The downhill is usually discussed in terms of time, not length—thus a 2-minute or a 2.5 minute downhill.

The two main tools of the downhill racer are the tuck, which cuts wind resistance, and the prejump, which enables the racer to remain close to the snow over a bump. One key to how well a racer is doing is to observe how long a tuck is held in a rough section of the course. Another key is to observe how closely the skier remains with the contour of a bump. A mistake here would send the racer flying through the air and cost valuable time. Well-waxed skis are extremely important in this race.

The *giant slalom* requires the racer to cross and recross the fall line while seeking the fastest way down the course. The racer must pass through each gate. Gates are usually about 20 feet wide. The terrain varies in such a way that a premium is placed on the racer's ability to choose the fastest line and hold it. Edge control plays an important part in this race since an edged ski will travel faster in a straight line than a ski that slips sideways.

It is important for the giant slalom racer to be able to do step turns as well as conventional turns. Since the speed the racers travel always forces them to the outside of a turn, the step turn has been developel to help the racer hold close to the inside of the gate. The step turn is accomplished by stepping uphill before the turn and then bringing the inside ski close to the outside ski. As the turn is completed, the racer again steps uphill to find a faster traverse toward the next gate. Often the racer will finish the turn on the uphill ski in order to maintain the high line. Not all turns in a giant slalom require a step turn; the racer must decide which is the right turn to use.

The *slalom* race is the only Alpine event the spectator can watch from start to finish. In both slalom and giant slalom the racers run the course twice (the second time the racers ski in reverse order). The total of the two runs determines the winner.

Slalom gates are a minimum width of 9 feet, 6 inches and one gate must be set at least 30 inches from the next gate. There are two basic types of gates— open and closed. An open gate is one in which a line extending from one upright to the other is at right angles to the fall line. The closed gate is one in which such a line would parallel the fall line. By combining these two gates

Fig. 7.2.   Part of a typical slalom course

in certain sequence figures, such as hairpins and flushes, the course can be put together. The maximum number of gates in a slalom is 75.

Both the racer's feet must pass through every gate. Failure to do so will disqualify; however, the racer may go through the gates from any direction and in any position. Many course setters may try to trick the racers into a fast line through a flush which may cause them to come out on the wrong side for the next gate. This causes the racers to lose a most important factor—their rhythm.

In watching the Alpine events, concentrate on the racer's feet. Watch for excess skidding in the turns, how the skis behave over bumps, and the way the legs react when the going gets tough. These points will tell you a lot about the racer's chances of winning.

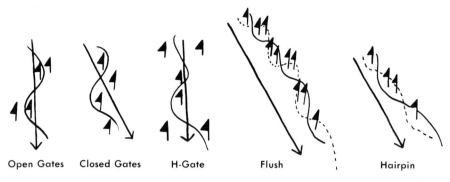

Fig. 7.3.   Different kinds of racing gates

Recently an interesting variation known as *dual racing* has been added to the slalom and giant slalom. It has been popularized by the professional ski racers and is now moving into the amateur ranks. A dual race is held on a hill where the terrain allows for two courses to be set side by side. The two courses must be as equal as possible in difficulty and speed. Instead of the traditional two-pole gate, a single pole that the racer must ski around is used. Skiers are disqualified if they miss a gate or ski into the other course. The professionals build jumps into the courses to make the race more exciting and challenging.

A dual race follows one of two formats. The *professionals* race in a single-elimination tournament. In this kind of race the two racers of a pair run the first heat and the difference in their times is recorded. Then they switch courses and run the second heat and the difference in their times is again recorded. The winner, who is determined by the two differences in times, advances to the next round where the process is repeated. Eventually only one person is left and that person is declared the champion.

In the *amateur* ranks, a different format is used because the number of entries is usually much greater. The two racers of a pair run the first heat and the time for each racer is recorded. Then they switch courses and run the second heat and the time for each racer is again recorded. The two times for each racer are combined and the winner of the meet is the one with the lowest combined time. Ocassionally a variation is used where only the winner of each heat is recorded. If there is a tie after two heats, a third heat is held and a flip of the coin is used to determine who races on which course in the third heat.

NORDIC EVENTS

The nordic events have grown rapidly in popularity but still are not as popular in the United States as are the Alpine Events. As a spectator sport, jumping is increasing in popularity, but cross-country is showing little progress in this respect. Again, the reason is that the spectator can view jumping from start to finish, while in cross-country the race may take an hour to finish and the skiers are in view during only a small portion of the race.

Jumping requires the greatest precision of any ski event. The jumper is evaluated not only on distance but also on form. The meet is evaluated by five judges and each jumper is allowed two jumps in competition. The scores on these two jumps are totaled for the final score. Each jump has a possible 120 points. Sixty points are based on distance, and 60 points are based on form.

After each round is completed, 60 points are awarded to the longest jump. The rest of the competitors are scaled down according to the distance they obtained. Actually a competitor may acquire more than 60 points for an exceptionally long jump. The distance is measured from the lip of the jump to the spot where the skier's feet land.

The style points are awarded over the whole jump. The jumper is carefully observed descending the in run, taking off, flying through the air, landing, running out, and stopping. Each of the five judges starts with 20 points and for each error observed, a judge reduces the number of points. Then each judge marks the total points awarded to the jumper. The highest and lowest awards are eliminated, leaving the 3 middle ones to be added for the total style points.

The cross-country events require many of the same skills as distance running. The terrain is selected to include both flat and hilly areas. The up- and downhills should not be excessively long or steep or the flats too short.

The course is usually laid out in a circular fashion so the race finishes near the start. Often the course will cover the same terrain twice before returning to the finish. This is done to keep racers in a smaller area and provide the spectators with a greater view of the performance.

The purpose of cross country is to test endurance, strength, ski technique, and tactical ability. The race is usually designed to cover five to fifty kilometers with five to fifteen kilometers being the most common. As in all racing events (except slalom where the course is cleared after each racer), the cross-country racers are started at time intervals of about one minute. The racer from behind has the right of way and can call the racer ahead to move out of the way. The course is set to require the racers to pass through or go around specified check points. Between check points the racers may choose their own course.

Identify the physical demands of cross-country skiing. What types of conditioning exercises would be most beneficial?

FREESTYLE SKIING

During the recent past a new form of competitive skiing has become very popular. It is called freestyle and includes three events—moguls, ballet, and aerials. The winner of each event is determined by either five judges (three middle scores count) or four judges (all four scores count).

Mogul competition is held on a rather steep slope that is covered with large moguls. There is a start and a finish line, but the competitor has the choice of where to ski between the two lines, and the time it takes to complete the course is not a consideration. The points are awarded by the judges according to how well the skier remains in the fall line, maintains speed and control, carves the skis as opposed to swiveling them, and whether or not the skier does any jumping during the run (jumping must be spontaneous and not planned).

Ballet is, as the name implies, similar to figure skating. A shallow and smooth slope is used. Again there is a start and finish line and the competitor has freedom between these two points. Judging is based upon continuity of motion, smoothness, variety of stunts, and variety and difficulty of ballet maneuvers. Additional points are awarded if the skier shows excitement or personal flare.

Aerial competition consists of three successive jumps, which a skier must complete in a prescribed time period. This event is an outgrowth of Gelande jumping which has been popularized in recent years. The competitor files a flight plan for the first jump. Each of the three jumps includes a stunt, such as the daffy, front flip, back flip, 360° turn, 720° turn, mobius, spread eagle, and others. Any kind of double flip is illegal. Contestants are judged on their take-off, height of the jump, degree of difficulty of the stunt, performance of the stunt, and the landing.

THE RACING CHALLENGE

Almost everyone who puts on a pair of alpine or cross country skis soon has the urge to test himself on a race course. The increased popularity of NASTAR and citizen races are witnesses to this fact. The cross country citizen races are very much like the local weekend five to ten kilometer jogging races across the country. Sex and age group categories exist, and the race is open to everyone. There is usually a small entry fee and everyone who finishes is a winner.

The National Standard Race (NASTAR) is a little more complicated. Most local resorts conduct NASTAR races several times a week over a rather easy giant slalom course. Gold, silver, or bronze medals are awarded in each sex and age group category to individuals who succeed in exceeding a standard time established within each category. Each course requires a pace setter who has been handicapped in relation to the national standards. The pace setter's time and handicap allows every racer's time to be adjusted in relation to the national standard. Those who accumulate a number of gold medals can advance to national championship. Every racer pays a small entry fee and can run the course several times.

Racing is a natural way of testing your progress in skiing and each year more skiers are enjoying the challenge and thrills of competition at all levels.

ski touring
8

Winter touring on cross-country skis is a delightful activity for vigorous individuals who want to experience nature's winter scenes. This form of skiing involves relatively easy-to-learn skills, except when the skills must be perfected, as in competition. Hence ski touring is easier to master than downhill skiing. The following are descriptions of the basic techniques used in ski touring.

SKI TOURING TECHNIQUES

Lost somewhere in antiquity is an event where a man clothed in bearskin first found that he could walk over snow without sinking if he had a long board under each foot. This man's successors devised a stable binding of hide or skin. Later sticks were used to aid in balance and to push the skier along on top of the snow. Hence, with the most crude equipment a ski technique, of a sort, was born. Through the ages skiing has evolved into much improved forms, and the equipment has become precisely designed and well constructed.

Skiing today is of two kinds: *Alpine* (downhill) and *Nordic* (cross-country). Our concern here is cross-country skiing, or ski touring.

Diagonal Stride

The basic method of travel on cross-country skis is the diagonal stride, which is simply a modification of walking. This means that you use the leg and the opposite arm simultaneously. The arm pushes with the ski pole while the leg pushes off or "kicks." The diagonal stride can be learned best by starting with an ordinary walking stride on skis. Then gradually increase the force of the kick and the push with the opposite arm. The upper body bends forward more and the arms swing through a greater range of motion.

Just as in walking, the kick in the diagonal stride is the primary force that propels the skier forward. The push from the pole helps to do this more force-

Fig. 8.1.   Side view of diagonal stride

Fig. 8.2.   Front view of diagonal stride

fully. The important characteristics of a good diagonal stride are a smooth but forceful stride; a long, smooth arm movement; and a long glide with the weight balanced on one ski.

Except for the faster tempo of the racer, there is little difference between good touring technique and good cross-country racing technique.

Double Poling

Both poles can be set simultaneously to provide variation in movement and to increase speed under certain conditions. This technique involves a vigorous push with both poles followed by a glide. After planting the poles forward of the body, bend the upper body forward to throw additional weight onto the poles, then push vigorously. Toward the end of the push the body straightens. This technique takes a great deal more energy under normal conditions than the diagonal stride.

Describe the important characteristics of the diagonal stride as used in cross country ski touring.

Double-Poling Stride

Double poling can be used in combination with the diagonal stride. This is done by combining the arm movements of double poling with the leg movements of the diagonal stride. The stride is taken during the glide, following the thrust with the arms.

The double-poling stride can be modified by taking two strides between each double-poling action. This technique is characterized by the pattern push-stride-stride, push-stride-stride, and so on. It is especially useful on a slight downhill slope when the skier wants to conserve energy.

Uphill Techniques

There are several techniques that can be used to ski uphill. The preferred technique is dependent largely on the snow conditions and the steepness of the slope.

Diagonal Stride. If the slope is gentle and your wax is right for the snow conditions, you can use the diagonal stride uphill in the same way as on level terrain. In order to get sufficient glide uphill, a hard kick and a vigorous pole thrust are required. This calls for a slightly crouched body position and a more forward lean than normal. Both the stride and the glide will be short, so the tempo will have to be quicker to compensate.

Trot. This technique is similar to the diagonal stride with the glide eliminated. You move up the slope with short walking-running-type strides, placing the skis softly and using a relatively quick tempo. The arm actions are the same as in the diagonal stride. The body should be slightly crouched with more forward lean than usual.

Fig. 8.3.   Side view of double-poling technique

Traverse. The traverse is probably the ski tourist's most common method of getting uphill. It is usually done with a single-stride technique with a sidestep effect added. The skier zigzags up the slope, setting the traverse at the steepness desired. Either herringbone turns or kick turns are used to link the traverses. The trot technique can also be used in traversing, as can the diagonal sidestep in the case of a steep traverse.

Herringbone. The herringbone technique is a fast, but very tiring, method of going straight up a slope. However, if you are strong and the slope is short, this might be the preferred technique. The legs and arms alternate as in the single stride, but there are several important differences. First, in the herringbone there is no glide. Second, the ski tips are spread apart to form a V, or herringbone, pattern. Third, in order to hold from slipping, you must set the inside edge of the supporting ski (see fig. 2.3).

Side Step. The straight side step is relatively difficult on touring skis because the heel of the boot does not attach to the ski. Diagonal side stepping works much better. To do this stand with the skis across the slope at a right

Fig. 8.4. Double-poling stride

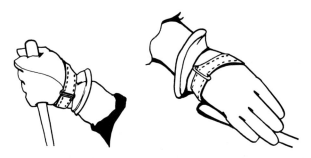

Fig. 8.5. Techniques of gripping the pole at the beginning and completion of the poling action

angle to the fall line. Place the uphill ski 6 to 12 inches up the slope as you step forward. Set the ski firmly in the snow, then bring the lower ski up beside it. Set the lower ski in position and repeat the step pattern (see fig. 2.3).

Identify the uphill techniques most suited to the following terrains: a gentle uphill slope, a short steep slope, and indicate the conditions under which each would be used.

Skiing Downhill

Skiing downhill on touring skis is a bit more difficult than on alpine skis because the equipment is not designed specifically for this task, whereas alpine equipment is. Nevertheless, with some modification of technique and lots of practice you can become very proficient at skiing downhill in all types of snow conditions. Basically the same techniques apply to the various maneuvers already outlined in Chapter 3 in connection with the skiing skills. However, since touring bindings allow substantial heel movement and boots allow considerable ankle movement, while the skis are not so stiff and often lack metal edges, you cannot be as vigorous in applying turning pressures as you can with alpine equipment. The following modifications of touring technique will be helpful.

1. Be more subtle with turning pressure.
2. Use more rotary motions for steering the turns.
3. Use more vigorous up unweighting movements.
4. Keep your weight more towards the outside of the turn on the outside ski.

The construction and design of cross country skis and bindings make down hill skiing more difficult than with alpine equipment. Which are the differences in touring equipment that present problems?

In recent years, the ancient Telemark turn has been resurrected by touring enthusiasts. This turn is probably the most graceful of all touring techniques. To make a right turn, slide the left ski forward turning it gradually toward the right and edge it on its inside edge. At this point, the binding of the left ski should be close to the tip of the right ski, while most of your weight should be on the forward ski. The trailing ski acts as a stabilizer and aids in maintaining balance.

SKI TOURING EQUIPMENT

The specialized ski equipment used in touring (cross-country) includes skis, boots, bindings, and poles. During the last few years all of this equipment has gone through drastic changes in concept and materials and is still changing rapidly.

Fig. 8.6.   Telemark turn

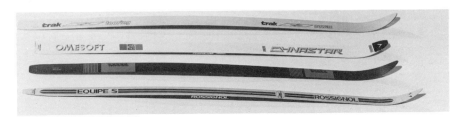

Fig. 8.7.   Comparison of a general touring ski, **top;**
top center, alpine ski; **bottom center,** cross country ski; **bottom,**
cross country racing ski

Skis

Touring skis can be divided into four classifications: racing skis, light touring, touring, and mountaineering. Racing skis are very lightweight, about 44 millimeters wide and shaped like a javelin. They are designed strictly for running in a set track. Light touring skis are about 46-50 millimeters in width with a straight side cut; they are primarily for use in a set track. Touring skis are heavier, wider, have edges and side camber and are designed for skiing in all kinds of snow conditions. Mountaineering skis are almost as wide as alpine skis and have most of the same design characteristics. They are used as the name implies—for rugged adventure in mountainous conditions.

Almost all touring skis are now constructed of carbon fiber or fiberglass, with the heavier skis adding metal for strength. A plastic base similar to that of alpine skis is used for a running surface. The skier can now choose between waxable or no-wax bases. The recommended length of a touring ski is about 8 to 12 inches longer than the person's height. Anything shorter than this may cause problems when the skier stretches out into long strides. Most touring skis have the following characteristics:

1. A soft tip with a stiff tail to cause forward spring.
2. Plastic bases with a choice of waxable or no-wax surfaces.
3. Hard plastic or metal edges.
4. Light and sturdy construction.

Like most other equipment, touring skis vary considerably in quality and price. Each person should choose skis that are affordable and suited to his or her particular need and preference.

Bindings

Nordic, or touring, bindings are designed so that the heel is free to lift off the ski. The bindings should afford maximum freedom of the feet and still provide the proper amount of control of the skis. They should be sturdy, yet as light as possible.

There are several different models of *toe-clamp bindings* for cross-country racing and light touring. On these skis the 50 millimeter binding has virtually replaced the 75 millimeter binding. These bindings are very lightweight and share the characteristic of the boot, being attached only at the tip of the sole in front of the toe. Great progress has been made in heel devices which insure that the heel of the boot always returns to the heel of the ski. This arrangement allows for optimum foot movement.

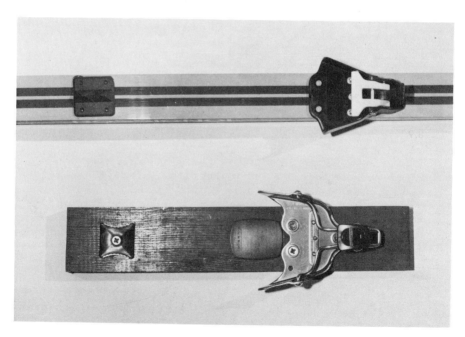

Fig. 8.8.   Cross country bindings: **top**, racing; **bottom**, touring

Light toe-clamp bindings should be used only on light skis because they are not substantial enough to be used on heavier skis for long distances. The general touring bindings are heavier and usually in the 75 millimeter width category. Often they are used in combination with cables for rougher touring conditions. While using these bindings instead of racing bindings the skier sacrifices some freedom of movement and lightness, while gaining durability of the binding and possibly better ski control. These bindings are recommended for general and long-distance touring.

Boots

There is a variety of boots being made for racing and touring. The intended use should be the determining factor in selection. Racing and light touring boots resemble jogging shoes and use much the same materials in construction. The sole of the boot is harder and extends in front of the toe to fit into the binding.

Touring boots tend to be higher topped and stiffer in their construction. More care is taken to provide padding and warmth for longer treks in the snow.

Fig. 8.9.   Touring boot placed in toe-clamp binding. Notice the freedom of movement

Fig. 8.10.   Three styles of cross country boots: **left,** racing; **middle,** touring; **right,** mountaineering

Fig. 8.11.   Tip characteristics of two types of cross country
ski poles: **two left,** racing; **right,** touring

Poles

The bamboo pole is almost a thing of the past. Racing and touring poles are
made mostly of aluminum, carbon fiber, or fiberglass. The length of the pole
should extend from the floor to the armpit of the skier.

When compared to alpine poles, Nordic poles have some interesting
features. Nordic poles are used more for pushing than for balance, thus they
are longer and not intended to come much farther forward than the foot. The
tip of the pole is curved forward so as to hook the snow and penetrate it. The
basket on a racing pole is shaped like a horsehoof so that the front edge will not
drag in the snow. The basket on a touring pole is more traditional, so as to
keep the pole from sinking into the soft snow. The baskets are made of strong,
durable plastic. The grip is designed to accommodate the changing hand position as the pole moves through its long arc of motion. The strap is adjustable
to fit the hand size of the particular skier.

Waxing

The new plastic bases have made many of the old waxing techniques obsolete.
Skiers are now using alpine racing waxes on the tips and tails of their skis to
enhance the glide. The kicker area under the foot is still waxed with the conventional waxes. The intracacies of kicker waxes for racers are beyond the
scope of this book; you will be able to find that information in a book on cross-
country skiing.

For the touring enthusiast, the wax manufacturers have devised a three
wax kicker system. They are: hardwax for cold temperatures, soft wax for warm
temperatures, and klister for melting snow conditions. The kicker wax is applied to the base, under the foot, about equal distance in front and behind
the toe-piece of the binding.

No-wax skis are becoming very popular among tour enthusiasts. The plastic base has an area under the foot that either have holes of fish scales extending toward the tail of the ski. These allow the ski to bite during the kicking phase, but slide forward in the gliding phase of the diagonal stride. The no-wax ski is usually not so efficient as the waxed ski except in snow conditions of zero degrees centigrade.

Climbers

As a substitute for waxing, some people use ski climbers made of sealskin or mohair. These items can be purchased in certain mountaineer shops, but in most localities they would need to be special ordered. Climbers made of sealskin are preferred because they are more durable and grip the snow better than mohair. However, they are considerably more expensive and this might be prohibitive for some people. In both sealskin and mohair climbers, the grain of the hair runs back along the bottom of the ski so that the ski will run fairly well on a downhill slope, although not really effectively, and will grip the snow when going uphill, thus preventing slippage.

CLOTHING

Clothing worn by the touring skier is somewhat different than that of the downhill skier. Figure 8.1 shows a typical cross-country ski outfit. One piece suits are now as popular as the usual pant and blouse suit. They share the characteristic of being more loose than the downhill pants, and permit freedom of movement. The long socks add warmth and help protect the legs from the dampness of powdery snow. Clothing on the upper part of the body should be applied in layers and be the kind that can be loosened or tightened about the neck, making it possible to adjust conveniently for warmth. Sometimes the cross-country skier works very hard, thus producing much body heat, while taking it rather easy at other times. The skier must therefore have clothing that can be conveniently adjusted to suit different levels of exercise. Unless the weather is unusually warm the skier should wear thermal underwear, a sufficient number of heavy socks to keep the feet warm, warm mittens or gloves, and a hat that can be adjusted to cover different amounts of the head, depending on the temperature. Of course in stormy weather a water-repellent outer shell is essential.

choosing safe skiing terrain

9

So far as terrain and environment are concerned, there are three kinds of hazards that a skier should be cautious of: (a) heavy wooded areas, (b) cliffs or slopes that are too steep for skiing, and (c) potential avalanche areas. The first two kinds of hazards are quite obvious and can easily be avoided by an alert skier who uses good judgment, but the third hazard is much less obvious. This is because many people neither recognize the characteristics of an avalanche area nor are cognizant of potential avalanche dangers. There are many dramatic stories about people who have lost their lives because they permitted themselves to be at the wrong place at the wrong time by not knowing enough about the avalanche hazards that surrounded them. The rule of thumb is to be knowledgeable about the conditions that result in avalanche hazards and to take no unnecessary risks.

AVALANCHE CONDITIONS

An avalanche will occur whenever gravitational pull on the snow is great enough to break the cohesion between the snow layers or between the snow and the ground. The probability of an avalanche is dependent upon the following snow and terrain characteristics:

1. Size and shape of the slope—the larger the slope the greater the hazard
2. Steepness of the slope
3. Bonding characteristics of the ground surface—large rocks, trees, and shrubs increase the bond
4. Depth of the snow—the deeper it is, the more likely it is to slide
5. Moisture content of the snow—the more moisture the heavier the snow.
6. Internal cohesion of the snow layers.
7. Presence of cornices
8. Recent and present weather conditions—the danger increases as the temperature becomes warmer.

Describe the markers used by major ski areas to indicate avalanche danger and extra caution.

Kinds of Avalanches

The four kinds of avalanches are known as *dry snow, wet snow, wind slab,* and *ice* avalanches.

Dry snow avalanches are the most frequent. They usually occur after a very heavy snowfall, especially when deep new snow has fallen on top of crusted snow. Dry snow has very little cohesion initially, and the cohesion becomes even less soon after the snow has fallen and the crystals begin the process of transformation. The transformation eliminates the bond provided by the interlacing of the branches of the crystals and this permits the snow to flow. If the loose snow falls in heavy amounts on a frozen crust, it has little opportunity to become bonded to the hard, frozen surface, and this contributes to the possibility of an avalanche.

Factors that determine whether a dry snow avalanche will occur are the following:

1. The amount of new snow that has fallen. The more snow, the greater the chance of an avalanche.
2. The snow surface on which the new snow has fallen. The smoother and harder the surface, the greater is the chance of a slide.
3. The weather conditions following the snowfall. If the slope is exposed to warm sunshine soon after the storm, the avalanche hazard will be high for a few hours, but if the sunshine continues, most of the danger will be over within two or three days. Conversely, if the slope is not exposed to warmth and sunshine, avalanche conditions will continue a longer time—maybe two or three weeks. Generally, south and west slopes will avalanche first and subsequently become safe again because of their exposure to the sun; whereas north and east slopes receiving less sunshine will remain dangerous for a longer time.

Wet snow avalanches may occur when a large amount of new, wet snow has fallen or when old snow becomes damp because of warmth or rain. Water in small quantities increases the cohesion, but when present in large quantities, it decreases the cohesion much the same as in the case of sand. Dry sand slips easily, damp sand is sticky, and wet sand tends to flow.

Wet snow avalanches are usually slow moving and do not proceed very far. They occur because the snow becomes so heavy with water that its weight cannot be held by the internal cohesion. The snow flows much like mud, but there are usually large, rolling snowballs associated with this kind of slide. These slides usually occur the same places year after year at approximately the same time of the season, but there are exceptions to this rule, influenced by unusual weather conditions.

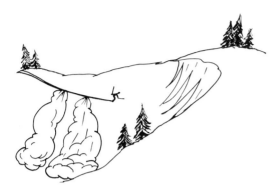

Fig. 9.1.   Dry snow avalanche triggered by skier

Fig. 9.2.   Wet snow avalanche

Fig. 9.3.   Wind slab or ice crust avalanche

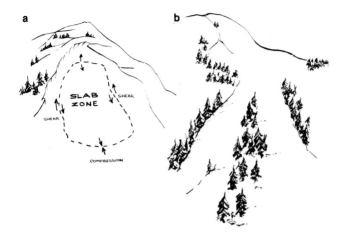

Fig. 9.4.   Two different areas of terrain where avalanches
would be likely: **a,** a large open slope with very little
ground covered to bind the snow to the surface; **b,** a steep
slope with natural channels for snow slides

A *wind slab* is built and formed by wind blowing loose snow over the surface of other snow for a prolonged period of time. The friction created between the loose, moving snow and the snow surface causes some of the shifting snow particles to cling to the snow surface. This process results in a building up of a hard slab over a period of time.

A wind slab avalanche may occur at any time after the formation of the slab until it has become well bonded to the underlying snow. Sometimes the weight of the slab will cause the whole slab to begin sliding. However, it will usually not slide until it is broken, either by settling from its own weight or by the weight of additional snow or people. Sometimes the weight of a single skier will cause a slab to crack, and this might break the bond of the lower portion of the slab. The initial phase of this kind of avalanche consists of the slab sliding over the snow surface. As the slab breaks up, large blocks of icy snow tumble down the mountain, thus breaking other snow loose and causing the slide to be much larger than the slab itself.

Ice avalanches of great proportion often occur at the end of glaciers high above the valley floor. As the glacier progresses down the slope, the protruding ice eventually becomes so great that it breaks off, tumbling down the mountain and clearing everything in its path. If there has been heavy snowfall on the slope below, the ice might trigger an accompanying snow avalanche. Mountaineers who go into areas where such conditions exist ought to be well informed about such hazards and how to avoid them.

Where the terrain is more mild and glaciers are nonexistent, there is still some chance of ice avalanches. Water from melting snow or from seepage may freeze on cliffs and overhangs and over a period of time may build up to a con-

Fig. 9.5.   Typical forms of new snow crystals

siderable thickness. Sooner or later a thaw will cause the ice to break loose and the falling ice may trigger a snow avalanche. Except in glacier regions, ice avalanches are infrequent, and areas where they might occur are easily identified and can be avoided.

Contributing Snow Characteristics

A snowflake is composed of tiny crystals. Crystals are of three basic kinds—plates, prisms, and star-shaped (see fig. 9.5). The platelike crystals are the simplest, and the star-shaped are the most complex. Snow crystals of the plate type form loosely into snowflakes, while the more complex crystals are bonded together by the intertwining of their branches. Therefore, an avalanche is not likely to occur immediately after a snowfall made of branched crystals; while snow made up of plate crystals will flow more easily.

Identify the four kinds of avalanches and the snow and weather which are most likely to cause avalanche.

Soon after snow has fallen, a transformation of the crystals begins. Due to snow pressure on the individual crystals, combined with warm weather in certain instances, the tiny branches of the crystals melt and cause the crystals to lose their original shape. Some of the smaller crystals combine with the larger crystals. The result is a gradual transformation from branched to platelike crystals, with some of the crystals combining. By this process, *new snow* is gradually converted to *old* snow, or what is sometimes termed spring snow. The rate of this transformation depends largely upon the weather, but it goes on continually. This accounts for variations in the internal cohesion of the snow at different times during the season.

During the early phase of the transformation, the melting of the interlocking branches results in a loss of cohesion. But as the crystals continue to combine, the snow settles and packs, and cohesion increases again. Then as spring comes, warmer temperatures and higher humidity causes wet crystals and a thin film of water to form between crystals. This acts as a lubricant and reduces internal cohesion.

The effect of wind on the snow varies considerably depending on whether the temperature is above or below freezing and whether the humidity is high or low. If temperature and humidity are both low, then the snow will

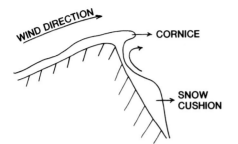

Fig. 9.6.   Snow cornice—a likely trigger for an avalanche

remain dry and the wind will not cause very much crusting. If the temperature is low, but the humidity is high, a wind crust or wind slab will form. If the temperature and humidity are both high, the snow will become slushy on the surface.

As far as avalanche hazards are concerned, the wind has two obvious effects. First, by blowing over a ridge or mountaintop the wind will cause the buildup of cornices, which may break off and trigger a slide. Second, in some cases the wind will build up snow to such a depth that the snow cannot hold and a slide will result.

Slope and Ground Characteristics

The steepness of the slope is one important characteristic. All else remaining equal, the steeper the slope, the greater is the chance of an avalanche. It is a rare occasion when an avalanche occurs on a slope of 20° or less, but it is possible if the snow and ground characteristics are conducive to a slide.

The *ground surface* is an important factor. Smooth dirt, slick rock, or grass-covered surfaces provide for a poor bond between the surface and the snow. Shrubs and brush, especially of the rigid type, add considerably to the bondage. Large rocks add greatly to the snow's stability, especially if some of the rocks are high enough to protrude through all of the different snow layers. Thick groves of trees are very effective in stabilizing the snow; and the presence of the trees indicate that avalanches have not recently swept through that area.

The *contour* of the mountainside also affects the stability of snow. On a concave slope, the snow on the lower (flatter) portion of the slope tends to support the snow on the higher (steeper) portion. Conversely, on a convex slope, the steep portion is at the bottom and the snow on that area would tend to break away into a slide.

SAFETY PRECAUTIONS

1. When in country where avalanches are likely, or even possible, be very observant of potential slide areas and of snow conditions. Make the best interpretations possible about where slides might occur and avoid those areas.
2. When a slide area must be crossed, select the safest route. These guides should be considered:

    a. A route along the top of a ridge is the safest, provided cornices are avoided.

    b. The center of a broad valley is reasonably safe, although it is possible for a large slide to carry well into a valley.

    c. If a hazardous slope must be crossed, it is safer to cross near the top rather than in the middle or toward the bottom, unless the slope is concave, causing the top portion to be steep.

    d. Avoid walking either over or underneath cornices.

    e. The members of a party should cross a hazardous area one at a time, being spaced well apart (100 to 200 yards) so that there is a minimal chance of more than one person being caught in a slide. This procedure also reduces the chance of triggering a slide.

    f. In getting off a dangerous slope, it is safer to go straight up or straight down than across the slope, since going across might cut the bond of the snow and trigger a slide.

    g. All necessary steps should be taken to facilitate quick removal of skis (or snowshoes) and poles in case a slide starts, since having these items bound to the feet and hands makes escape almost impossible.

    h. The probability of being found if caught in an avalanche is greatly increased if one end of a colored cord 30 to 40 feet in length is fastened to the body.

3. Keep in mind that loud noises sometimes trigger avalanches, therefore the amount of noise by members of the party should be controlled in accordance with the avalanche hazards.

4. It is important to know how to conduct yourself in case you are caught in a slide. The rule is quickly to remove all equipment that may drag you under. Leap into the slide with the back facing the snow, keeping the feet and head high, then perform a vigorous backstroking action in an effort to keep on or near the surface of the snow. Even though this action may not prevent you from being overtaken by the slide, it will likely put you in a better position to be rescued. In the case of small slides, it might even keep you from becoming covered with snow.

5. If you find yourself in the path of a slide and choose to try to escape rather than free yourself of equipment, your best chance is to ski diagonally away from the slide, rather than down the fall line, as your chance of outrunning the slide is poor.

AVALANCHE RESCUE

When a victim is caught in an avalanche, it is very important for other individuals to be alert in observing the path of the victim in order to know the most likely area to search when the avalanche comes to rest. Those best able to observe the position of the victim should remain in place to direct others who should move quickly to mark the search area. The search should be expertly organized and start quickly. The procedure involves systematic probing with the best instruments available. Long slender poles are preferred, such as the poles used to mark a race course in skiing. However, these are not usually available except at ski resorts, so ski poles or skis might be the best instruments at hand. If ski poles are used, the baskets should be removed, or the poles should be reversed and the leather straps at the handles removed. The probing should be as deep as possible.

The searchers arrange themselves in a line 3 to 4 feet apart; they move forward abreast keeping in perfect alignment, probing first in front of the left foot then in front of the right foot, with the probe marks being approximately 1 foot apart. The probers must be highly sensitive to the feel of the victim with the probing instrument. If the victim is not found in the marked area, the searchers expand beyond that area a specified distance in each direction. This procedure should continue until the total area where the victim might be found has been searched.

If the victim is not found by the probing method, the next recommended procedure is the digging of trenches 8 to 9 feet apart. This permits probing horizontally from one trench to the other and diagonally downward from the bottom of the trench into the deeper snow.

Naturally while all this is being done, additional help should be requested, if this is the practical thing to do in terms of the number of people available and the accessibility of additional help. Once a victim is found, immediate and proper first aid is essential. First aid will probably involve treatment for overexposure, frostbite, shock, and suffocation. Sometimes there are injuries to bones and joints that require treatment.

Describe the procedure you would follow in trying to escape from the path of a slide.

---

mechanical analysis and definitions
10

MECHANICAL ANALYSIS

The following mechanical analyses are not meant to be all inclusive, but rather presented here for the further enlightenment of the more serious skier. Additional definitions are also included to acquaint the novice with some of the specific terms often used among skiers.

Angulation

Angulation in any of the body regions discussed below contributes to edge control, pressure control, and balance. Angulating should be thought of as on-going movement rather than a position which is statically maintained.

Angulating in the Feet. As our primary sensors, the feet are usually the place where a skier makes his first corrective and balancing movements. Even inside the rigidity of ski boots, the feet are actively moving and adjusting. As more experienced skiers can tell, a tightening or relaxing in the feet, as well as extending or bending the ankle (calcaneus) laterally, are significant movements while skiing. Like a rider guiding his horse almost invisibly with thigh pressure, a skier can guide his skis to a great extent with his feet. With the improving fit of boots, such action merits greater attention.

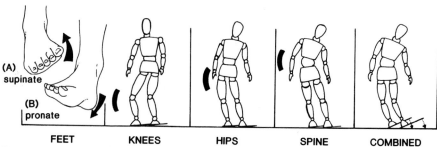

(A) supinate

(B) pronate

| FEET | KNEES | HIPS | SPINE | COMBINED |

Fig. 10.1. Ways in which to angulate

Angulating in the Knees.   Angulating and de-angulating in the knees is mostly a rotation of bent legs in the hip sockets. A person is actually able to bend "sideways in the knees" only to a very limited extent, and this sideways movement is due to some tibial rotation in the knee. Such movement makes the knee joint vulnerable, and can be done only under small loads (pressure). What this means in terms of edging and turning is that so long as the rotation of the legs is minimal and does not exceed the amount of rotation that is actually available in the knee joint (as much as the tibia can turn under the femoral head), a skier will begin to pressure the side of the foot toward which he has displaced his knees (edge). If the rotation is carried further, torque will be transmitted through the joint to the feet and skis. Whether or not the skis will turn under these conditions will depend upon the difference between the torque generated and the resistance from the snow and skis.

When watching skiers in the last phase of their turns, we often can see them drastically increase knee angulation. Such movement is usually short in duration and is part of the "wind-up movement." Although the increase in knee angulation temporarily enhances the bite of the edges, the severity of such movement also generates torque, which actually creates the effect of a preturn. Such movement is typical for most turn initiations in skiing, much as a baseball pitcher will wind up before moving his arm and hand in the direction of the pitch. Thus, while a skier may show extreme knee angulation at the finish of one turn (through which he may temporarily increase the edge bite), this movement must also be understood in terms of the upcoming turn. In contrast, we seldom observe knee angulation of this severity during the controlling phase of the turn. Indeed, observations indicate that prominent angulating movements in the knees last only for short moments. At the beginning of a turn, such angulating indicates leg rotation transmitting torque to the feet and skis. In the latter phase of a turn, such movement typically creates the preturn (wind-up movement) and the subsequent edge setting to launch a new turn.

Angulating in the Hips.   Angulating forcefully in hips and knees usually does not occur until one attains more skillful levels of skiing. Until then, angular movements come predominantly from the feet and spine.

Angulating in the Spine.   Angulating in the spine is done mostly in the lumbar (lower) region of the spinal colmun.

Anticipating

A movement in preparation for turning, during which upper and lower body are brought into a twisted relationship. The resultant stretched muscles are quicker and stronger in contracting and causing movement.

A skier can anticipate by twisting the torso toward the center of the intended turn, as is generally the case in longer radius turns, or by turning the skis beneath the torso as is literally done in short radius turns. Realistically, both movements will interact to some extent, with one generally being dominant. Often we will be able to observe a movement toward anticipation made with sufficient momentum to "kick off" the turn with a touch of rotation, in which case purists can no longer call such a turning initiation "anticipation release."

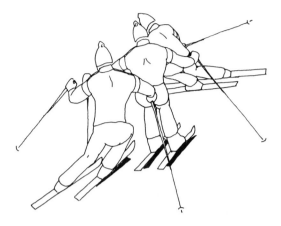

Fig. 10.2.   Anticipation

Carving

A turning of the skis with little lateral movement of the skis over the snow is carving.

Skiing requires that the skier perform all the functions illustrated in the following figure.

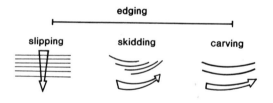

Fig. 10.3.   Ski motions on the snow

Sliding: the movement of the skis in the direction of their longitudinal axis.
Slipping: a movement of the skis sideways.
Skidding: the composite result of skis moving forward and sideways and pivoting.

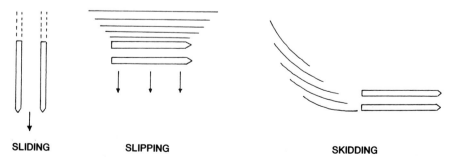

Fig. 10.4.   Ski motions on the snow

Edge Angle

The degree of tilt of the ski about its longitudinal (vertical) axis in relation to the supporting surface is the edge angle.

Edge Bite

The edge bite is the extent of the forces generated by edging.

Edge Change

The action of tilting the skis about their longitudinal axes from one set of edges to the other is the edge change. This action suggests that contact with the slope is established when leaving one set of edges and again when engaging the other set. It is the most fundamental aspect of turning; it can be performed while the skis are in contact with the snow, or it can be performed without ski/snow contact.

Edge Control

The action of adjusting the edge angle of the ski to the task at hand is the edge control.

Edging

Edging refers to the interaction of the ski with the supporting surface (snow) and, more specifically, relates to the angle between the running surface of the ski and the slope.

Pressure Control

The action of actively adjusting the pressure exerted by the skis against the snow (supporting surface) is pressure control. This includes such movements as shifting pressure from one ski to the other (weight transfer), applying pressure from one ski to the other (weight transfer), applying pressure to the front, back, or middle of the skis (leverage), and adjusting the magnitude of the pressure by vertical displacements of the body mass (unweighting, absorbing, pressuring).

Terrain unweighting is an additional form of pressure control in which inertia plays a dominant role. The experienced skier will usually seek out the help of terrain to start turns, though this is seldom a conscious effort.

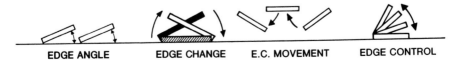

EDGE ANGLE   EDGE CHANGE   E.C. MOVEMENT   EDGE CONTROL

Fig. 10.5.   Edging

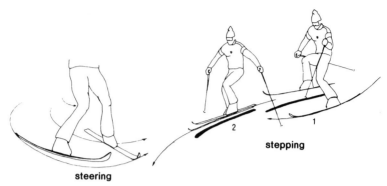

stepping

steering

Mere "pedalling" or "transferring weight" from one ski to the other are not considered to be qualifying conditions for step turns.

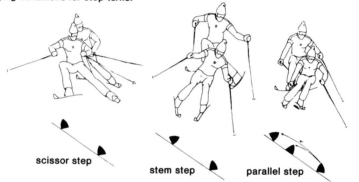

scissor step   stem step   parallel step

Fig. 10.6.   Forms of SELR

Sequential Leg Rotation (SELR)

The action of using one ski as the support from, or against, which the other ski is turned is referred to as sequential leg rotation.

The reason for distinguishing these turns from others is that they utilize mechanical principles associated with changing one ski's edges and then the other's. Such movements rely principally on a lateral pushing off from one ski, or using one ski as a fulcrum for the other ski, to initiate a turn. These devices allow one to ski with greatest economy of motion of the torso and arms, minimizing the need for unweighting, and facilitating the development of leg action in skiing.

Simultaneous Leg Rotation (SILR)

The act of turning both legs at the same time is referred to as simultaneous leg rotation.

We speak of SILR-type turns whenever we refer to "braquage" (rotation of the legs in an open stance), rotation, counter-rotation, or a rotary push-off or rebound from both skis.

Stepping:

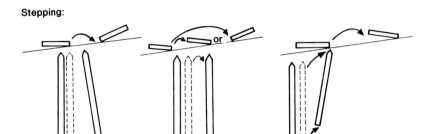

Fig. 10.7.   Edging associated with types of stepping motions

These types of turn initiations tend to be associated with pronounced vertical movements (unweighting). Braquage, perhaps, is an exception to this statement insofar as both skis need to bear pressure in order to permit them to pivot. But, even then, we can see an intuitive dropping of the center of mass to facilitate the pivoting once turning momentum exists (unweighting).

SILR-type turns are especially useful in deep snow, crud, crusty conditions, high-speed skiing, or moguls. When teaching these turns, a useful method is to emphasize "rhythm"; shouting "now-now-now" in the rhythm of the turns or clapping hands to provide a rhythm can be very helpful.

Why do we distinguish SELR and SILR turns? When comparing the mechanics involved in "1" and "1-2" movements, it is clear that they are essentially different from each other. Both movement groups are unique, and either may be more suitable when given special consideration and emphasis during the mechanical development of a skier.

Step Turning

Step turning is a type of turning where, during the preparation and/or initiation of the turn, the skier steps from one ski to the other and displaces the ski being transferred to forward and or to the side in a convergent, divergent, or parallel position.

DEFINITIONS

Arlberg.   A mountain region of Austria that fostered the Arlberg and Austrian techniques.

Avalanche cord.   A bright-colored nylon cord approximately 100 feet long that is tied to a skier traveling in avalanche terrain and used for the purpose of locating a skier who is buried in an avalanche.

Camber.   A curve in the ski contour from tip to tail.

Checking.   The action of slowing or stopping the skidding of the skis on snow.

Christie.   A light brushing of the tails of the skis against the snow as in the end phase of a basic christie turn.

Counterrotation. A quick turning motion of one part of the body, resulting in a counteraction in another when resistance is markedly reduced.

CSIA. Canadian Ski Instructors Alliance—the association that sets standards for instruction and certifies professional ski instructors in Canada.

Downhill race. One of the three forms of Alpine racing in which the skier competes against time in a downhill course following the natural terrain restricted by only an occasional control gate.

Down-unweighting. A flexion of the body by quickly bending at the ankles, knees, hips, and waist.

Fall line. The shortest line down a slope; the line that a freely moving body would follow if influenced only by gravity. The fall line is referenced to the skier's immediate location.

FIS. Fédération Internationale de Ski (French terminology)—this is the international ski federation that supervises and regulates international ski competition.

Gate. Two flags or other markers between which a skier must pass during a race.

Giant slalom. One of the three forms of Alpine racing; it combines the elements of downhill and slalom racing.

Gondola. A ski lift consisting of enclosed cars suspended from a cable.

Herringbone. A method of traveling up a slope on skis, so named because of the pattern the skis leave in the snow.

Hotdogging. Performing stunts and unusual ski maneuvers of the acrobatic type.

Inside ski. The ski that describes the inside arc of a turn.

J-bar. A ski lift consisting of a series of J-shaped bars suspended from an overhead cable. The skier sits or leans against the bottom of the J and is pulled along on his skis.

Kick turn. From a stationary position with the skis parallel, the ski on the side of the turn is picked up, turned 180°, and placed parallel to the other ski. The other ski is then brought around as the body turns and is placed alongside the first ski.

Leverage. The application of pressure foreward or backward or on the middle of the skis.

Methodology. The procedure or way of teaching, the manner used in working toward a maneuver.

Mogul. A mound of snow formed by many skiers following the same track and thus pushing snow from the track into a mound at each turn.

NSPS. National Ski Patrol System—a national organization in the United States of volunteer skiers trained to serve as ski patrolmen. Their main functions are to enforce safety rules and administer treatment and transportation for injured skiers.

Outside ski. The ski describing the outside arc of a turn.

Parallel christie. A christie turn executed with both skis close together and parallel at all times.

Poma lift. The same as a J-bar except with a disc at the bottom of each bar instead of a hook. The skier straddles the bar, sits against the disc, and is pulled along the snow on the skis.

Rebound-retraction.   A type of unweighting produced by a temporary relaxation of the legs.

Release binding.   Binding designed for safety due to the fact that it will release under a certain amount of stress.

Rope tow.   A ski lift where the skier holds to a moving rope and is pulled along on the skis while in a standing position.

Rotary heel thrust.   The displacement of the ski tails by down motion and the turning of the legs.

Safety binding.   Same as release binding.

Safety strap.   A strap attached to the ski or binding and wrapped around the ankle to keep a loose ski from running away.

Schuss.   Skiing straight down the fall line without using any turns or checks.

Short swing.   Consecutive parallel christies without a traverse between turns.

Side camber.   A part of the design of a ski. The relative dimensions of shovel, waist, and tail of a ski produce a sweeping curve along each side of the ski. The wider shovel leads into a gentle curve, followed by the narrower waist and the wider tail. Coupled with the ski's basic width, these design features produce varying performance characteristics.

Sitzmark.   An impression made in the snow from the fall of a skier. Sitzmarks should always be leveled, otherwise they serve as hazards to other skiers.

Ski position.   Relative position of one ski to the other: closed, open, wedged, stemmed, or advanced.

Slalom.   One of the basic forms of Alpine ski racing where the skier must follow a course marked by a series of gates formed by flags, singly or in pairs, and must pass through each gate.

Snowplow.   The stemming of both skis at the same time at identical angles; also called wedge.

Steering action.   Turning force resulting from twisting of the feet combined with forward lean, causing lateral and torsional movements of the knees.

Stem christie.   A christie turn initiated by stemming one ski.

Stemming.   Lateral displacement of one ski tail.

T-bar.   Same as poma, except having a short bar horizontally across the bottom instead of a disc. The skier straddles the vertical bar and leans against the horizontal bar. A double T-bar is one with a long horizontal bar so that two skiers can be pulled along, one on each side of the vertical bar.

Torsion.   The turning or twisting of one part of the body against another.

Total motion.   The placement of specific body movements into correct sequence, resulting in a total motion with the whole body. Use of the total body in performing skiing skills.

Track.   A path made by skis. Also a warning to another skier that you are coming up from behind and plan to pass.

Tramway.   One or more large cars mounted on a moving cable used to transport skiers.

Traverse.   Descent at an angle to the fall line.

Unweighting.   An upward motion of the body caused by a smooth straightening of the legs and trunk resulting in momentary lifting of the body from the snow. During this brief moment the skis are highly maneuverable. See also down-unweighting, rebound-retraction, and up-unweighting.

Up-unweighting.   A quick extension of the body upward; an extreme lift will produce a hop.

USSA.   United States Ski Association—this is the national ski organization of America; it is a member of the FIS.

Wedeln.   A playful execution of consecutive parallel turns without traverses between the turns and only slight setting of edges.

opportunities unlimited

11

For a skier with imagination and a spirit of adventure there are unlimited opportunities for excitement through participation in this sport. In the United States and Canada one can find practically every kind of ski condition, in a great variety of settings. Well-known ski areas are found as far north as Alaska and as far south as Tennessee, Virginia, and North Carolina. They are located in every state in the northern half of the United States and every province of Canada.

CHARACTERISTICS OF DIFFERENT AREAS

Ski areas differ greatly. Each area has a unique personality and offers opportunities not found at any other area. Those who enjoy skiing with plenty of company and on packed snow are inclined toward areas located in the East, especially the Eastern seaboard and New England states. The snow is wet and heavy, and the large number of skiers keep the slopes solidly packed. The thick woods of the East contribute to a beautiful landscape for the skiers' enjoyment, but the woods largely confine skiers to trail skiing. Eastern slopes are typically medium in length and offer a limited variety of skiing.

In the midwestern states, skiers find more flat lands and rolling hills. Except that the snow is typically less moist and the woods less thick, skiing is essentially the same as in the East. The density of the population also provides plenty of company on the slopes. Because of the low elevations of the eastern and midwestern states, the snowfall is relatively light. In the past this has resulted in short seasons of skiing on thin snow. In recent years the seasons have been lengthened considerably by use of artificial snowmaking machines. This practice has become very popular in the heavily frequented areas and has greatly enhanced skiing throughout the United States.

Ski areas in the Rocky Mountains are at high elevations and in a relatively dry climate. This results in a powder skier's paradise. Nowhere is powder skiing better than at the high Rocky Mountain resorts. Also, the Rockies offer a great variety of skiing terrain. One can find a slope as steep or as gentle and as long or as short as is desired. On these high mountain slopes the snow is deep, the seasons long, and the trails varied. The rugged mountain scenery adds much to the skiers' enjoyment.

To the west are the high Sierra and Pacific Coast mountains. This region provides a greater variety in skiing than any other region in North America. On any given winter day, depending on which area is visited, one may find wet or dry snow, large crowds or only a few skiers, deep or shallow snow, and steep or gentle slopes. Because of the location of the Sierra and Pacific Coast Mountains, their climate is relatively wet on the west and relatively dry on the east.

If you are looking for good skiing and eastern personality, the well-known areas of Vermont, Connecticut, New Jersey, New York, or Pennsylvania are best. Areas in the midwestern states of Wisconsin, Michigan, Ohio, and Minnesota offer a less traditional atmosphere and less emphasis on style of dress. If you prefer a taste of southern hospitality, try skiing in North Carolina, Virginia, or Tennessee. If you are looking for deep-powder skiing, long runs, and a variety of terrain, go to the Rockies. If you want good skiing combined with living at a faster pace during the nonskiing hours, try some of the well-established areas near the West Coast. If you enjoy privacy and adventure, resorts in most of the regions of the United States and Canada now offer the solitude and challenge of helicopter skiing in remote areas. Regardless of where you go, once you become a good skier, you will like the skiing. As expressed by one old timer, "The skiing is always good, but sometimes it is better that other times."

Moving from the eastern to the western coasts, the Canadian ski areas closely parallel those of the United States in the type of skiing they offer. Typically, the Canadian areas are less crowded and the climate colder, causing the snow to be dryer.

OPPORTUNITIES FOR INSTRUCTION

Through the trial-and-error process, it has been discovered that high-quality instruction is a significant step in learning to ski. Instruction is especially valuable at the beginning stage, where one must learn the fundamentals on which to develop the more advanced techniques. Instruction by certified ski instructors is available at practically all ski areas on either a private or group basis. These instructors must pass vigorous tests in both skiing performance and teaching technique, thus assuring their students of high-quality instruction. Many communities sponsor ski schools for the residents of the area, and a large number of colleges and universities now sponsor extensive ski-instruction programs. Usually top-quality instruction can be obtained through any of these sources.

PROFESSIONAL OPPORTUNITIES

The limited opportunity to earn a living as a full-time ski professional does not discourage many from becoming instructors, coaches, or ski patrolmen. Many ski professionals use their ski earnings to supplement other incomes or to help finance new equipment and ski passes. Most ski schools offer classes, clinics, and apprenticeship opportunities to aid prospective instructors, develop teaching skills, and prepare for certification. Certification exams for associate and fully certified instructors are conducted yearly by the local divisions of the Professional Ski Instructors of America.

The ski patrol, once a voluntary position, is now moving more towards paid personnel. A person must have a first aid card, be sponsored by a current ski patrol member, and serve a year in training before being voted into the national ski patrol. In the west many resorts now require ski patrol members to have avalanche experience and emergency medical training.

RAPID INCREASE IN SKIING

The increase in skiing in North America has occurred at an almost unbelievable rate in recent years. Operators of established ski areas have been forced to expand their operations, thus providing more and better ski facilities. New areas have developed at a rapid rate. Numerous ski areas have been expanded to become year-round resorts, and many of them are now emphasizing vacation opportunities for nonskiing members of families or other groups. Americans' rush to the great outdoors is making its mark on the exciting sport of skiing; this trend will continue as long as we continue to increase our mobility, income, leisure time, technology, and population.

selected references

ABRAHAM, HORST. *The American Teaching Method, Part I.* Boulder, CO: P.S.I.A., 1976.

ABRAHAM, HORST. *Teaching Concepts A.T.M. III.* Boulder, CO: P.S.I.A., P.S.I.A., 1978.

ABRAHAM, HORST. *Teaching Concepts A.T.M. III.* Boulder, COs P.S.I.A., 1980.

CAMPBELL, STU. *Methodology.* Boulder, CO: P.S.I.A., 1978.

GALLWEY, TIMOTHY and BOB KRIEGEL. *Inner Skiing.* New York: Random House, Inc., 1977.

JOUBERT, GEORGES. *Skiing: An Art . . . A Technique.* LaPorte, CO: Poudre Publishing Co., 1980.

JOUBERT, GEORGES. Teach Yourself to Ski. Aspen, CO: Aspen Ski Masters, 1972.

LIGHTHELL, STENMARK. *Skiing for Women.* ETC Publications, 1979.

Ski, Magazine, Universal Publishing and Distributing Corp., 800 2nd Avenue, New York, NY.

Ski Magazine, Universal Publishing and Distributing Corp., 800 2nd Avenue,

Ski Racing. Ski Racing, Inc., Box 70, Fair Haven, Vermont.

WITHERELL, WARREN. *How the Racers Ski.* New York: W. W. Norton & Co., 1972.

questions and
answers

1. New innovations and concepts are constantly being introduced to standardize teaching techniques. (p. 9)

2. Beginning students should use a shorter ski to increase their learning rate and to reduce their potential for injury. (p. 10)

3. It is the intent of the ATM (American Teaching Method) to perfect the basic skills as an end unto themselves. (p. 11)

4. Minor differences in skiing styles result from varieties in body build, temperament, and other influences. (p. 9)

5. To move into the basic wedge position, the student should push the heels out as the toes are being pointed together. (p. 11)

6. In the basic wedge position, the weight is equally distributed on both skis. (p. 11)

7. The skier should visualize the wedge as a basic straight running position with double stemming, or with both skis stemmed at the same time. (p. 12)

8. Sideslipping is relatively unimportant in learning to skid the skis. (p. 15)

9. In order to completely develop the christie, there must be a feeling of using a weight transfer to turn out of the fall line and to decrease speed. (p. 17)

10. The ultimate goal of the christie is to learn to use the legs to develop more effective turning. (p. 17)

11. It was once thought that stemming showed a weakness in a person's skiing skills and classified one as less than an expert skier. (p. 10)

12. Racers work to improve a step-out action in order to skate or drive from one ski to the other, causing the skis to accelerate and enabling them to hold a faster line. (p. 55)

13. Angulation is the leaning away from the slope with the upper body in a traverse or toward the outside of a turn. (p. 78)

14. Anticipation is a preparatory movement affecting the middle part of the turn. (p. 79)

15. Carving is the skill of reducing lateral slippage throughout the turn in an attempt to ski the arc that the ski produces when edges are pressed into the snow.
(p. 80)

16. GLM (Graduated Length Method) refers to teaching skiing starting on a shorter ski and progressing gradually to a longer ski.   (p. 10)

17. Method is how a technique is practiced.   (p. 84)

18. Pole plant is the effective use of poles to enable the skier to use a pole as a crutch to swing around a turn.   (p. 16)

19. Short swing consists of consecutive parallel christies with a long traverse between turns.   (p. 85)

20. Snowplow is the stemming of both skis at the same time at identical angles, now commonly referred to as the wedge.   (p. 85)

21. Stem christie is a christie turn initiated by stemming one ski.   (p. 85)

22. Technique refers to a philosophy that does not include the mechanical description of a skiing system.   (p. 9)

23. Turning means changing direction on skis.   (p. 12)

24. Up-unweighting is the only form of unweighting used in skiing.   (p. 84)

25. Wide track is the "feet apart" attitude to aid lateral stability.   (p. 11)

26. Effective muscle conditioning will not necessarily improve your skiing or help you to reduce your chance of injury.   (p. 30)

27. Strength can be improved by applying the principles of strength overload and progressive resistance.   (p. 30)

28. Practically every muscle in the body is used to some extent in skiing.
(p. 31)

29. To encourage flexibility, the muscles should be stretched gradually and slowly until the stretch pain is felt and then held in that position for several seconds during each repetition.   (p. 31)

30. An exercise program developed for skiing should be designed to encourage muscular strength, endurance, and flexibility in specific muscle groups where these traits are needed.   (p. 30)

31. Vigorous participation in sports that require much starting and stopping and changing of direction is not desirable to prepare for vigorous skiing.   (p. 35)

32. Troops on skis have played an important part in the outcome of many wars.
(p. 2)

33. Early Scandinavian travelers were influential in introducing skiing to other countries.   (p. 2)

34. Waxing is most important to the racer, but the beginner has no need to wax.
(p. 52)

35. Cutting the pie, sidestepping, and herringbone are all hillclimbing skills.
(p. 7)

36. Expert skiers generally prefer longer skis.   (p. 45)

37. Bindings are the most important piece of equipment to keep in good shape.
(p. 46)

38. A binding seldom needs adjusting once the proper setting has been achieved. (p. 46)

39. Ski boots are the most important piece of ski equipment the skier will buy. (p. 47)

40. Ski clothing should fit snuggly, but not too tightly. (p. 49)

41. Dacron-filled parkas are the most expensive and provide the greatest warmth. (p. 50)

42. Too many skiers are more concerned about style than warmth when they purchase their ski clothing. (p. 50)

43. Since most ski days are cloudy or snowy, a skier need not worry about protection from the sun. (p. 40)

44. The downhill race is the most highly regarded of the Alpine events. (p. 55)

45. A jumper's success is closely related to an ability to use air currents to obtain distance. (p. 58)

46. The different forms of skiing today are classified into two kinds, Alpine (downhill) and Nordic (cross-country). (p. 53)

47. The herringbone is a climbing technique that is fast, but difficult and tiring. (p. 63)

48. Under normal ski touring conditions, double-poling is considered faster, easier, and more efficient than the diagonal stride. (p. 61)

49. Because of the vigorous use given to cross-country racing skis, they are ordinarily wider, heavier, and more rugged than general touring skis. (p. 65)

50. As a general guide, the length of the touring ski should be from the floor to the wrist when the arm is stretched above the head. However, recreational skiers often want skis slightly shorter than this to enhance maneuverability. (p. 65)

51. Three of the most important characteristics of cross-country boots are flexibility, lightness, and durability. (p. 67)

52. It is possible that people may suffer frostbite on certain areas of the face without knowing it, unless someone tells them about the pale and glossy appearance of their skin. (p. 40)

53. Equipment dating 4,000 to 5,000 years has been found in the Scandinavian countries. (p. 1)

54. The first evidence of the use of ski equipment for warfare involved the Austrians and Germans in the fifteenth century. (p. 2)

55. Factors that have had significant influence on the vast popularity of skiing are improved equipment, including mechanized ski lifts, as well as more time and money available to the population in general. (p. 89)

56. Usually sidestepping is a good method of climbing a short, steep slope. (p. 8)

57. The herringbone is another way of traveling up a slope on skis. (p. 8)

MULTIPLE CHOICE

58. The American Teaching Method's primary concept is to
    a. develop the christie   c. eliminate the wedge turn
    b. develop better racers
    (p. 10)

59. The major difference between the American Teaching Method and the American Ski Technique is
    a. the perfecting and finishing of forms
    b. the emphasis placed on students progressing to higher levels without perfecting final forms
    c. giving skiers more confidence in their equipment
    (p. 10)

60. Ski racers and racing techniques have had a decided effect on
    a. making skiers who were once racers better teachers
    b. teaching techniques
    c. encouraging all beginning skiers to try racing
    (p. 10)

61. If pushing the skis out to the wedge position is too difficult, the skier can accomplish this by
    a. unweighting one ski and pushing that tail out, then doing the same with the other ski
    b. getting on a steeper slope where speed is increased
    c. hopping to a wedge, or Spartan, position while skiing down a gentle slope
    (p. 11)

62. Keeping the skis in a wide-track position (approximately 12-14 inches apart) allows the skier to
    a. go faster
    b. feel weight equally on either ski
    c. maneuver through a slalom course at a faster rate
    (p. 11)

63. A short swing turn is a maneuver used by experts, usually on steep hills or difficult terrain, for the purpose of
    a. getting more "air" off the bumps or moguls
    b. controlling their speed with short turns
    c. learning to be less aggressive
    (p. 19)

64. The expert skier is characterized by
    a. an ability to go fast
    b. being able to "show off' or "hotdog" in front of other skiers
    c. being able to approach all snow conditions and different terrain problems with confidence
    (p. 25)

65. In order to handle speed properly, the skier must
    a. first learn how to ski rather slowly on gentle terrain and then increase the speed as confidence to handle more difficult terrain increases
    b. get on a gentle slope and go as fast as possible
    c. try to ski fast through congested areas
    (p. 26)

66. The character, size, and shape of bumps, or moguls, has drastically changed because
    a. ski areas can't use their big equipment to knock them down on steep places
    b. the length of the ski (short ski) and the changes in boots and bindings in the last couple of years have made them sharper and steeper
    c. edges have become sharper on skis
    (p. 26)

67. In order to maneuver well in deep snow, the skier must
    a. be able to distinguish the difference between the different types of snow one must encounter
    b. not be concerned about speed but just let 'em go
    c. try to keep the skis above the surface of the snow at all times   (p. 28)

68. One of the most important things to remember while skiing deep snow is
    a. to use longer skis that are fairly stiff
    b. to keep weight equally balanced on both skis
    c. not to use any pole action at all   (p. 28)

69. The man responsible for the vitality of modern ski technique was
    a. "Snowshoe" Thompson
    b. Hannes Schneider
    c. Roald Amundsen
    d. Mathias Zdarsky   (p. 3)

70. Which does not contribute to a ski's stability at higher speeds?
    a. groove in ski bottom
    b. width and side camber
    c. short length
    d. camber   (p. 44)

71. In buying ski boots it is most important to consider
    a. the color of the boot
    b. the height of the boot
    c. comfort
    d. forward lean   (p. 47)

72. Which is not an important consideration in the selection of poles?
    a. length
    b. durability
    c. weight
    d. grip and basket   (p. 48)

73. An example of a Nordic competition is
    a. the 20-meter jump
    b. the slalom
    c. the downhill
    d. the ballet   (p. 57)

74. An event in freestyle competition is
    a. the giant slalom
    b. the cross-country
    c. the dual slalom
    d. the aerials   (p. 58)

75. Which of the following is not a contributor to snow blindness?
    a. ultraviolet light
    b. dazzling visual rays
    c. thermal heat
    d. infrared rays   (p. 40)

76. The most basic stride in cross-country skiing is
    a. double poling
    b. double-poling stride
    c. diagonal stride
    d. none of these   (p. 60)

77. Which of the following is not a climbing technique on skis?
    a. side step
    b. herringbone
    c. uphill christie
    d. side step traverse   (p. 62)

QUESTION ANSWER KEY

True or False

1.	T	13.	T	25.	T	37.	T	49.	F
2.	T	14.	F	26.	F	38.	F	50.	T
3.	F	15.	T	27.	T	39.	T	51.	T
4.	T	16.	T	28.	T	40.	T	52.	T
5.	T	17.	F	29.	T	41.	F	53.	T
6.	T	18.	F	30.	T	42.	T	54.	F
7.	T	19.	F	31.	F	43.	F	55.	T
8.	F	20.	T	32.	T	44.	T	56.	T
9.	T	21.	T	33.	T	45.	T	57.	T
10.	T	22.	F	34.	T	46.	T		
11.	T	23.	T	35.	F	47.	T		
12.	T	24.	F	36.	T	48.	F		

Multiple Choice

58.	a	62.	b	66.	b	70.	c	74.	d
59.	b	63.	b	67.	a	71.	c	75.	c
60.	b	64.	c	68.	b	72.	c	76.	c
61.	a	65.	a	69.	b	73.	a	77.	c

ANSWERS TO EVALUATION QUESTIONS—SKIING

Page   Answer and Page Reference

8   To set the edges of the skis roll the ankles and knees toward the hill When sidestepping is done correctly, a clean linear impression is left with each step. Unsuccessful sidestepping results in a broader sliding impression.   (p. 8)

7   Wagon Wheel-Sequentially; One Step Glide-Sequentially in the step and simultaneously in the glide; Hop-simultaneously.   (p. 7)

12   When the knees are rolled in, edging is increased and the skis bite into the snow and slow down the pace (p. 12). When gliding in wedge position the skis run over the snow; when edges are set, skis cut a deeper line in the snow.

15   In wide track running position, skis are parallel to fall line; skis glide on their bases; weight is distributed evenly on both skis. In traverse position, skis cross fall line; edges of both are set equally towards the hill; weight is more on downhill ski.   (pp. 11-14)

17   The hockey stop leads to awareness of weight transfer from ski to ski, the importance of edge set, and pressure on the skis which alters the shape of the ski causing it to carve into the snow.   (p. 17)

21   The upper body remains facing directly down the fall line, and, while appearing to be passive, the body really sets up a torque or block which assists the rebound of the legs when the completion of one turn becomes the preparation for the next.   (p. 20)

Page

21   The uphill stem allows for an easy change of edge and a tentative initiation of the turn. The downhill stem with the edge set helps to check speed and creates a platform which allows the ski to rebound into the turn. A wide stem results in a short radius turn; a narrow stem, in a long radius turn.   (p. 21)

24   Moving from a traverse position into a parallel step christie, the uphill ski is stepped out and placed flat or on the inside edge. Simultaneously the weight sinks and is transferred from the downhill ski allowing it to close parallel.   (p. 24)

28   *Reploiment* is used when skiing over short choppy bumps. *Avalement* is used when skiing at greater speed over bigger bumps. This is a much more dynamic technique.   (p. 26)

32   Answer specific to the student.

42   Frostbite usually occurs in extremities. The affected part first becomes slightly flushed and then white or grayish-white and glossy. Warning symptoms of snow blindness are burning sensation underneath the eyelids, spasms in the muscles surrounding the eyes, bloodshot eyes, and watering eyes. Sunburn is prevalent in skiing and the redness of the skin and extent of burns is not noticed until some hours after leaving the slopes. Mountain sickness can happen when a skier ascends rapidly from a low to a high elevation. The victim often feels dizzy, weak, and nauseous. Hypothermia is a very serious condition resulting from overexposure. The victim becomes drowsy, incoherent, and staggers. Movement becomes difficult and unconsciousness follows.   (pp. 40-44)

47   The skier must provide adequate maintenance and periodic readjustment if bindings are to aid in the prevention of injury.   (p. 51)

58   Cross country skiing makes similar body demands as does distance running. In the pre-conditioning phase, emphasis should be on endurance exercises, but the program should also contain exercises which improve strength and flexibility.   (p. 58)

62   The diagonal stride is a modification of walking, legs and arms work in opposition to produce a smooth, forceful stride, a long, smooth arm movement, and a long glide when the weight is transferred onto the gliding ski.   (pp. 60-61)

64   A gentle uphill slope can be ascended by using the diagonal stride technique, provided you wax and the snow conditions are favorable and do not cause slipping backwards. The herringbone technique is a fast and efficient method for ascending a short steep slope. This is a tiring technique, however, so it demands considerable strength.   (pp. 62-63)

64   Touring bindings allow the heel to move freely, touring boots permit much ankle movement, and the skis are more flexible and often are not edged with metal.   (pp. 65-67)

71   An avalanche area is indicated by an orange octagon; extra caution is indicated by a red diamond.   (p. 39)

Page

74   The four kinds of avalanches involve dry snow, wet snow, wind slab and ice. Dry snow avalanches are the most common and usually occur when a fresh layer of deep snow has fallen on top of existing crusted snow. Wet snow avalanches may occur when a considerable amount of wet snow has fallen, it has rained, or there has been an increase in temperature. A wind slab is formed by the wind blowing loose snow over existing snow until a hard slab of ice builds up. Ice avalanches of sizeable proportions often occur at the end of glaciers at high altitudes. Eventually the ice protrudes to such an extent that it breaks off causing a serious avalanche situation.   (pp. 71-73)

77   If trying to out race an advancing slide, ski diagonally away from it, not down its direct path.   (p. 76)

index